THE
THIRTY
NAMES
OF
NIGHT

ALSO BY ZEYN JOUKHADAR

The Map of Salt and Stars

THE THIRTY NAMES OF NIGHT

A Novel

ZEYN JOUKHADAR

ATRIA BOOKS

New York   London   Toronto   Sydney   New Delhi

ATRIA
BOOKS

An Imprint of Simon & Schuster, Inc.
1230 Avenue of the Americas
New York, NY 10020

First Atria Books hardcover edition May 2020

ATRIA BOOKS and colophon are trademarks of Simon & Schuster, Inc.

For information about special discounts for bulk purchases, please contact Simon & Schuster Special Sales at 1-866-506-1949 or business@simonandschuster.com.

The Simon & Schuster Speakers Bureau can bring authors to your live event. For more information or to book an event, contact the Simon & Schuster Speakers Bureau at 1-866-248-3049 or visit our website at www.simonspeakers.com.

Interior design by Erika Genova

Manufactured in the United States of America

1   3   5   7   9   10   8   6   4   2

Library of Congress Cataloging-in-Publication Data is available.

ISBN 978-1-9821-2149-5
ISBN 978-1-9821-2155-6 (ebook)

For those who name themselves

ONE / ██████

Tonight, five years to the day since I lost you, forty-eight white-throated sparrows fall from the sky. Tomorrow, the papers will count and photograph them, arrange them on black garbage bags and speculate on the causes of the blight. But for now, here on the roof of Teta's apartment building, the sheen of evening rain on the tar paper slicks the soles of my sneakers, and velvet arrows drop one by one from the autumn migration sweeping over Boerum Hill.

The sparrows thud onto the houses around me, old three- and four-story brownstones, generation homes with sculpted stoops, a handful recently bought from the families who have owned them for decades and gutted for resale. Nothing has stayed the way it was since you died, not even the way we grieve you. Downstairs in Teta's apartment, I've drawn the curtains, tucked Teta's glasses back into their drawer so that even if she wakes, she won't look down on this street dashed with dying birds. Five years ago, when your absence stitched her mouth shut for weeks, I hid your collection of feathers, hid the preserved shells of robin's eggs, hid the specimens of bone. Each egg was its own shade of blue; I slipped them into a shoebox under my bed. When you were alive, the warmth of each shell held the thrill of possibility. I first learned to mix paint by matching the smooth turquoise of a heron's egg: first aqua, then celadon, then cooling the warmth of cadmium yellow with phthalo blue. When you died, Teta quoted Attar: *The self has passed away in the beloved.* Tonight, the sparrows' feathers are brushstrokes on the dark. This evening is its own witness, the birds' throats stars on the canvas of the night. They clap into cars and crash through skylights, thunk into steel trash cans with the lids off, slice through the branches of boxed-in gingkoes. Gravity snaps shut their wings. The evening's fog smears the city to blinding. Migrating birds, you used to say, the city's light can kill.

A sparrow's beak strikes my hand and gashes my palm. I clutch the wound, the meat of my thumb dark with my own blood. You taught me a long time ago to identify the species by the yellow patches around their eyes, their black whiskers, their white throats, and their ivory crowns. You were the one who taught me to imitate their calls—*Sam Peabody, Peabody, Peabody.* In your career as an ornithologist, you taught me two dozen East Coast birdcalls, things I thought you'd always be here to teach me. I reach down to scoop the sparrow from the rooftop with my bloodied hands. He weighs almost nothing. There is so much of you—and, therefore, of myself—that I will never know.

Tomorrow, when the ghost of you enters my window with the smell of rain, I will tell you how, since you died, the birds have never left me. The sparrows are the most recent of a long chain of moments into which the birds, like you, have intruded: the red-tailed hawks perched on the fire escape above Sahadi's awning, or the female barred owl that alights on Borough Hall when I emerge from the subway. For all my prayers the night you died, the divine was nowhere to be found. The forty-eight white-throated sparrows that plummet from the sky are my only companions in grief tonight, the omen that keeps me from leaning out into the air.

My gynecologist is using purple gloves again. They are the only color in this all-white examination room. I set my feet in the stirrups with my knees together, only separating my thighs when he taps my foot. The paper gown crinkles. The white noise of my blood thrums in my ears. There is no rainbow-colored ceiling tile with dolphins here like the one at Teta's dentist. Last spring, I got my teeth cleaned while she had a root canal just so I could hold her hand.

I clench and unclench my sweaty fingers. The speculum is a rude column of ice. I focus on a pinprick of iodine staining the ceiling tile and force myself to imagine how it got there. I will myself out of my body the way I used to do when I was bleeding. The summer after you died, my periods were the heaviest they'd ever been. I spent the rainless evenings standing in fields at sunset, waiting to be raptured into the green flash of twilight, wishing there were another way to exist in the world than to be bodied. It had been less than a year since I'd closed my hand around those eggs in the nest, and still I wanted nothing more than to disappear into the weightless womb waiting inside each round, perfect eggshell, that place of possibility where a soul could hum unburdened and unbound. The man between my legs checks for the string of my IUD, and I am flooded with the urge to return my body and slip myself into a different softness: the stems of orchids, maybe; the line of sap running up the trunk of a maple; the fist of a fox's heart.

Instead I am jolted back to my body by the shiver of lube running down the crack of my ass. He pulls off his gloves and tells me to get dressed. There are never enough tissues, so I use the paper gown and ball it up in the trash. My gyno returns just as I tug my T-shirt over the shapewear compressing my chest.

"Everything looks good," he says, sitting down at the computer. He adjusts the pens in the pocket of his lab coat, though none of the doctors in this place write on paper anymore. "I can't find any reason for your pain."

"But I've been spotting and cramping ever since I got this thing."

By the look on his face, he doesn't take this seriously. He hands me a pharmaceutical pamphlet on the IUD, the kind with women laughing on the glossy front, shopping or hiking or holding their boyfriends' hands. He urges me to wait a few more months until things stabilize, then asks me if I'm using backup protection. I say yes, though I haven't had sex in years. For some reason, my first crush pops into my mind, the white girl in my high school biology class who loved acoustic guitar music and coconut rum. It's been so long since I've allowed myself to want anyone or anything.

"I thought this thing was supposed to stop my period." I pick at a hole that's starting on the knee of my jeans. "And my chest is sore. Didn't know that was a side effect."

"Sure, breast tenderness can happen in the beginning." The gyno looks at me like I am a puzzle he's lost a piece to. "It might make your periods heavier, too, but that should settle down after a few cycles." He asks me about my moods, but I can tell bleeding, cramping, and sore breasts aren't going to be enough to convince him to take the thing out. In his mind, a woman should be used to these things. There is no way to explain the eggshell or the fox's heart. My insufficient, unnameable suffering is my own problem.

I hop off the table. I say, "It's probably just that time of year again."

He softens. You went to him before I did, and you still hang between us in the waiting room when I come for my appointments.

He asks me if I'm back to painting, trying to make small talk, but I don't know how to answer.

"You need to get inspired. Get your mind off things." He suggests an exhibit at the Met on Impressionist painters. I try not to roll my eyes. He pats me on the shoulder as I leave. On my way out, the receptionist calls me *miss*.

The sun is low when I step outside. It will be angling red through the window when I arrive home, and Teta will be dozing in her armchair. I can't stand the thought of another summer sunset in that silent apartment, so I take the 6 uptown to the Met. Now that I'm taking care of Teta, their pay-what-you-wish policy for New York residents makes it one of the few museums I can still afford. Maybe a change of scenery would be good, I tell myself.

The grandness of the Great Hall, with its columns and its vaulted ceilings, makes me hate the undignified way my sneakers squeak on the polished stone. I wander into the Impressionist exhibit, which turns out to be more than just Impressionists. *Representations of the Body: From Impressionism to the Avant Garde* is essentially a study of nudes, a departure from the plein air landscapes typically associated with the Impressionists. I pause in front of Degas's toilettes, Cézanne's bathers, Renoir's nudes. The women's bodies are not overly posed or idealized; at the time, this was a provocation. I look for Mary Cassatt, for Eva Gonzalès, for Berthe Morisot, but I don't find them. Gauguin is here, though, and the plaques beside his paintings of brown-skinned Tahitian women make no mention of his dehumanizing gaze, nor of the pubescent girls he had sex with in Tahiti. Matisse, too, is here, with his 1927 Orientalist fantasy, *Odalisque with Gray Trousers*: "I paint odalisques in order to paint the nude. Otherwise, how is the nude to be painted without being artificial?" In that moment, my body and the bodies of all the women I know are on the wall as sexualized ciphers for the desires of white men. I don't know why I am here in this place where I should feel belonging but am, instead, an outsider. I'm grateful that the Met has little contemporary art. I know all the names, know who will be at the Venice Biennale this year and who was featured in the contemporary art magazines, but I can't imagine my name listed among them. I'm not the only one, of course. The last time I saw one of my male classmates from art school, he consoled me about my artist's block by telling me how few of the girls we studied with were painting anymore. It is one thing to have a body; it is another thing to struggle under the menacing weight of its meaning.

I stop to wash my hands on the way out. The museum's bathroom is decorated with a print of a white woman posed over a clawfoot tub, her belly and breasts perfect pink globes. This is not Impressionism. She turns to regard the viewer at such a severe angle that it's as though the artist has painted, instead of a woman, a porcelain bowl for holding pears.

By the time I get off the subway in Boerum Hill, it's the golden hour. There are no signs of last night's sparrows, just hot pavement and sweating brick. I make the left onto Hoyt from Atlantic and pass the Hoyt Street Garden and the peach stucco of the Iglesia del Cristo Vivo with its yellow sign. At the intersection with Pacific, I nod to the crossing guard in front of the Hopkins Center. I'm one building down from Teta's apartment when I spot the owl feather, white against the green ivy that snakes over the brick posts on either side of Teta's stoop. The tangled down at the base of its hollow shaft and its brown striping give the owl away. The feather is a fat, weightless thing, the tip oiled with soot, the down still warm from the leaves.

Brooklyn simmers in September, when the urine-and-soot stink of the subways sifts up through the sidewalk vents and Atlantic is noisy with restaurant-goers who don't know that hummus is Arabic for chickpeas. While I fumble with my key chain, a white family pushes a stroller down the sidewalk, and the toddler inside reaches for the Swedish ivy bursting from Mrs. King's window boxes. Lately I've been wondering how long Teta will be able to stay in this building. It's the same story in every borough these days: the weekends bring the expensive strollers and the tiny dogs, the couples who comment on how much safer the neighborhood has gotten. Rent goes up and up and up. The family-owned bodegas keep on closing, replaced by artisanal cupcake shops and overpriced organic grocery stores whose customers hurry past the homeless and the flowers laid on street corners for Black boys shot by the cops. Some people go their whole lives in New York shutting their eyes to the fact that this city was built for the people who took this land from the Lenape. Sometimes I wonder why you never spoke of this—maybe you thought I was too young to understand, or you were just desperate to eke out an existence here. Now I am old enough to understand that we live on land that remembers. I hear the voices when I touch the brick or pavement, catch fragments of words exchanged hundreds of years before the island of Manna-hatta was paved. I sometimes think about the Arabs and other im-migrants who came here a century before my own family, hoping they wouldn't be devoured by the bottomless hunger of the very forces that drove them from their homelands, hoping they could survive in this place that was not built for them.

Teta's been baking: the stairwell is perfumed with walnuts and rose water. Inside the apartment, a fresh pan of bitlawah steams on the counter. If I'm honest, no matter how much I long for the apartment I had in Jackson Heights before Teta's back pain got worse and she needed someone to take care of her, I'd miss the smell of her house if I left it. It's just the two of us now, fielding the occasional call from Reem up in Boston. I can't blame my sister for not wanting to be reminded of what we've lost; the gears of memory lock their teeth every time I remember.

I slip off my shoes by the door, allowing the purls of Teta's

Persian carpet to separate my bare toes. Asmahan gets up from the living room couch and stretches, then shakes the sleep from the ruff of fur around her neck. It wasn't long before that horrible day that Asmahan came to us, but Teta and I never stopped calling her your cat.

"Better let the bitlawah sit, habibti," Teta calls to me from her favorite armchair without looking up, "it's hot. Get us a cup of coffee, eh?" The afternoon light catches on the white brow feathers of the scarred old barred owl that sits on the sill watching Teta every evening. Teta meets its gaze, but I pretend not to see.

Asmahan follows me into the kitchen. On my way, I pick up the half-empty plastic cups on the coffee table. Asmahan loves to drink from unattended water glasses, so Teta indulges her by leaving cups of water around the house. Asmahan knocks one over now and then—thus the plastic. The way Teta spoils that cat.

In the kitchen, I retrieve the electric bill and the unpaid rent notice I tucked in the top drawer, fold them, and stuff them in my pocket before Teta sees. I get out the tiny cups you brought with you from Syria when you and Teta came over to the States years ago. The painted blossoms look almost new. I don't know how Teta keeps them so pristine, how she makes sure they don't get dropped or chipped in the cabinet by the plates or the forty mismatched jars of spices we've got knocking around in there. We always make our own spice mixtures, just like the women in our family have been doing for generations. Teta's got everything labeled neatly in Arabic, so those were the first few words I learned how to read. She has her own chai mixes, her own baharat, her own fresh za'atar. She makes them from memory, never measuring anything out, just estimating by the handful or the scoop or the pinch. The mothers and grandmothers of the other Arab kids I knew in school never wrote a recipe down, either; it was something you learned by heart. I'm sure Teta thought you would be around to teach me when I got older. Instead she had to teach me herself.

I fill the long-handled coffeepot with water and add the ground coffee, sugar, fresh-crushed cardamom. Out the window, impending rain hangs like dusk. Asmahan trots over to the kitchen table and hops up. Someone's staring at me from one of the chairs. I don't have to turn to know who it is.

"It's okay, Mom," I say without turning my head. "You don't have to get up."

But you do, and I know you're coming over to me even though I can't hear your footsteps. When I turn, you are gazing out the window with your hands on the countertop. You're always smiling, smiling at everything like there's still too much world to be experienced. I let the ring of electric coolness that surrounds you raise the black hairs on my arms, wishing, as I do every time, for some sign that you are real: a touch, a sound, a shadow. Instead the scent of fresh thyme fills my mouth as though you're holding a clipping under my nose, and I want to cry. You turn your head and smile at me. I smile back in the tired way the living have of appeasing the dead. How are you supposed to smile at a ghost without feeling lonely?

The coffee froths up, and you wait while I pour off the froth into our cups. You reach down and offer your hand for Asmahan to sniff. I almost put out three cups instead of two.

"You've been around more often," I say, turning my face as though I expect the scent of thyme to weaken. It doesn't. "Summer must be getting on."

You look at me—that stricken look. This is our agreement: we don't talk about the night of the fire, not even as its anniversary hurtles toward us like a planet and you continue your wordless visitations. Every year, the end of summer is the same. You'll come in the morning and sit in your favorite kitchen chair, the one you always used to sit in when Teta had us over for dinner. Teta can't cook like she used to, so I'll be in the kitchen, bringing her spices or making sure the onions don't burn. It's been four—damn, five years ago now—since we lost you, and nothing has tasted the same since. You'll watch me cook, watch me clean or read or make coffee for everyone but you. Sometimes you'll lean in close to my ear, and the earthen smell of thyme will offer up the names of things in Arabic to me, calling the coffee *ahweh* and the oil *zeit*, and in this strange and silent way we'll talk until it gets dark and you disappear.

The coffee froths up the second time. I shut off the gas range and pour it out into your tiny cups, gentle so as not to slosh them and disturb the grounds. I leave the coffeepot on the burner, avoiding our reflections in the window above the sink. You consider the long handle and the dark liquid in the pot like you want to join us.

"Yalla," I say, beckoning with my eyebrows toward the living room. It's no use: outside, dark has fallen. Teta coughs, and Asmahan trots toward her between my legs. When I look up, you're gone. In your place is that scent of fresh thyme, the kind you used to grow on the fire escape to make za'atar from memory.

I bring the coffee and a diamond of bitlawah to Teta in the living room, setting it on the table beside her armchair. She's fallen asleep with her favorite blanket folded on her lap, a lavender underscarf wrapped around her head like she always wears in the house, even though we don't get visitors anymore. She winces and opens her eyes, and I help her sit upright in her chair, arranging the pillows behind the small of her back and her shawl around her shoulders. It's been a few years since her multiple myeloma went into remission, but she never regained the bone density she lost, and her back is a knot of constant pain.

"Keef halik, Teta?"

"Alhamdulillah." She squeezes my hand. "Sit, sit. I never see you sleep anymore. Where you go all night?"

I kiss her papery forehead. "Let me get the heating pad."

When I come back, Teta's nodded off again with the coffee in her hand. I set it on the table, but my hand slips trying not to wake her, and it spills on my jeans. The cup clatters back onto its dish.

"Storm of the storms!" Teta exclaims while I curse under my breath and wipe myself with a napkin. She's been calling me that ever since I broke one of her teacups as a kid. She must have heard it on the news at some point, *storm of storms*, maybe. Somehow it journeyed through Arabic and was resurrected as *storm of the storms*, and now my clumsiness has its own nickname. Teta means it lovingly, but my face burns. I inspect the cup for chips.

When I slide the heating pad behind her, Teta furrows her brow at me. I bend forward, a force of habit, and hope my loose tee hides the fact that I'm using the shapewear she gave me to flatten my chest, rather than smooth the belly and hips Teta thinks I'm self-conscious of. I take a breath, and the cloth pulls across my ribs. This, too, is a border I am transgressing. Last week, I slashed the polyester at the rib cage to flatten the passengers on my chest that hide the surface of me. I have not told Teta this. I wouldn't know where to begin.

"Hope I didn't wake you banging around in the kitchen," I say before she can question me again. I sit down across from her on the sofa, a gorgeous old Damascene thing with a wooden frame and rolled arm pillows whose damask patterns have long since faded into gold and burgundy splotches, an heirloom from the bilad.

Teta holds my eyes for half a second before glancing away out the window. She laughs, shifting her back against the heating pad. "I sleep heavy these days."

There's no way she didn't hear me talking to you, but this is the response I expect. Though we both see you, we never admit it. You are first on the list of things we don't talk about, questions we don't ask, ghosts we don't count. I've never told her about the others, but I know she's seen you.

The envelopes in my pocket crinkle when I cross my ankle over my knee. This is the second thing we do not speak of: money. I'm Teta's only caretaker now, the one who pays the bills and the rent, and though Teta often tries to write out checks for birthdays or for food shopping, both our savings are dwindling. It's an ugly thing, but your social security only goes so far for two people in the city. Teta and I have reversed roles now; when you and my father were still together, she changed my diapers and babysat me until you both came home from work. She cooked meals for us, took me to the playground, quit her odd jobs when the family needed her. Now, long after your divorce, after your death, after my father has stopped even feigning promises of help, I've done the same. Though we both thank God for the Medicare that covers the bulk of Teta's medical bills, we are still paying off the cost of chemo and radiation a year later. I scold myself for it, but I've begun to hope Reem will start helping out now that she's finally taken a corporate job, though I know Teta's pride would never allow her to accept Reem's money. Here in this city whose lifeblood is the dollar, our solution to its weight is silence. It's not that Teta doesn't think about money—that's a privilege our family will never know—but to discuss her anxieties with me would be 'ayb. It would be a mark of shame; she'd feel like she'd failed me. The children and grand-children of "real Americans," the ones who made it, shouldn't need to fear poverty. But Teta has found walls in this country that she never could have imagined.

I drain my demitasse and roll the warm ceramic between my hands. I'm sitting in that way you used to correct me for, legs spread like a boy, elbows on my knees, leaning forward so my hair drops in my eyes. I clear my throat and try to draw myself up, mussing my hair out of my face, but the movements are wrong. They are always wrong: my elephant feet, my way of closing cabinets with a bang, my bad posture. Do you see? I've memorized even your comments that used to drive me crazy.

"Mom would've been fifty-five this year." I glance up to meet Teta's eyes. "Wouldn't she?"

Teta sets the half-empty cup of coffee on the side table and folds her thick arms over the blanket in her lap. She shifts her weight forward and then back, rivulets of pain cabling her face until she settles into the heating pad. "It was beautiful, the day, until the rain."

The cup in my hands yields its heat to my palms. "Beautiful."

"When I was young," Teta says, and a smile sneaks onto her face, "we used to stay inside and play tawleh when came the rain. My father, Allah yarhamu, when he was alive, all the men in our town used to come to our family café to smoke arghile and talk politics. Immi kept the coffee hot all day. When it rained the men start to come, until we had the place full."

I want to ask her how my great-grandfather died, but it is one of the stories Teta has never told me, one of the many she keeps in her locked trunk of memories. His death, too, is on the list of things we don't discuss. "How old were you when he passed away?"

"Seventeen," she says, and then she drains her coffee and falls silent.

It's no use. The television drones from the corner, too low to be heard. "Tell me again about the bicycle woman." I look up from the sludge of coffee grounds at the bottom of my cup. "The one who flew."

Teta perks up in her chair. She's always preferred to tell fantastical stories rather than recount the past, and this is one of her favorites, a fail-safe. The first time she told it to me was after Jiddo died. In that first version, Teta spoke of a woman in her village in Syria who built a flying machine out of a bicycle and two sets of linen wings. She peddled hard to gain speed, then hit a ridge and became airborne for a quarter mile before crashing in a field outside the village. The story didn't bring me any comfort then, but it felt real, and I never quite believed the version she told after that, the one where the woman on the bicycle escaped gravity, never to be seen again. As a kid, it was more comforting to imagine this woman ending up somewhere warm and colorful, like San Francisco or Miami, but it was too easy an ending. Teta never said where the story came from. I knew better than to ask.

"It was my friend saw her go up into the air," Teta says when she's finished recounting the story. She's told it so many times I could probably relate it by heart. "No one else in the village thought she could do it. Immi kept me home that day, but I heard every detail. We were all of us amazed." She ends with the same bewildered shake of her head and a reminder to believe in the un-believable.

"They called her Majnouna," she says, wagging her finger.

"I know, Teta. The crazy woman." I take our cups and pat her hand. She is cold, has always been that way, and her circulation has gotten worse these past few months. This, too, the myeloma took from her. We don't get much sun in this western-facing apartment, and the nights are starting to turn cool. I've told Teta a thousand times to turn the heat on at night to keep her blood flowing, but she knows how much it costs. In the winter, it will be worse.

I smile to keep Teta from reading all this on my face. "If Asmahan starts drinking our coffee, Majnouna will be the least of our worries."

After I get up, Teta clears her throat and calls out to my back, "Fifty-four." When I turn to her, she directs her eyes to her hands. "November," she says, "she would be fifty-four."

I retreat to my room. Your presence is still here, everywhere, your hand on everything. The photo albums I saved, stuffed with pictures, my first days of ninth grade and high school graduation, shots of you braiding my wet hair before bedtime and making goofy faces at the camera. An old, half-empty bag of henna powder in a ziplock bag, the last one you used to make my hair soft and shiny. Your prayer rug that I keep in a place of honor, draped over the bench that sat in front of your worktable where you kept your bird-watching supplies and journals. You always said you'd replace the scarred worktable someday, but here it is, covered in your stray pen marks and smears of acrylic paint. It's cluttered with the books that were in your study when you died—bird-watching manuals, Audubon's *Birds of America*, a few Arabic ornithology texts I can only read the short sentences of. Everything I know of birds, I learned from you. When you were gone, I learned from these pages turned by your hands. These books taught me the names of birds in Arabic, things you must have thought you'd have time to explain. Your last sketchbook sits in the corner, a couple of your colored pencils still lodged inside as a bookmark, deforming the binding. I remove a pencil, and a photograph slips out onto the floor. It's the two of us posing in front of my elementary school door: me in patent-leather Mary Janes and a polka-dotted dress you'd picked out for me, you with that unguarded grin that showed your gums, your arm pressing me to you as though you could fuse us forever.

When you came with me to first-grade parent-teacher night, I was so excited to have you meet my teacher that I'd begged a friend's dad to take this picture beforehand. You'd somehow gotten the money together for a private school. You wore your best silk blouse that evening and dressed me in a new outfit, hoping we'd both make a good impression. I had the sense, without being able to name it, that we didn't quite belong. We arranged ourselves in front of the school's wooden door, me tugging down my hideous dress while you laughed and hugged me to you, my shoulder curving into the space above your hip. We held the pose while my friend's dad fumbled with the camera. We pressed into each other with the rise and fall of your breath. Then came the flash, blinding.

I tugged you inside, the warm stripe of your touch still painted on my shoulder. Mrs. Wilson greeted us at the classroom door, the blackboard free of chalk and her can of pencils still full, a pristine leather handbag perched on her desk. Then Mrs. Wilson's face twisted into shock, and when you started to speak, my teacher frowned and leaned in as though she couldn't understand your accent. She forced a smile, looking from me to you and back again.

"It's lovely to meet you," Mrs. Wilson said. "But I was expecting— well. It's only that she looks so—"

My fingers twitched in yours, our knuckles interlocked. You pursed your lips and knit your brows. Mrs. Wilson pushed her chin forward above my head and raised her voice, taking your unease for a lack of understanding.

"She must look more like her father," Mrs. Wilson said, slowing and separating her syllables. "You understand?"

I dropped my eyes to the floor. You tensed and shifted your thumb against my hand, the nail scraping my skin like nicked leather.

Then you smiled without parting your lips. "A colleague told me that once," you said in smooth English, "when she saw the picture of us in my office, next to my master's diploma." Then you squeezed my hand and steered us away.

You said nothing more of Mrs. Wilson that day. You shut the door that night when you ran the water for your bath, and I laid my head on the wood. I listened for the squeak of the faucet turning off and wished I never had to leave this little studio apartment again, tried to imagine a home where other people's words couldn't separate us as cleanly as any wall.

I run my fingers over the burnished pine. I vowed I'd paint at this table after that day half a decade ago now, to honor your memory. But the sight of it made Teta cry, and I couldn't paint at all when I sat down at it. Our sadness had seeped into the wood. Soon I couldn't paint anywhere else, either. I'd just graduated art school when you died, but your death rendered all those years of planning useless. Art school had kept me away from home in what turned out to be the last years of your life, and though people told me not to blame myself, a dark thought took root: that painting itself had separated us. Every time I lifted a brush, the undertow of my guilt tugged me down. The following year, Teta fractured a vertebra pulling thistles from around your grave, and we discovered multiple myeloma had made her bones weak. Still, I nearly had to confine her to the apartment to keep her from returning to her gardening: she was adamant that the thistles were choking the roots of her roses. It turns out that even when you plant roses, sometimes thistles come up instead.

Asmahan tangles herself between my ankles, the walls tighten with grief, and your memory threatens like rain. That burning stench begins to rise from the nails, from the carpets, from the floorboards, summoning the one moment I refuse to remember. I drag my fingers over the worktable, and the black scars of fire spring up across the burls in the wood, as though even the lightest touch of the living is enough to scorch the dead.

I throw on my canvas jacket and my Converse. "Yalla bye, cutie." I rub Asmahan's chin, trying to make my voice upbeat. "Back in a few."

On the way out, Teta's gentle snoring follows me from her bedroom. As I shut the front door, I turn the knob so it doesn't click.

It's because of your textbooks that I know so many birds by their Arabic names. Sometimes it takes a minute for the English to come, and other times it doesn't come at all. There is no nightingale among my index of birds, only the bulbul; in Farid ad-Din Attar's Sufi poems, Solomon's confidante is called not the hoopoe but the hudhud, crowned by the other birds to lead them to the legendary Simorgh. Many of these birds I grew up naming without seeing. The cinnamon-colored hudhud with its crown of feathers, for example, isn't typically found in North America, but the books you left behind taught me that the European and north Asian subspecies migrate across the Mediterranean to breed, and once, after reading about the hudhud's migratory flights over the Himalayas, I dreamed of a flock of thirty birds emerging from a cloud bank, the gold of them as real as any photograph.

I walk down to the Barclays Center and take the R toward Manhattan to Rector Street, then walk down to the tenement building at 109 Washington, where I've been working on a mural of a hudhud of my own. I avoid the gauntlet of catcallers near the subway exit, crossing the street to avoid a man who shouts repeatedly for my name, then my tits. The main thing, I have learned after more than a quarter century in this body and this city, is to keep moving.

The lower West Side, especially near the 9/11 Memorial Museum and One World Trade Center, is crowded with souvenir shops, cafés, and bars these days. A couple blocks down from the new bone-white Oculus transportation hub, the new hotels stop and old brick buildings begin. The transition feels stark and surreal. What used to be a neighborhood of tenements inhabited mostly by Syrian immigrants is now nearly obliterated, much of it lost to eminent domain and the demolition that cleared the way for the Brooklyn–Battery Tunnel in the forties. The rest was brought down for the construction of the World Trade Center two decades later. Most of the inhabitants were forced out to Brooklyn's Atlantic Avenue, others to New Jersey, Ohio, Michigan, and beyond. The only exceptions are this five-story tenement, still occupied and sporting a new restaurant on the ground level, and the community house connected to it, empty for years and recently condemned. The local historical society has been trying to get them declared landmark sites or a historic district for years, but with the exception of St. George's Syrian Catholic Church, the white terra-cotta chapel next to the community house, they haven't been successful, and the inside of the church is now home to an Irish pub. Eventually, these buildings, too, will probably be swallowed by the pace of development in Lower Manhattan. Despite all the work you did to try to save them, the history they represent has never been deemed worthy of protecting.

The bars around the corner are filling with twentysomething finance-sector employees beginning loud rounds of beer pong. I leave the sidewalk and stalk through the empty lot next to the tenement and around to the back of the building. Back in the thirties and forties, this empty lot held a front and back tenement separated by a sliver of courtyard that functioned as an airshaft, providing ventilation and light to the two cramped buildings. The back building had already been demolished for years by the time you tried to save the front one, the older and more beautiful of the two tenements on the block; what a waste it seems now. That second tenement, too, was pulled down just a year after you died. The scarred brick of the building next door and a weed-infested lot are all that's left of your fight, a flattened piece of earth awaiting the construction of another high-rise hotel.

You'd laugh at the way I look everywhere for reminders of you—even in the old community house, I still check the locks and try to get up the courage to slip inside. I haven't succeeded yet. Maybe it's for the best; though I've scoured newspapers and art history books about the painter you loved who used to live here, Laila Z has always remained obscure, reduced to a line I once found in an article about how she lived for a while on the fifth floor of the community house doing social work and providing "cultural activities" for recent immigrants, one of the few decent jobs a woman could get in those days.

I've never dared to break in and look for signs of Laila Z's presence. Tonight, like all the other nights I've come down here, I settle for the satisfaction of paint on brick. I pull out my chalk and sketch the next area of the mural I want to get done, the hudhud's black-and-orange crown. I wind my bird around old spray-painted tags and crumbling, gouged wall. I know the risks, but it's the only way I can paint anymore, the only time I'm not blocked. It's my way of reminding this neighborhood of its past.

I miss the city I knew as a child: the subway cars graffitied down to the last inch of wall or door, the rank phone booths, cigarette butts at the sidewalk edges, kids running through the fountains in Central Park in the summertime or dancing in the rainbows of busted fire hydrants. That Manhattan is invisible now, a city that lives only in the memories of those of us who were there.

Time slows down when I'm painting. I read that article you gave me back when I still said I wanted to go to MIT and major in physics—trying to be a good first-generation child—on the state of flow, how a person is supposed to know what they love to do by how time blurs when they're doing it. The problem, I guess, is that time has always been blurry for me. Maybe that's why I made such a lousy physics student. I learned a long time ago that things that happened years ago never really go away. They live in the body, secreted away inside liver and fingernail and bone, alive on street corners and in wallpaper glue and the yellowed water in Brooklyn basements.

I stroke my brush against the brick, and its memories rise to meet me: years of car exhaust, and beneath the soot, decades of chicken fat and frying onions, the clang of a cracked cast-iron pan being flung out a window, a girl's happy shriek, the purple-black curl of a scab being tugged off a knee.

You were the one who first brought me down here as a child and told me there was a whole community here years ago, a Syrian enclave that doesn't exist anymore, scattered across the country from Brooklyn to LA when Little Syria was demolished to build the entrance ramps for the Brooklyn–Battery Tunnel. I used to think there was some secret here, something that drew you to these buildings, some collective memory I could include myself in. That's why I chose Washington Street to paint on, even though you and

Teta came to the States twenty years after it had been leveled. I'm addicted to the memories that live on in the mind of New York, the flood that comes when I place my hand on a wall or a window or a stoop, the knowledge that death and time are both illusions because we and every stone are made of the same ever-shifting particles. If we live, it's only because some distant galaxy lent us its dust for a while. Ghosts are more honest than the rest of us: they can't help but be what they are. You taught me that revelation has its price in a world that prefers the comfort of closed eyes. Maybe that's why I'm still convinced that the painter you loved left an echo of herself behind here, waiting to be heard.

A soundless shape glides by over my head. Pricks of cold air rise on my skin. You were the one who first showed me, when we found that disembodied snowy owl wing hiking upstate one winter, how owls' feathers make no sound when they cut the air.

I pack my paints and follow the bird back around the building and out to the street. A whisper of feathers, and the owl lands on the lintel above the community house door, its arrival ruffling scraps of posted paper. There's no mistaking: it's the scarred owl that visits Teta's windowsill each day—there are the shorn feathers on the left wing, the white brow. The owl gives a slow blink to the streetlight and peers down at the door, the dull green of a neon bar sign reflected on its talons. There are new notices posted on the front door today. I finger the corner of one stapled page, the illegible signature of some inspector at the bottom, and for a second, the presence of the owl gives me a strange sort of courage. Up the stairs to the fifth floor—what harm could it do to have a look? I touch the door.

It's unlocked.

It swings inward when I press on it, revealing nothing but dark. There is a chaos of wings at my cheek, and I duck to cover my face as the owl dives inside.

I fumble in my pocket for my phone and use it as a light.

Scraps of old paper and crumbs of ceiling tiles litter the floor inside the foyer, and my feet scuff stained tile. This community house has been empty for years, but at one time it was a rich resource with a health center, space for musical productions and plays, classrooms, a food pantry. Now, it's hard to imagine the life these rooms once held. I sweep the light of my phone toward the back and discover a narrow staircase leading up into the belly of the second floor.

The owl has disappeared into the darkness. I tiptoe toward the stairs. The floorboards groan and sag under my feet, but they hold. The stairwell stinks of ancient wallpaper paste and lead paint. The rooms on the second, third, and fourth floors hold overturned desks and rusted bedframes, wallpaper slashed from corner to corner, old filing cabinets with their drawers pulled out by looters or squatters. On the fifth floor, the empty socket of a light bulb greets me in what was once a living room, the plaster now flaked down to bare brick.

The old bedroom walls are covered with peeling wallpaper that probably used to be orange, now a rusted, water-stained goldenrod. A lace doily that must have once covered the upended desk lies wrinkled on the floor, decorated by the red carapace of a dead cockroach. The matching curtains have all but disintegrated, as though they'd turn to dust if I touched them. The desk's single drawer has been jammed shut by years of Manhattan humidity, and a candle burned down to a stump has slid off the surface of the desk onto the floor, leaving a ring of wax on the wood. The wallpaper bulges and sags on one wall of the room, near the carcass of a twin bedframe. I peer closer—the peeling corner of the wallpaper is trembling. A puff of air escapes a slot in the wall formed by two missing bricks that must have been papered over at one time, revealing a rectangular cavity, a hidden shelf.

I brush my fingers along the inside of the opening, and they come away filmy with cobwebs. I squeeze my eyes shut and reach in. My fingers brush something firm and soft, and when I open my eyes, I've slid a leather-bound notebook out of the hidden compartment.

The spine creaks as I open it to a sketch of a little yellow bird, a woman's shaky handwriting on the facing page. It must be some artist's old nature journal, each illustration accompanied by a diary entry. A black-and-white photo slips out of a young woman, her black hair in braids. Behind the photo is a watercolor painting of a bird with a frill of white feathers at his chin—a white-throated sparrow.

I slip the notebook into my backpack and shut the papered door on my way out. On my subway ride back to Teta's, I study the photograph inside the front cover of the notebook. In the light of the subway car, the subject looks a bit like Teta when she was a girl. The young painter has her black hair over each shoulder, her strong chin raised, her eyes dark and hooded, her eyebrows thick with a soft unibrow. She and Teta could be sisters.

I turn back to that first sketch. It's signed in Arabic, bold and rising to the left: Laila. ليلى The ink is blotched on the final curve of the last letter, the alif maqsurah, leaving a smudged black mark. Later on, the signatures switch to English, and the handwriting gets smoother and smaller. When I was young, I, too, used to hoard my Arabic name like a treasure, trying to convince myself that this name, too, existed.

On the page that faces the watercolor sparrow, Laila Z's notebook begins: *The day I began to bleed was the day I met the woman who built the flying machine—*

TWO / LAILA

DEAREST B▓▓▓▓▓,

The day I began to bleed was the day I met the woman who built the flying machine. My mother would say this isn't a seemly way to begin a journal—she would prefer a list of mundane tasks, I'm sure, or news of visiting friends, or gratitude for the fact that our family has survived the hunger that has overtaken the city since the stock market crash. But Khalto Tala told me I should use these pages to write down the truest things I know of myself, and anyway, since no one else will ever read them—and I can't imagine why anyone would—then I suppose I'm free to say what I really feel, which means I can write to any audience I please, real or imaginary. That's why I'm addressing this diary to you, B. You're the only one I can imagine reading my secret thoughts over my shoulder. No matter that it's too late now to tell you all this; never mind the thousands of miles of ocean between us. Here, in this notebook, I can call you back into my mind and write the words I'd never dare to say.

Until I met you, I had few friends. Back in the days when I knew you in Syria, my mother was beloved by everyone. Both the village midwife and dresser of the dead, she walked hand in hand with the shadow world, and the otherworldly became my constant companion. I played by myself in the fields, tracing the golden line of the steppe. Beyond were the ancient pillars and temples of Tadmor, the Bride of the Desert. It was on this desert road that the Bedouins sometimes approached our village to sell wool or livestock, though they came less often in those days than when I was small. On the day I began to bleed, I thought I'd grown beyond the age when magic approaches from the corner of one's eye.

There, at the edge of the world I knew, I met a woman from my village who loved winged creatures more than people. To my mind there wasn't anything strange about this, though our neighbors regarded her as quite the oddity. I came to learn her name was Hawa, like the first woman, and that she was building a flying machine.

Amongst themselves, our neighbors whispered about her and called her Majnouna. My mother's friends gossiped about her flying machine as they picked pebbles from the freekeh one afternoon. I began to watch her while my mother was out delivering babies. Those who saw me returning to the village laughed and warned me away, but day after day, I went out into the fields to watch Hawa gather her materials. She built the double wings and the body of the machine first, then added the two wheels and the two rows of fabric draped across its back.

I never spoke to her until after her fateful flight. That was the day of the blood. Though my mother would have been ecstatic, I hid it. I didn't want to tell her, maybe for fear she'd keep me home that day; or maybe it was the fear of what else it would mean, the new things I'd have to learn as a woman, the vague fear I had of marriage, the feeling that something was ending and would never come again.

The whole village came out to watch the spectacle of Hawa's flight—all but my mother, who had been called away a few hours earlier by a neighbor whose wife had gone into labor with her first child. Though the baby shouldn't come until after sundown, my mother said, the woman was nervous, and her husband insisted she come.

For my part, I was thrilled. I rushed out to the edge of the village. A crowd had gathered, a circle with Hawa at its center. Her flying machine was an ungainly contraption with pedals and wheels and adjustable wings, little more than linen stretched over wooden broom handles. People whispered that it was a strange amalgamation of a bird and a bicycle. I was the only one who believed she could fly. To me, Hawa's linen wings looked like God's angels.

Hawa pedaled hard, gaining ground and speed. As her path diverged from the crowd, I lost sight of her. I ran along behind her until I escaped the crush of people. By the time I caught sight of her again, she had reached the crest of a small ridge, and then she was airborne. The crowd went silent and stopped their taunting. No one followed her. The village whispered prayers and murmured fearful things.

Only I followed. I tracked Hawa overhead, into the fields. When I looked back, the crowd and the village were far behind us, nearly out of sight. Hawa's wings held; I held my breath. Her shadow rushed over me. She hadn't gained much height, but she was in the air, and that, I thought, counted as a miracle.

Because of my faith in her, I was the only one to witness her death. It began with an upward gust of air. Her wings wobbled, then dipped. The linen tore and separated from the wood. She didn't cry out as she fell, only angled her body toward the earth, smiling as though she were going to meet an old friend.

I rushed to her, but I didn't have my mother's skill at dressing wounds and setting bones. I cried out for help. We were too far for anyone to hear.

Before I could rise and run to get someone, Hawa gripped my wrist. "Allah calls to his daughter," she told me, "and soon I must go to Him." These are the only words of hers I can remember now. Time has reduced the rest to the mist of dreams. Hawa pressed my hand to her chest and related to me startling things, visions that had been revealed to her before she hit the earth, wonderful and monstrous events that were to come: dark clouds, rippling flocks of shadows, winged flashes of light.

"But madame," I said, for what she had told me had disturbed me, and I was afraid, "are these visions of blessing, or a curse?"

Hawa did not answer. Above us, the gray kites drifted into the south. Hawa's eyes fixed themselves on the sky. I closed them each with a finger.

I treasured up her words as I returned home. My mother met me along the way, coming from her delivery. She was early, but I kept my curiosity to myself. I told her Hawa's flight had ended in tragedy, but kept quiet about the visions she'd related. I was sure she'd be sorely angry with me for following Hawa into the fields, but she said nothing. At first I was relieved that she was too tired to chastise me. But as the first shadows fell over our faces, the fading light caught my mother's skirts, marred with blood. Then I began to fear her silence. I asked her, as I was accustomed after a delivery, whether the baby was a little boy or a little girl. My mother bit her lip.

"Ya 'albi." She called me "her heart" only when she was overjoyed or gravely sad, and I knew then without having to ask that neither mother nor baby had survived. "The night falls over all of us the same," she said, "but also the light, praise God."

When I was born, my mother named me Laila so I would not fear the night. "Allah, in His infinite wisdom," she used to say, "has created the darkness to remind us that He has given us the light."

But in truth, I have always been afraid of the night and the doubt it brings. When we arrived in Amrika and I picked up a paintbrush for the first time, I was sick with terror, and more than terror, guilt. Who was I to pick up a brush and freeze the soul of something, knowing the world was ever-changing and nothing would appear this way again? Even a piece of fruit ages and dies, and there I was, trying to capture a robin or a hummingbird, seizing time in one hand.

Months have passed since I wrote here about Hawa. I sketch more birds than I write these days, maybe because I've never been one to raise my voice or speak my mind. But if I fill this book with drawings and say nothing of myself, I fear I won't recognize my own hand when the colors have dried. So as I set out with my paints and these pages, I will write down where I come from. And to keep the fear at bay, I will imagine you here again before me, little wing, and this time I will tell you everything.

Let me start over. I was born on a sunny day in early March of 1920, the day Emir Faysal declared Syria to be an independent Arab state, in a village not far from Homs. You never knew my birthday, did you? My mother tells me my grandmother took all the flour and oil and clarified butter in the pantry, went down to the butcher, and had a lamb slaughtered. She gathered all the women of the village together—for in the bilad my mother and her family knew everyone; my mother had delivered every last one of their children—and together they baked bread and kibbeh and prepared huge trays of kunafeh while the men drank ara' and danced the dabke as though it were a wedding. All this celebration was for Syria, not for my birth, though my mother always says the rejoicing and zagharit went to my head.

The French saw to it that the young kingdom didn't last six months. When the French army took Damascus in July of that same year after a ten-day siege, my father's textile business took a sharp downward turn. My mother's milk dried up. But I was the kind of child who struggles, and my mother had already birthed two other children, twins who would have been my older brothers. George had died of pneumonia in childhood, but God had spared my brother Issa. I grew up to be a skinny, scab-kneed girl with teeth too large for my mouth, and for years Issa would tease me that I had gnawed my way out of death's grasp, until well into adolescence when my features had balanced themselves and I had gained some plumpness in my cheeks.

You knew my mother as a wise woman, the kind of woman who would listen to anyone with a problem, who always had coffee in the house to serve a grieving family who had lost a loved one in the night and enough flour and ghee to make a tray of bitlawah for the celebration of a birth. She was the keeper of life and death. Her face, creased by years and by the sun, was the first thing most people had ever seen—and the last. People recognized her at once, even children who met her for the first time. The elderly and ailing, those who had lost the ability to recognize even their own loved ones, still knew her. Perhaps it was this mystical power that set her apart from the other women; perhaps it was this that separated her from me. For as long as I have been her daughter, my mother has been the loneliest woman I have ever known.

My mother used to say her loneliness arrived with the locusts. She said they came as a dark storm from the heavens, descending upon the crops until they had eaten every fig to its stem, devoured the bark from every olive tree, and reduced the fields of wheat to dust and a fearful hum. This was during the Great War, before my parents met; you would not have been born yet, ya ayni. The Ottoman armies had begun conscripting Christian men in those days, stocking their ranks with my mother's brother and father, with uncles and husbands and neighbors' sons. Throughout the province of Syria, particularly in Mount Lebanon, people suffered from the taxes and from the famine that followed the locusts. In those days families had little, and what little they had stored up for hard times was quickly depleted. My grandfather, already ancient, stopped eating so that his remaining children would not go hungry.

The way my mother tells the story, she had only just started out on her own as a midwife when the famine began. In those dark days, weeks went by with more miscarriages than births. Those who had been ill when disaster struck succumbed to their illnesses. Friends and relatives began to disappear, either leaving for Beirut or Tripoli or vanishing into their hunger. At first the women mourned their dead, wailing as the funeral processions went by. But as time went on, all became too weak with hunger and too crushed by loss to wail.

The war had taken more from my mother's village than it could bear. And so when news arrived of an Arab uprising against the Ottomans, the village rejoiced. Some of the young men spoke of joining the revolt. If you ask my mother, she will tell you that my father, then a scrawny young man prone to philosophizing, declared one day that he was going to join the fighting. They barely knew each other then, though my father had a reputation for lofty political ideas and larger-than-life stories. He was laughed at by the other boys his age, and my mother, too, scoffed at his outlandish promises. But when he vanished one morning, the mothers murmured that he had finally made good on his promise.

He didn't make it out of the province before the sound of warplanes sent him running down a hill to hide in the brush of the nearest orchard. The planes passed overhead without incident, but my young father tripped on a root and went sprawling head over knees down the hill, breaking his leg. He was promptly returned to the village by a passerby, where word spread that he had survived an air raid, though this was only partially true. Soon, the story became more and more embellished by the village youth, who quickly claimed—despite my father's halfhearted protestations—that he had been attacked by a dozen or more men and fought them off himself, that he had popped out one of their eyes with a branch, that he kept the dried eyeball like a desiccated persimmon under his bed. By the time the Arabs took Dera'a and then Damascus, my father had become a local hero without ever lifting a weapon, and because my mother had taken a liking to teasing him about the absurd tales of his misadventure, when he asked her to marry him, she said yes.

But despite the promises of the Allied powers and Emir Faysal's declaration, France and Britain divided up our land according to their whims, and my father grew sullen and jaded. The failure of independence had broken something in him, my mother used to say, and he was never the same hopeful, rambling intellectual after that, with his big plans and uncompromising ideals. He settled into my grandfather's textile business and became resentful of the revolution that had failed his hopes, resentful of the world that had disappointed him.

Five years later, the smallpox came. The epidemic arrived in the spring and was followed by an ill-timed drought. My mother buried many infants and children who succumbed to the disease, and she quarantined me to the house for most of the spring and summer, healthy and forlorn. Our neighbors began to flee disease and lack of water, until it was clear there would not be enough people to harvest even a meager crop.

I had just turned five. The scent of lightning was thick in the air when we received word from the Bedu elders that Sultan Pasha al-Atrash had declared revolution against France in Jebel ad-Druze. The Druze revolt grew in strength, until many cities were in open rebellion, and sympathy for the rebel cause began to grow in Homs and Hama and, finally, in our village.

Do you have any memory of those years, little wing? Perhaps

you were too young to remember them. We were lucky; our village was of little importance to the French, so we were spared the violence France rained on Hama from the air. The aerial bombardment reached us when my father's business suffered, though, and when the French cut back Abu Rayan's orchards to prevent ambushes.

On the first of October of that year, my father set down a bite of bread and lentils at supper and announced that he intended to join his kin in Hama in the fight against the French. My mother told him he was a lunatic, that he had two small children to support, that we would starve if he were lost. My father accused my mother of her disbelief in his ideals, and she accused him of being naive. To this day, this was the bitterest fight my parents have ever had.

My father left that night, dissolving into the dark with only a goat-hair jacket and a bag of bread and dates. We would not hear from him for eight days. The fighting lasted only four, but it was dire. The French, who had few troops in Syria, brought in additional forces from Morocco and Senegal to quell the uprising, and surprised the rebels. The revolt in Hama was over. Preparations were made to bury the dead.

When we did not hear from my father after six days, my mother began to fear the worst. She became frantic, searching the orchards at night for survivors who had been missed. Still, there was nothing. After a week, Imm Rayan, who lived next door, tried to console my mother with herbal teas and the revolutionary songs my father loved to sing, but my mother was in too tight a knot. My mother opened her mouth to scream in frustration when, to everyone's shock, the door opened and my father fell into the foyer.

After we had cleaned the scratches on his legs and arms and given him a little ara' against the pain, my mother spread old linens on the good couch and set him down in the sitting room, demanding he tell her what had happened.

My father had cheated death a second time. Senegalese mercenaries under French command had surprised them in the orchards, and the Hamawi forces had run this way and that, afraid to fire on their countrymen amid the trees and the dark. Two bullets grazed my father in the confusion, impossible to say whose. One bullet had torn a line of flesh from his back, and another had taken a chunk of his ear. Bleeding and stunned, he had stumbled in the dark and struck his head on a stone. He'd lain in the brush like a dead man for the remainder of the battle, too weak and confused to rise. When he finally came to, the fighting was over, and he'd crawled his way to the closest house, where a sympathetic widow had cleaned and dressed the wound on his ear. The damage to his spine was harder to remedy. He had lost the use of one of his legs, to which most of the nerves had been severed, and would walk with the aid of a cane for the rest of his life.

The season of my father's political idealism was over, and with it, Hama's revolt. Merchants stopped coming to our village for a time, and trade nearly ceased. A pervasive sadness filled the streets and the homes of my neighbors, a hopelessness that made people whisper again about leaving. They spoke of relatives who had gone to Amrika and come back to build houses, sons who sent good money home, a cousin here or there who had decided to stay and make a life where there was a good living to be made. Why were we here when our sons were reaping their harvests elsewhere? Though Amrika had begun to close her doors to immigrants from outside Europe the year before, children were occasionally able to bring their parents or their siblings to join them, and hopes were high that the measure would be reversed. Perhaps there was a way, they said, and even my father spoke of such things when he thought my brother and I weren't listening. When he began to talk of abandoning not only his business and his village but also his country, I knew my father had lost all hope.

Years went by like this, my father withdrawing into himself, business dwindling, the young and the strong being drained from the villages to find work elsewhere. On one particular evening, I lay awake as my mother mended clothing by the window. We'd gone to bed hungry again; my father hadn't sold anything in weeks, and my mother had served us the same watery lentil soup from the night before. An owl had come to roost in the tree in our garden, and it called out into the falling evening. Beyond the window, the orchards outside of Hama were visible against the sky. My father shut the window; he could not take the owl's cries. He used to say they were the spirits of those who had died unjustly, haunting the living.

"Come now," my mother said to my father. "Do you believe such things?"

"I've seen many things I would not have once believed."

My mother set down her sewing and scolded my father that he was lucky to be alive. Though she raised her voice, I pretended to sleep.

"You have your life and two healthy children. Can't you be happy with that?"

My father breathed in through his nose. The night lay still, uninterrupted by the usual sounds of evening, the happy noises I'd once heard: the neighbors in their gardens, telling stories, laughing over glasses of ara' or cups of coffee. There were no such sounds from our neighbors now. Imm Rayan and her husband had left to join their son in Amrika, leaving the house to a cousin in Aleppo. The village had taken on a brooding quiet.

The owl sent its mourning cries into the dark. My father looked up from his account books. He fixed his gaze out the window on the empty house next door and said nothing, and I knew then that there was more than one way to imprison a man.

Little wing,

Today Khalto Tala snuck me away after my chores were done and took me to see a talkie at the Roxy movie palace off Times Square, on the condition that I not tell my mother. You'd like Khalto Tala, B, I'm sure of it. Sometimes I can hardly tell she's my mother's sister, they're about as different as dandelion and hibiscus.

Khalto Tala left Syria long before my parents got up the courage to follow her. She was always the braver of the two sisters, so when she boarded a steamship bound for Amrika, no one was too surprised, even though it was rare for a woman to travel alone. Before we arrived in New York, I only had vague memories of her. I used to take solace in her letters, though, and in her tales about the land of plenty beyond the dark Atlantic. Khalto Tala sent back trinkets from time to time, baubles she bought for me or my brother with the money she made peddling. Khalto Tala had found someone in Amrika who was teaching her to read and write, and in her letters she built fantastical worlds for us back home.

None of the older women in my family knew how to read, not even my mother, who I used to believe knew everything. My father read the letters to us while my mother cooked or sat with my brother in her lap, and I would listen. That's how I learned to read English, from reading the bits of it in her letters over and over. When my parents decided to invest in English lessons for Issa (who was, in fact, not well suited for languages), I would eavesdrop while I washed grape leaves for wara' einab or mixed burghul and lamb with my hands for kibbeh, and after Issa's lessons were over, I'd whisper what I'd learned to myself as I went about my day. And anyway, what did I have that was more interesting in those days than Khalto Tala's stories? Khalti wrote of deep pine forests and ice-laden cold, of prairies flat as a palm and of sky melting into heaven, and these were my dreams in those days, the fantasies I escaped to when I was alone.

That's what I was thinking of when I met you the day after Hawa's death. At first, I didn't even see you. I was walking home from school when I looked up and noticed a small gray bird fighting with a hawk. Though the bird put up a bold and desperate fight, the hawk tore the feathers from his wings and dropped him. I broke away from the cluster of schoolchildren and ran to the place where he'd fallen. It was a kite, one of the same birds I'd seen when Hawa crashed. His eyes were closed and his beak was open, his head tilted at an angle so that he looked like a holy man opening his mouth to pray.

You ran up to me as I scooped the kite into my hands, another girl in the same awkward stage of middle adolescence. We locked eyes—do you remember? We looked just alike back then, our hair the same shade of almost-black, our arms and legs the same gangly length, our strong chins all but identical.

You reached out to touch the kite's feathers and asked me if he was dead. I thought he was; I couldn't feel him breathing. We studied his feathers and the shape of his wings, the talons on his scaly feet. For a time neither of us wanted to speak. You asked if you could hold him. He seemed to belong with you. I was jealous, though I didn't say so. You had the look on your face my mother once described to me of new parents—a wondrous silence. Finally you said we should give him a proper funeral, then picked up the feathers on the ground that had been torn out by the hawk. I thought of your hands months later on the ship to Amrika, how the feathers were longer than your fingers.

We buried the kite in my mother's garden. We stood side by side for our prayers, but the heat of you so close distracted me, and I had to start over twice. I said the Lord's Prayer over the bird's body and crossed myself, and you said: "Surely we belong to Allah, and to Him we shall return." We both said, "Ameen."

Something about your face made me feel I was looking at my-self. I'd been lonely so long. I put my arms around you and kissed you twice on each cheek, the way I'd been taught to greet the women in my family. I felt strange and light, but I pledged my sisterhood, because I had no words then for what that lightness meant.

You didn't come to me with your gift until weeks later, tapping on my window before school one morning with a bundle wrapped in old linens. Your mother had been ill, as I recall, and you'd stayed home to take care of her. She was pregnant. You were hoping for a sister you could sew tiny dresses for. Back then, neither of us knew what lay ahead.

I unwrapped the linen bundle, curved like the seed of a mango. You'd stitched the feathers of the kite into a magnificent silver-white wing. You held your breath while I lifted it to the sun, and I thrilled at the thought that you cared for my approval. It was the most beautiful thing I'd ever seen.

I brought the wing with me to school that day, hidden among my things. I took it everywhere with me, carried it in the folds of my skirt and tucked it beside me when I slept at night. With the wing under my pillow, I once dreamed that God visited me in the form of a bird. I don't know why I think of it now. He was a slender starling, his feathers smoothly oiled, his iridescent plumage speck-led with pearls. He perched on the window my father kept closed to the owl. I opened it, and there the King of Kings sat with the moon for a crown, preening his feathers. For the first time in many days, I felt peace.

When I awoke, it was to my father once again poring over his account books and my mother's whispered prayers. My Lord's visit had changed the inside of me, but out in the world, it had changed nothing. I lay with my eyes shut and your silver feathers beneath my head. I clutched their softness tight. I've showed your wing to no one since then, B, not even when I folded it into my steamer trunk when we left for Amrika. It reminds me that something pure still exists in this world, that something immortal can be lifted even from a harvest of torn feathers, and of all your qualities, little wing, that is the one I have always loved best.

THREE /

ON THE SUBWAY, THE first sign of dawn is a girl in a striped blouse who breaks the quiet of the empty subway car where I sit reading Laila Z's diary. I've been riding the system all night since I missed the stop for Teta's apartment. I've been sitting on this orange plastic bench, people shuffling forward and back around me, until all human presence trickled away to silence. Down here, I can almost pretend I've escaped the passage of time.

But it's later than I thought, and Teta will be worried about me. I'll have to find some way to make it up to her. I get off at Borough Hall and emerge into the reddish light. An elderly Black woman is feeding pigeons in the park, and grandmothers in saris, scarves, or Yankees caps are walking their kids to school, laden with their backpacks like blossoms heavy with bees. Black trash bags are lined up on the sidewalk for collection. We used to make this walk, too, on our way to the Islamic community center. You used to take me to their after-school Arabic classes, though I was far from the best in my class. You liked the location because it was close to Teta, so we could drop by for dinner afterward. It's housed in a beautiful old two-story building and has been missing the Arabic half of its sign for years because of fears of arson. A few years after you died, the women's entrance was scorched by fire one night, and I felt like telling you, Look, see where this silence has gotten us.

I walk down to the bodega and grab a newspaper to kill time. I am bleeding again, and the farther I walk, the worse my cramps get. I'm convinced my body is rejecting the piece of plastic in my uterus, no matter what my gyno says. I stop by the local bakery to pick up a man'ousheh for Teta, trying to assuage my guilt. The woman behind the counter can tell I haven't slept. She says nothing; she doesn't have to.

When I leave the shop with my paper box, I spot two men walking down the sidewalk across the street holding hands, checking the brunch prices in a restaurant window. The man on the right laughs at something the other man says, flipping his black hair over his shoulder. His partner rubs the back of the man's hand with his thumb. They look at each other.

I drop my eyes. The man with the long hair reminds me of Sami, and on this morning, of all mornings, my unrequited crush is the last thing I want to think about. But I can't help myself: I see Sami in the linen shirt this man is wearing, remember our thrift shop fashion shows and the day I held Sami's hand when he finally got up the courage to get his ears pierced. Now he is using his art with laser focus to keep the memories of his community alive, and I am trying to forget him.

I turn away and head back to Teta's apartment. A man in a crisp polo shirt passes the two men on the street and turns to stare. The knot of their fingers unravels when they drop each other's hands.

Teta's living room is cool and dark. The curtains are half drawn, blocking the usual rectangle of morning sunlight. Teta is in her chair, reading under your framed print of John James Audubon's American Redstart, one of his paintings from the *Birds of America*. Next to it, hanging in a place of honor above the china-filled break-front like a religious icon, is the most valuable thing in the house: your prized Laila Z aquatint of a hudhud in its walnut frame.

Teta motions to the sofa opposite her chair, and I sit down, unwrapping the man'ousheh for her. The apartment smells of disturbed dust, but the sounds of the city don't find their way in. Apartment 4A is Teta's stronghold against the repeating past.

"Hazy today." Teta accepts the man'ousheh with a napkin on her lap to catch the stray za'atar. The bread is still hot from the oven.

"Summer in Brooklyn." I don't add what we are both thinking: that time of year again. Teta holds the man'ousheh between her lap and her mouth. You are on the tip of her tongue, but she won't invoke you. Your death is an enchantment neither of us is strong enough to break.

I glance toward Teta's days-of-the-week pill tray in the kitchen. "Did you take your meds?"

Teta scoffs between bites. "They raise the price one time more," she says, "and I cut them in half."

"You can't do that. Those are your maintenance meds, Teta. For the myeloma. They're important."

We've broken two of our unspoken rules: I've questioned Teta's frugality, and I've made her feel frail. Every month, as we get close to refilling her prescription, Teta starts cutting her pills in half. I've seen her do it, even though I tell her it's dangerous and unnecessary. She's never forgotten war and hunger, never forgotten hoarding medicine for her own sick mother during the French bombardment of Damascus in the late spring of '45, and I've had to accept that sometimes to feel secure is its own medicine. Still, by now she must have found the spot where I stash the bills. She must know I don't always have the money to pay them.

We eat in silence, and then Teta folds the napkin into a tiny square and pushes herself up on the arms of the chair. "The kazbara," she says, as though the cilantro on her fire escape explains everything, and turns to the window.

"Teta, you're not supposed to—"

Before I can stop her, Teta hikes up her wool skirt to slip a stockinged foot onto the fire escape. She knows I won't pull her back, for fear of knocking her down, which is why she turns and smirks at me over her shoulder.

"Oh, you know what you're doing," I call after her as she lifts her other foot over the windowsill. Asmahan saunters over, curious.

"Don't sass me," she retorts. "I stood up to armed men with a bucket of water before you were born."

There's little I can say to that. "I already watered the kazbara, Teta. Come back in. Let's play tawleh."

But there's no arguing with Teta when she has her mind set on something, and anyway, she's been climbing out onto the fire escape to water her garden when I'm not home for months. She never grew thyme after you died, but she's kept the garden ever since.

"First Christmas after you were born," Teta says over her shoulder as she takes up the watering can on the windowsill, "your father, he wanted a tree. Astaghfirullah! He demand a tree, and I'm the only one home. I carried the tree on my back to surprise them. You remember, eh?"

Asmahan puts out a paw to test the situation, and I shoo her from the window. "I know, Teta. Twenty blocks."

"Twenty-four!" This number has increased over the years.

I set one foot on the fire escape and freeze. It's been years since I've been able to stand on one of these without panic. "Come inside. It's about to rain."

Teta waves the watering can for emphasis. "I took you to Prospect Park so we could walk and walk. Thirty, forty blocks." Teta sits down on the window ledge and wipes her brow. "We used to walk and walk until I had the feet like two stones. You remember?"

I laugh. "Ma fi benzene." The first thing I ever learned from Teta, who never got tired first, was how to tell her I was out of gas.

Teta cackles. She pinches a silver tuft of sage between two fingers. "To Allah belongs the east and the west." She's reciting Surat al-Baqarah. "So wherever you turn, there is the face of God."

Surat al-Baqarah reminds me of the afternoons I used to spend with you during Ramadan, when I'd start out trying to fast during the school day and come home cranky and exhausted, and you'd recite it to me. Teta memorized the whole Qur'an as a young girl, something you used to say impressed everyone around her, given that her education was cut short by poverty. You always denied it, but I think you knew it by heart, too. You used to tell me, during those long afternoons, how fasting could bring you closer to God if you let it. You used to say that not worrying about your next meal made you feel more present to the world around you. I wonder how it would feel to inhabit my own body so fully that even the ache of fasting would feel miraculous.

I lean out the window and lay my forehead on Teta's broad back. If I close my eyes, I can remember being carried in the thick branches of her arms. "I wish I was as strong as you."

She slips a furred sprig of purple sage behind my ear, then cuts a bit of kazbara for later. She angles her bulk back through the window. Teta is a sturdy ship in the too-small harbor of this apartment. I gather up the remnants of our man'ousheh while Teta sets the fresh cilantro in a cup of water. She sets the cup on top of the fridge to discourage Asmahan from drinking it. As I crumple our oily napkins, my gaze drifts from Teta to your Laila Z, the sun glinting off the wooden frame. It's a hair crooked, and I rise to straighten it. I've been studying the bird since Sabah gave it to you, but I still can't tell what species of hudhud it is. I thought about asking Sabah once, but I didn't want to make a fool of myself to your best friend. I was supposed to be the ornithologist's kid, supposed to absorb everything you knew. I failed, though to your credit, you never gave up on me. You were still teaching me up until the day you died.

A second set of fingers strokes the frame. You never come two days in a row. This is not supposed to happen. I am not supposed to have to miss you so much.

"Teta," I call out into the kitchen, "you want me to do the dusting before dinner? The frame needs it." Maybe if I go about my day as though you aren't here, you'll leave. Out of the corner of my eye, you seem wounded.

"Ma'alish," Teta calls back, "leave it." She fills the teapot with water and lights the stove. She looks up at me and then squints at the dusty frame of your Laila Z, and it's impossible to tell if she is only pretending to look through you. "It wasn't so common those days, a woman painter. And to paint with all those details, like a scientist—it was rare, yanay. Beautiful, her birds."

I roll and unroll the hem of a doily on the end table. "Mom never really accepted her disappearance."

"No." Maybe Teta doesn't see you after all. She is rubbing the leaves from a cutting of sage, preparing to make tea. "By the time we arrived, she was missing nearly twenty years."

You tap the corner of the frame, and underneath the illustration is a signature in Arabic, one I've seen before. I could go to my room and pull out Laila's notebook, let the words pour out of me, tell Teta about the community house and the watercolor sparrow. But in my mind's eye I can hear what Teta will say, the way she will turn her face from me, the way she will plead with me not to root around in the past the way I do, the way you did. Teta has lost too much to the hunger of memory. I've given up trying to force that lock.

But those birds. The details on the tail feathers, the beak, the scales on the toes. "It's hard not to imagine what might've been. If things were different."

"Eh." Teta nods her agreement. She fills her silver tea egg with sage, then stops so long I nearly ask her if she's all right. "I was in love once," Teta says, "before your jiddo." She pauses, even her hands. "There was someone."

I wait for Teta to fall asleep in her easy chair for her afternoon nap, then tuck Laila Z's notebook under my shirt and open Teta's walk-in closet. A quarter of the space is dedicated to the frames wrapped in brown paper that house prints of Laila's illustrations, along with two rare aquatints. All your things are here, just as Teta was keeping them for you when you died.

Though Laila Z was never able to secure gallery representation, she did do some illustration work for publishing houses, mostly for birding guides and conservation campaigns. One of her aquatints, like the hudhud in Teta's sitting room, was a gift from Sabah. The other you saved up for years to buy.

I understood, even as a child, how much you loved Laila Z's birds. Once, while you were saving up to buy that second aquatint—the yellow-crowned night heron—I offered you my life savings in my ceramic piggy bank, but you refused. When you got tenure, not a year before your death, you bought that print to celebrate. Sabah was the only curator of Arab American art that we knew in those days, so she was the one who helped you find it. Aquatint, a variant of etching, isn't so widely used anymore; it produces tone rather than color, with lines etched to create detail and depth. Laila Z insisted on hand-coloring her prints with watercolor, creating startling images with hyperrealistic anatomical details.

They have a surreal, flattened look to them, with all the detail of pen and ink and the ethereal wash of watercolor. There are still a few galleries that show Laila Z's work—what little of it is still circulating these days, produced before her disappearance back in '46— but being a naturalist, observational painter, and a woman besides, she's generally been relegated to the obscurity of time. Just a few weeks before your death, you had Sabah over to pick her brain about Laila Z's last painting before her disappearance, trading theories on what was known to exist—and what might have happened to her.

Sabah, along with most of the art world, was beyond certain that everything we'd ever know about Laila Z had already come to light. Her disappearance coincided with the city's destruction of Little Syria, all records of her vanishing, and so everyone took this dead end to mean death. You were one of the few who refused to let her memory die.

You loved Laila Z long before you started campaigning to save the remaining half of the old tenement on Washington Street, the one that's been reduced to an empty, weedy lot since your death. But by the end, you became so passionate about saving the building her family lived in that even for me, it was hard to remember which obsession came first. Maybe the painter's activist spirit inspired you. Maybe that's what fueled your desire to save the nest of rare birds you found on the old tenement's roof during the building inspection, the birds that set everything in motion. Either way, you took the nest as a sign, adding it to your long list of reasons to save the building. When you joined forces with the local masjid in trying to buy the old tenement, the fact that the purchase would not only save the home of both painter and birds but also create space for the local Muslim community made you even more determined. It couldn't all be a coincidence, you said, all these reasons popping up like crocuses. You believed that God was the remover of obstacles; you used to talk about the future as though it were something we could build for ourselves. It was an omen that the birds had chosen that building to roost on, you said. There were only two tenements left on Little Syria's stretch of Washington Street— history was slipping away. You reminded me of the power Allah gave to Solomon to understand the language of the birds, the way that all things were signs for those who look. But you read those signs wrong.

I shuffle through the frames tucked in their brown wrappers, peeking under the taped corners of the paper. You once looked with love on these paintings; your passion made me want to create beautiful things when I grew up. But I didn't grow up to be a Laila Z. I wonder, if you were still alive, if I could take you with me on the subway, walk you down to Lower Manhattan and show you the murals I've been working on, the hudhud and her crown.

When I open the corner of one of the packages, I find you sitting beside me in the narrow closet in the dark, examining the edges for dents or rips, your legs crossed under you like you always sat with me on the old Persian rug on your bedroom floor. You've got your hijab off, your hair mussed as though you've slept on it, the white hairs in your part preserved forever from the last time you dyed your hair black with henna and indigo. Two generations before you, our ancestors were nomadic. You used to sit like this and tell me stories about my great-great-grandmother, the one who killed scorpions with her bare heels and slit the throats of the goats on Eid. You and Teta Badra before you and Teta's mother before her— my great-grandmother Wafaa, daughter of the scorpion-killer—you were the bearers of bravery in our family. You were the one who fought to save the neighborhood I'm now sneaking into to paint each night. But you failed to realize that America has only ever deemed certain heritages worth preserving. If the Lenape were forced from their ancestral home on the island of Mannahatta, the eviction of Little Syria's impoverished immigrants is no surprise, and it's hard for me to imagine that things will ever be any different.

Even I believed, by the end, that what you imagined was really possible—that this abandoned tenement, the older of the two left on the block and the place where Laila Z and hundreds of other Syrian immigrants had once lived, could really become a place of prayer, a place of history, with a protected home for the birds who miraculously built a nest on the roof. But futures so beautiful are rare for people like us. You lost your battle and, in the process, I lost you to someone else's anger. There was a confidence in everything you did that I never learned to emulate, a belief in everything you loved, as though victory was secured, as though it wasn't a fool's errand to believe in justice. You weren't afraid when the death threats came, and you don't look afraid now. For a ghost, you are strong-shouldered, the glow of middle age still gleaming on your brown hands. With no one else in this closet but us, I could be the one who died in the fire, not you. I am left with these paper-wrapped frames and the reminder you always gave me with a raised eyebrow: *Don't believe them when they tell you who is dead and who is living.*

I stack Laila Z's paintings back against the wall and rise to dust fuzwahs off my knees. I bang the top of my head against a low shelf. The shock of pain stuns me, and the shelf's contents tumble to the floor: a stack of your leather-bound sketchbooks.

The first begins with dozens of pages of notes, followed by hand-drawn maps of Lower Manhattan. A block of Washington Street is indicated by a darkened rectangle, then inset in a larger view on the next page. The inset block reveals the second tenement next to the one still standing at 109 Washington Street. You've outlined the front of the building, drawn a red arrow to the westernmost window on the top floor. A sketch of a nest, the silhouette of two birds.

The sketchbook explodes into drawings—graphite, ink, charcoal, colored pencil, watercolor. The birds in this nest are birds I've never seen, bearing an unrecognizable name. *Geronticus simurghus—third documented sighting,* your notes read. The pages of notes spill over into another four notebooks, hypothetical migration routes that might have taken them to New York, the number of eggs in the nest, the coloration of the wings in the dawn light. And, throughout, references to the other two known records of this bird so rare it was once thought to be a fable: the century-old field notes of an ornithologist named Dr. Benjamin Young and an aquatint by Laila Z, hinted at only in a letter to a private collector you found buried in the archives of the New York Historical Society.

Though I never heard even Sabah mention the existence of an aquatint like this, I've seen sketches of a similar bird before. I dart out of the closet and into my bedroom, returning with Laila's notebook. I flick through the pages. The entries are written in English but from the rightmost page to left, as in Arabic. I stop at an entry accompanied by a sketch of a cream-colored bird with hints of iridescence in its breast feathers, little more than a streak across the page.

I still remember the TV interview you did, the one that preceded the first wave of threats. I knew it was going to be a problem while you were filming it. At the time, I was convinced that it wasn't the fact of the hypothetical masjid that set people off. It was the conviction in your voice when you talked about the birds. The newscaster must have done her homework; she brought out every look-alike species she could think of. You held fast. In the years since, I've been afraid of the knot of shame that was tied in my belly then: the shame of earnest belief. *Don't let them see the thing you love,* I wanted to shout at you, but it was too late. I wanted to cover your mouth. I'd already learned from my father and my bullies that believing in something, for people like you and me, was a punishable crime.

And yet, here: your evidence waiting for someone to take up where you left off, your secret inkling that you, Dr. Young, and Laila Z all saw the same miraculous event that quickened your belief in the rare, in the impossible. You tried to tell me while you were alive, but I wasn't ready to believe you. One of your sketchbooks has fallen open at your feet, revealing a watercolor inset of this rare bird's pale breast. Your cross-legged ghost is no longer looking at me. Both our eyes drift to your sketch, a mirror half a century after Laila's. You sit unmoving, your palms curved around the sketchbook. I lift it from the mist of your touch and cradle it as though it might shatter in my hands.

Sabah doesn't pick up her office phone, so I walk down to her father's shop on Atlantic to find her. The sidewalks are packed with girls in gauzy midi skirts and crop tops, boys in tropical print T-shirts and bright sneakers with unscuffed soles, men in plump middle age talking loudly on their phones. The restaurants, shisha bars, and coffee shops are packed with people whose apartments don't have air-conditioning. The painted electrical boxes thrum with effort.

Sami has expanded his project: the light poles at one intersection are encircled with thick silk cord dyed emerald or wine or adobe pink, each cord tied into an intricate knot—an endless knot, or a bowknot, or a sheepshank, or a lark's head. His efforts are working; I remember there was a police shooting not six months ago in this very spot that most people in this neighborhood, given the relentless pace of violence in this country, would have already stopped talking about. The knots are talismans against forgetting, and they work. I have not forgotten Sami.

The bell tinkles on the door of Sabah's father's shop when I push it open. I step inside into cool darkness. A path winds from the door to the back of the shop, past the ouds hanging in the window, the tawleh boards inset with mother-of-pearl, the brass coffeepots and trays assembled along the wall. The countertop is crowded with open boxes of roasted chickpeas and silver necklaces bearing Ayat al-Kursi, the floor with open canvas sacks of rice and bulgur wheat and fava beans that shoulder up against shelves of teas, halawa, and half a dozen kinds of pickled olives.

"As-salaamu alaykum," I call out into the dark, and something metallic dings to the floor as one of the cats startles up from her afternoon nap.

"Wa alaykum as-salaam," a deep cello of a voice calls back, and Sabah emerges from the kitchen behind the shop carrying a portable fan. Sabah is tall and broad-shouldered, a hewn marble slab of a person, but she maneuvers her square frame about the shop with surprising lightness. "Sit down. I'm brewing coffee."

I follow Sabah back into the kitchen behind the shop floor, and taxi horns fade away. It's rare to find the shop empty on a weekday afternoon. Sabah's father has been in business so long, since he came to the States from Aleppo, that the whole neighborhood knows their family, so there's always a steady stream of people who stop in to say hello and chat in Arabic. The delivery guys often stay for tea or coffee, arguing over politics with Sabah's father, and when Sabah is in, the old Lebanese ladies stop by to pick up fresh bread and give Sabah the latest neighborhood gossip, mostly regarding who's getting married and whose son just got into business school. Sabah always takes the news with a solemn nod and a grunt, and somehow this always placates the women, as though any response at all from Sabah is a precious thing. For as long as I can remember, Sabah's cousins have affectionately referred to her as a hassan sabi, a tomboy. Even the delivery guys, when they speak to her in Arabic, tell her "tfaddal" instead of the feminine "tfaddali" when they hold a door open for her. It might be a running joke, but she never corrects them.

"My sister had to take Dad in for a diabetes test," Sabah says as she lifts an orange cat off the uneven kitchen table, "so I had to cover at the store this afternoon."

"I figured you might be around today." I blink in the dark

kitchen. In the dimness, I make out the shapes of glass bottles on the counter stuffed with gerbera daisies. Her father has been bringing Sabah fresh flowers for years when she watches the shop for him, a token of affection and a way to brighten up the room, and Sabah changes the water and trims the stems of the daisies, gently, so as not to bruise them.

"Claudia's watching the gallery for me." Sabah moves off toward the windows, tying up one of the curtains to let a bit of light in.

"Any news about the spring show?"

Sabah motions to a pillowed chair and clears away a stack of books with one large hand. "I'm doing a studio visit in Detroit in a few weeks with an artist. I saw her solo show in LA a few months back. She makes maps of North American bird migration routes in handblown glass. Not my usual thing, but unique. I could pair her with someone more established. A double solo show, maybe for Frieze next May. People will call me crazy, but I don't care. I want something different, I want to combine energies. I'd really love to sign the artist who's doing those pop-up bird murals in Lower Manhattan, but they're never signed."

My face gets hot, but I don't take the bait. Sabah doesn't know that I haven't painted anything show-worthy in years; I've been too busy with my private experiments. The last time I painted a self-portrait, I tried to face myself in the mirror and paint myself nude. I ended up blotting out my breasts with black paint.

I clear my throat. "Who's gonna run the gallery while you're in Detroit?"

"Claudia and Sami can get by while I'm not there."

My stomach turns at the mention of his name. Sabah hands me a cup of coffee with two crushed cardamom pods floating in the foam. Her pinky finger is too big to fit into the tiny handle. She sets a tray of rosewater Turkish delights in front of us, dusting cornstarch off her hands as she sits down. Sabah used to run a bakery in her previous life, before she became a gallerist, but she still makes desserts for her father's shop on the odd week-end, especially now that his arthritis has gotten worse. She motions toward the tray, and I take the smallest piece, hearing my mother's voice in the back of my head, admonishing me to be polite.

"The gallery's not what I'm worried about." Sabah taps a tray of cookies cooling on a rack.

I pick at a loose thread in the chair cushion. "Who's going to fill in with the baking?"

"There's not many folks I'd trust to help Baba out. But I trust you."

"Me?" I've barely been out of Teta's apartment in the last six months, and nobody would say I know how to bake. But Sabah's got my number—she knows I've got nothing else to do while Teta is napping.

Sabah pushes her chair back and rises from the table. "I've had your teta's bitlawah. You've watched her make it." Anything Sabah asks is rarely a question. "You can take some ma'amoul home to her."

I follow her to fetch a pair of aprons from the cabinet. "How did I sign myself up for this?"

"I changed your diapers. You can bake some pastry."

We wipe down the table, then flour the wood. Sabah uncovers a bowl of dough and pulls it apart while I chop a sticky pile of Medjool dates.

"Listen." I rock the chef's knife back and forth. "You're the only expert I know on Laila Z's work. Did she ever paint a bird like this?"

I wipe down my hands and open my messenger bag. I've brought one of your leather-bound sketchbooks, which I open to your watercolor sketch of the nesting pair from Lower Manhattan. Sabah smears flour on her apron and finds her glasses atop a sack of lentils in the corner. She stares at the bird so hard and so long

I'm not sure if she has any idea what I'm asking. Then she takes off her glasses and massages the balls of her palms. Years of touching hot pans has left her with hardly any fingerprints. I wonder for a fleeting moment if Sabah, like me, finds it hard to stand being called a woman.

"I told your mother," Sabah says into her hands, "if it's out there, no one's ever seen it. Somebody may have fallen for a good fake along the way, but no one's laid their hands on one of Laila's. Not like this." Sabah turns away and takes up two paddle-shaped cookie molds, hand-carved, brought over from Syria by her mother. She begins to rub oil into the hollows in the center of the smooth wood. "Anyway, Laila painted real birds."

I flinch without knowing why. "What do you mean, real?"

"Birds that actually exist." Sabah nudges her head in the direction of the notebook. "Habibti, I respect your mother more than anyone, Allah yarhama. But she told me herself only one ornithologist had ever actually catalogued that species. He nearly lost his career—his colleagues thought he was inventing it. It's never appeared in any field guides or surveys, not Audubon's, not Sibley's. And you can't tell me a bird that rare just shows up in the middle of Manhattan fifty years later, just like that."

"But she wasn't the first New Yorker to see one." I draw closer to Sabah, the sketches in my hand. "She was never wrong on an identification. Never."

Sabah shakes her head. Her hair is pulled into a tight bun, exposing new gray at her temples. "Some of the most well-respected ornithologists checked your mother's sketches. Wallah, she talked to Aisha Baraka. Most of the bird people said your mother must have seen some common species, maybe an albino, and been mistaken. Or maybe it was a trick of the light."

I take up the knife again and chop dates, the veins in the backs of my hands pulsing. You follow the sun with your eyes. I could mark the hours by the longing to see you and the ache of waiting for you to dissolve into the dark. "I saw those sketches myself. You know how female scientists are dismissed."

Sabah says nothing. She doesn't want to talk about you. You are everywhere in this city: laughing in Abu Sabah's shop, waiting for a man'ousheh at the bakery, giving an interview for the evening news, sketching in Prospect Park, walking west into the sunset while finches scour the sidewalk for cockroaches and bits of hot dog. Sabah and I divide the dough, and you are there with us whether we conjure you or not, petting her orange cat as she eats Abu Sabah's tuna, making spirals in open sacks of dried chickpeas with your finger. You have no shadow and no weight to creak the floorboards. I knead the chopped dates into a paste. Your hands are on mine, the smoke traces of your skin leaving the scent of fresh thyme on the hairs on my arms. Then I blink, and you are nowhere.

I set down my towel. "Theoretically speaking, if there were a painting? If I could find it?"

"Could be worth a small fortune." Sabah presses the dough into the molds and fills them with date paste, then seals them and thumps the mold onto a towel wrapped over the table's edge to free the molded ma'amoul. "We're talking orders of magnitude more than her other works. Six figures, easy. No one's found anything in years. Definitely nothing like that."

There is a moment in which the weight of this, the maddening simplicity of it, clarifies itself. The largest amount of money I ever had in my bank account—this was before you died, before I moved back in with Teta, back when I still had the time to hold down a job—was $1,500. Beyond five grand, numbers start to lose their meaning. I argue with myself, scold myself, tell myself I am just thinking of what it would mean to me to see an artist like Laila Z represented in a museum. But it's too late for my excuses; shame runs icy down the length of my back. And yet, living in this country where my friends accrue scars and aches and ailments because they cannot afford medicine or rest or food or heat, I'm not sure what else I should feel. Money and power act on us whether we admit it or not.

I fish Laila's notebook out of my bag and open it to the water-color sketch that could be a replica of yours. "Laila Z and Mom can't both be seeing things." I flip back to the first diary entry, to the twin signatures in Arabic and English. "Mom cited Laila Z's sketches. She was looking for evidence."

Sabah unties her apron and holds the notebook to the light. Her eyes are wide and her voice quiet. "Ya Allah. Where did you find this?"

"Sabah." I seek out her eyes. "They can't both be wrong."

A long moment passes before Sabah is willing to relinquish the notebook. For a person who rarely gets worked up over anything, her hands are shaking. She slides the tray of ma'amoul into the oven.

"Let's say," she says, restraining the excitement in her voice, "that a painting like this does exist. Whoever has it must be keeping it to themselves, or it would have been discovered by now. But—" She interrupts herself, and her voice drops. "Look, I'm getting ahead of myself. What good would it do to look for this painting, 'albi? The old tenement is gone, the painter, your mother's birds, whatever they were—gone, all of them. Your mama would want you to move on more than she would want to be vindicated, habibti." Sabah lowers herself into a kitchen chair and settles her eyes on her own pile of bills, her father's plastic pill tray labeled with the days of the week and the bottles beside it, a leather-bound copy of the Qur'an in miniature on its wooden stand. A newspaper on the table, ringed with a chain of coffee stains, reports another school shooting in the Midwest. Well, I think to myself. America.

Sabah is murmuring. She's softened. "If you ever want me to go with you to the cemetery," she says, "all you have to do is ask."

I pack up my things, kiss Sabah goodbye on both cheeks, and

walk outside into a low, brassy sun. The lamppost on the corner, the one in front of Khoury's Fabrics, is decorated with a true lovers' knot in indigo cord. You are two blocks down, walking away from me opposite the sunset, striding one step after another toward the coming night.

FOUR / LAILA

B,

Some nights, little wing, when our stove breaks and we can't sleep for the cold, Khalto Tala tells us about the creatures who crossed the Atlantic long before ships ever did. The stories of fantastical creatures must have been passed down from my grandparents. My mother always claimed my jiddo was an educated man who once memorized al-Qazwini's *Marvels of Things Created and Miraculous Aspects of Things Existing*. But you know how slippery a story can be. The tale of the birds might have come from a distant uncle or great-great-grandmother rather than a thirteenth-century Persian astronomer, but that doesn't make the story less true.

The elders in my family have always said the birds went before us, long before the first of our families set off across the sea. Even before we left Syria, they'd spoken of these sixty wings, thirty arrow-shaped figures stark and snowy, an absence of color, shocks of light. Some said their wingtips were glossy blue-black, shimmering like the bellies of spiders; others said the white bodies and black markings were a myth, and that the only thing to interrupt their black plumage, dark as the moment after lightning, were their gilded breast feathers that gleamed like coins at last light. For all said that the birds took wing only at sunset. The setting sun was said to call them into the dark. They said the birds never stopped moving. It was agreed that the band of thirty flew west following the night, farther and farther with each day until they circled the planet without ever craning their necks to the east. Few had ever seen them, these birds that were the last of their kind, these birds that encircled the world like an unbroken ribbon. Most of my young cousins scoffed and denied it, and my aunties and uncles who had survived the plague of locusts shook their heads at the things their children now found too fantastical to accept.

Like all stories of things that are beautiful and true, whether or not they really happened, my mother found these stories difficult to believe. This lack of faith grieved her, because she looked for the sacred in everything. But she never, as far as I know, received a sign, not even when she held the hands of the old men of the village as they said their last goodbyes, not even in the eyes of the dying when the light went out in them. I asked her, once, what she saw when a soul passed from this world to the next, whether she saw the light of God's kingdom. She told me only that their eyes would lock on a spot in the distance that only they could see, and they would inhale with a sigh as one does before cut roses. But she didn't mention any light.

I still wonder how my father convinced her to cross the ocean for Amrika. When he brought up Khalto Tala's letters, my mother wouldn't listen. My father's business had been failing for years, but my mother had been able to earn a modest living as a midwife to keep our family afloat—babies come whether one's pockets are full or empty, she used to say. But my brother was of the age that yearns for adventure, and my father had heard that his son could earn a better living abroad than here in our village, where prospects were dwindling. And anyway, B, you remember the whirlwind each young man would kick up, returning to the bilad in a new American suit to find a wife and get married, only to leave the following month on a New York–bound ship from Beirut. The men who stopped in to speak with my father spoke of a city larger than Damascus, glittering terribly, her cobblestone streets filled with automobiles and rich men. The past couple of years had been hard, but they were still hopeful the good days would return, and still optimistic about the opportunities that lay ahead for them in New York. Soon my father was casually speaking at supper about the nine monthly steamships that could carry a family from one of the Syrian ports to New York. He began to repeat things I never thought I would hear him say, praising the virtues of Amrika the way some had once spoken of France, as though the Amrikiyyin possessed the education and wisdom to appreciate him in ways his countrymen did not. It was as though he thought our family was better than our neighbors. I'd long held my own unspoken opinions about my father's lofty ideals, but that was the first time I felt ashamed about his aspirations. With each passing week, his convictions grew stronger, until he was convinced that we owed it to ourselves to leave.

It was you who made me want to stay. I would have tried, if you'd asked.

How silly I feel this evening, B. If you were here, I'd ask you to forgive me for what I wrote last night. The truth is that, after that night, I don't blame you for not asking me to stay.

Maybe what Khalti says is true. Maybe if I write it down, I can stop carrying it.

I woke rubbing my eyes. My mother still hadn't come back from delivering Imm Shams's baby, and my father was nowhere to be found. He had taken, in those days, to nighttime walks around the village, as though he were saying his goodbyes in secret. As for my brother, Abu Anas had taken pity on the sorry state of my father's business and started paying Issa to watch his shop at night.

As this ink is my only witness, I confess that I was dreaming of you when you woke me. For this, too, forgive me. If you saw my pulse in my throat when I opened the door, you didn't show it. It was a dry summer night, but your hair was damp with sweat, and your palms were glossy with fresh blood.

My mother had taken the suitcase with her delivery kit. I threw open the trunk in her bedroom looking for supplies—a needle and thread, a spare tourniquet, old linens, a half bottle of laudanum she kept hidden for when her migraines struck. I threw my make-shift medical kit into a pillowcase and twisted the top into a knot. We ran from my house to yours, the sack bouncing. You sobbed soundless at my side. In my dream, you'd worn a yellow kerchief on your head. You'd stepped into my doorway with fresh bread from the village oven, handing me a warm piece as you might to a hus-band or a son. I dreamed I'd taken your hand and led you out into the fields, beyond the last houses, to where I'd seen Hawa and her flying machine fall. We knelt together where Hawa's shoulder had kissed the earth and began to dig with our hands. You smeared your yellow kerchief with dirt. When we'd dug a hole as deep as our el-bows, twilight was upon us, and the sounds of jackals started up in the distance, and I was afraid. Antares, the heart of the scorpion, shone above us. You reached into the ground and pulled out my heart, bloody and beating, and gave it to me to swallow. It tasted of copper and must. Reddish earth still under your fingernails, you leaned over and kissed me.

I expected to hear the shrieks before we reached your door, but there was nothing. A bad sign. We burst into the kitchen and found your mother on the floor, embroidered couch pillows beneath her, her thin dress and the floor smeared with blood. Your father had already gone for the doctor, but neither of them had returned yet.

I opened my sack and pulled out the wad of old linens, trying to stop the bleeding, but they were soaked through before I could stand. Your mother was in and out of consciousness. I tossed aside the soiled linens and checked for the baby's head—he was already crowning. You were frozen by the doorway, all color drained from your face. I had seen this reaction before during some of my mother's deliveries, when fathers or siblings came out of the bedrooms where women were giving birth, the same terrified look in their eyes. Controlling my voice, I asked you to get something to soak up the bleeding. Feeling you watching over my shoulder terrified me.

Your mother cried out. You dropped something. A contraction came, and I urged your mother to push. You ran back into the room with a jug of water and knelt beside me. Soon the dome of the head emerged, still wet, eyes squeezed shut. Then the tiny figure was on my mother's soaked linens, purple and unmoving.

We cleared the mucus away from the baby's mouth and turned it, waiting for a cough. It didn't cry, not even when I rubbed its back. We took turns blowing air into its lungs. When you began to choke on your tears, I breathed into the limp body again, and again, and again, until what felt like hours had passed and someone in the room was sobbing and a hand tugged me up by the shoulder, not unkindly.

"It's over," my mother said.

My hands and yours were on the baby's head, cupping it like a stone. I had been muttering the Our Father and the Hail Mary over and over without end, the ameen of one prayer running into the beginning of the next. You had been whispering beside me the Muslim prayer for the dead: "To Allah we belong and to Him we shall return."

It had been over before we'd arrived. My mother lifted my chin and told me to follow you outside. Your mother would survive, but not her child.

I found you by the corner of the house, shaking. You walked, stunned, down the path toward the fields. I realized I had never noticed the sex of the baby and wondered why this had ever mattered to me or to anyone. The air stank of metal. I bent over at the waist and vomited. When I looked up, you were staring out over the barren earth toward the retreating night, waiting.

B,

Sometimes a day passes where I forget. More often, I don't.

I don't know if my mother thinks about the sibling you lost. Sometimes I think she gave in to my father's dreams of Amrika because she thought it would shake me out of my guilt. But I don't like to think about that.

My mother was never a talkative person, it was true, but I knew as well as my father that when she declined to argue about his plan to join Khalto Tala in Amrika, she had as good as agreed to it. He went about making arrangements immediately, which wasn't too difficult. Everyone knew someone in those days who had a son or an uncle or a cousin who had left, and the young men who had returned from abroad—some temporarily, some indefinitely, and most all of them with enough money in their pockets to put a new roof on their parents' house or pay a sister's dowry— were full of advice for how to avoid the tricksters and the scams, the boats that would take a family not across the ocean but only to Greece or to Italy, where they would be marooned without funds to return.

My father found a young man who gave him a contact in Beirut, and my mother told us to gather a few things into a trunk. I didn't have much—none of us did—but I tucked in a book of

prayers and the rosary my mother had given me when I'd been confirmed, my two Sunday dresses, a pair of patent leather shoes my
mother had saved up for six months to buy. She had adopted my
father's stories: she told us that in Amrika we would have to dress
well, that American women were fair and elegant and rich like Pa-
risians, that I would have to practice gliding in my good shoes
down cobblestone streets. But I had never had good balance, and
as a child I tended to walk barefoot, all the better to remain out of
sight and in peace. On top of these things I laid your wing,
wrapped in its brown paper and tied with twine.

My mother convinced your father to let you go with us to Beirut, and to this day, I'm not sure why she did. She claimed it was
because your mother needed a special medicine, and she was in
touch with a supplier in Beirut who could get it for well below market price. I hadn't seen you since that night. Maybe my mother
thought we deserved a chance to patch things up between us. I'll
probably never know the reason. I think your father agreed because
he couldn't withstand both your grief and his own.

It had only been a few weeks since the stillbirth when you arrived at our house for the journey. You hadn't been to school in
weeks. Sometimes I'd slid the lessons under your door, but you
never came by to thank me.

The weather had begun to change the day we left to cross the
mountains, and the morning was cool. We shivered in the back of
the truck that would take us to Tarablus and then south along the
coast, wrapped in a blanket against the chill. The temperature
dropped as we rose, the cold air crisp with the scent of cedar. My
parents and my brother had long since drifted off to sleep, rocked
by the uneven road. I laid my hand on the seat in the back of the
truck, next to yours. Our fingers brushed with each bump. We did
not speak.

Beirut was a maze of cobblestone streets crowded with trams
and Pullman cars. Horse-drawn carriages carted piles of fruit and

sacks of rice and cracked wheat to the markets. As we descended toward the port, the breeze stank of smoke and salt. The tang of sea air was weak but inescapable, like a caress when one is dreaming.

We snaked our way through the narrow streets, past the brick and plaster houses of Gemmayzeh and then into Martyrs' Square, lined with young palms and squat automobiles. We passed cafés where old men in tarboushes smoked arghile and played tawleh, young men selling tea or watermelon juice, and clumps of French soldiers smoking cigarettes. We continued down until we spotted St. Georges Hotel sparkling like a fat white shell on the water, the harbor filled with boats.

My father hurried us down to Ras Beirut, where a man was waiting for us on the corniche: our contact, who would provide us our tickets for the ship that would take us to Amrika. The car let us out on a broad avenue where pastel houses on stilts abutted dark slabs of rocky coastline. Fishermen waded out into the water, and young men laid their broad backs onto old rugs tossed across the rocks, smoking shisha and trading boasts. You and I wandered off along the corniche, ignoring the blare of automobile horns until we reached a curve of seashore where the rocks jutted out into the green water. The sea lapped the silvery rocks like a baby's tongue on its milk teeth. It seemed all at once to be dreadfully quiet.

"Promise me," you said, "that you won't forget me, no matter what happens."

It was the first thing you'd said to me since that night. You placed your hands on my shoulders. Your skin was warmer than I expected.

The salt pricked at my eyes, and I blinked it away. I laughed when the water rose between my eyelashes, and the laugh became a sob. I didn't want you to remember me such a mess. I didn't want this to be the image you carried forever. I didn't wipe the salt from my cheek. I was afraid any movement might make you take away your hands.

I told you I should give you back your wing. When you squeezed my shoulders, lightning crackled behind my sternum. You must have told me to keep it; I don't remember. I reached for you and kissed you on both cheeks, and something in the belly of me boiled over. Did you hear the pounding of my blood in my ears? God forgive me the nameless thing I felt for you. I should write down that I am ashamed. I should write down that I repent. I do not.

The wind and the end of your kerchief were in my mouth. I held you close and fixed my eyes on the arch of Raouché Rock jutting from the sea. The huge cliff was surrounded by a cloud of white-and-gray rock pigeons whose nests lay in the crevices of the stone. On our walk along the corniche, a pair of boys had placed bets on which of them would have the courage to climb those rocks and jump. The sea below them was wild and sharp as glass, and the birds struggled against the wind that blew in from the open sea. The boys were nowhere to be found.

We parted. I wiped my face with the back of my hand.

"Tell me something beautiful," you said.

I opened my mouth and out came the only thing that I had ever known to be as beautiful as it was true: that I had once met a woman who knew how to fly.

You clasped my chilled hand in yours and lowered your gaze to our fingers. I hoped I'd said the right thing. My mother always used to say that people in mourning prefer not to talk about the earth.

"What a wonderful thing," you said, "for just one instant, to be so close to God."

The breeze tugged your hair across your lips. When my father had been injured in the revolt, I'd dreamed a flock of starlings had passed over our village, and their tears turned to pomegranate seeds. The seeds fell to the ground, but the earth was weary, and the seeds wouldn't take. The starlings circled, coaxing the earth toward fruitfulness. As they passed, the birds sang a psalm my mother had quoted to me many times, a line from the Song of Songs. I thought of it then, standing on the corniche so close to you that I could feel you breathing.

You are altogether beautiful, my darling. There is no flaw in you.

FIVE / ██████

THE FIRST FUNERAL I attended was held under a black froth of wings. The deceased was a crow that had been gashed in the belly by a red-tailed hawk. By the time the body dropped to the ground, the other crows in the neighborhood had already sent up their alarm calls. It was fall, and hundreds of them were gathered in the trees in Ruppert Park. This was back in Yorkville, across 2nd Avenue from our rent-controlled apartment, the one it took a fire to get us out of. The birds had been scolding earlier that morning, so the whole neighborhood knew there was a predator nearby. But the hawk had picked off a young crow, and the rest had mobbed him, screaming.

That was the day my body started conspiring against me. I'd gotten my period. It was so light I tried to ignore it, but you'd found the underwear I threw in the trash. I hoped this was a nightmare that would go away if I pretended it would. You called me into the bathroom to show me how to use a maxi pad. You said I should be happy. You said I was going to be a woman, and my body would change.

Up until that moment I had believed everyone was wrong about my body and what it could do. I knew what I was when I looked in the mirror, or when I hung from the monkey bars, or when I caught crickets in the park, or when I played street hockey with the kids on my block. I knew what I was when I read a book in the corner of the library or made fairy houses in the park with the girls from down the hall. I knew what I was no matter how I rolled or jumped or curled or stretched, and I knew what my body was supposed to feel like, even if I couldn't name it.

I tore the lump of the maxi pad from my underwear as soon as you left the room. I still believed I could will my body to become what my mind knew it should be: free and strong as a coil of brass wire. My chest and belly felt swollen and full, and every movement reminded me of how wrong I felt. I moved slower. A chasm had opened between me and my skin, as though I were fumbling around in a too-big pair of gloves. The only words I had back then were for what I knew I wasn't—a girl. But how to explain this feeling that my body was a tracing of something else, and not all the lines matched up?

The sound of flapping entered from the bathroom window, which faced the park. Through the glass, the rising tide of wings devoured the heads of the maples and the beeches, summoning a wind that swayed the traffic lights on 2nd Avenue. Beyond the iron fence, the tiny park was an ink blot of feathers. Our building was mostly home to immigrant families back then, families who'd lived in the same building for thirty years, and the old aunties down the hall had been complaining about the crows all day. Now they were afraid. This was a bad sign.

I rushed downstairs to see the commotion. The sky above our block was gray-green. I burst out the front door and sprinted toward the park, and tufts of black feathers flecked my cheeks.

The air was filled with the *caaw-caaw-caaw* of grieving crows. There were hundreds of them, one of the enormous flocks that sometimes gather in autumn in the northeast, congregating where there's food to be found. Behind the iron fence, in a clearing beyond the red-and-blue jungle gym, there was a circular gathering of several dozen crows. In the center was the mangled body of the young dead crow. Both its wings had been ripped from its body, hanging by thin slats of red muscle.

One at a time, each of the crows left the circle and hopped into the surrounding thicket, emerging with a small twig or a piece of dried grass. One by one, they placed their offerings on top of the body, hiding the twisted wings and the open beak that lay glinting like an obsidian shard in the low sun. More and more crows began to arrive, each bringing something to lay on the corpse, until the clearing was a sea of glossy backs. You'd told me once that crows mourn their dead. You'd never told me how.

Each bird laid their gift atop the dead crow and flew off. I did not yet know that, sometimes, it is impossible to mourn in the presence of others. When all the crows had left their offerings, the crowd dissolved into the twilight. The glittering wings gave way to an uneasy bruise of purple-and-green sunset. I was left alone in the clearing with the body, buried under twigs and leaves and grass, my blood slick between my thighs. Only the tip of one wing was still visible, a hole in the afternoon that swallowed the hint of light.

I haven't seen Aisha Baraka since the night you died. She was the one who warned you about the letters. She's the only one who would know if there was any truth to what you claimed in your notes—that you had spotted a rare species of migratory bird that most ornithologists didn't believe existed. Aisha was the one person you told everything.

You trusted Aisha because she was like you: a visionary, a

believer, and not only in the divine. Aisha had the foresight to tell you when you were onto something and when to call you on your bullshit. Not that you always listened to her. You got more than one anonymous death threat for trying to set up the Islamic community center, but Aisha warned you about the one that threatened fire. She asked you to lay low for a while, even offered to take us in until things calmed down. But you refused to let them break you, and that was the last time she saw you alive.

Finding Aisha is as easy as following my feet. The two of you used to go swimming every Friday after jum'ah at the 92nd Street Y in Carnegie Hill. Aisha has lived in Yorkville since before the wave of gentrification that reached the neighborhood in the late nineties, turning it into a clone of the rest of the Upper East Side, kicking out the tight-knit immigrant communities that used to live there. Her husband died when she was in her forties, and she never remarried. She's lived in the same rent-controlled apartment for almost thirty years now, and as far as I know she's never leaving that apartment, no matter how much money the landlord offers her.

At the Borough Hall subway station, I walk down to the 4 platform on the Manhattan-bound side. I ignore the cream-colored silk cords tied into repeated overhand knots on the turnstiles, and again ignore the thick braids of gray silk that decorate the square pillars on the platform. There was a suicide here not too long ago, a girl who threw herself onto the tracks, which I guess is what Sami's knots are trying to get us to remember. The knots sway when the trains go by. The trains are delayed; construction, as always. I don't want this languid time to think about where I'm going. I adjust my binder and ignore the deep twinge of pain starting in my right breast. I curse the swimsuit in my bag, curse the Y, curse gendered changing rooms everywhere.

By the time I get to the 92Y, I've almost changed my mind about going to find Aisha. I hurry inside the building and hand the woman at the front desk my ID, then avoid all eyes in the women's locker room and change into my one-piece swimsuit in a stall. I crumple my binder in the pocket of my jeans, tie up my hair into a swim cap, and struggle to cover my fat bun with the plastic. Jellyfish tentacles, twisted feathers, and eight-pointed stars doodled in black pen decorate my belly. I draw them when I'm alone late at night and feeling like my body isn't mine. Looking down at my chest still makes me feel distant and small. I reach to flatten it like I do after a shower. I suppress the urge to scream. Then something in me goes limp with resignation, and my mind quiets itself.

I walk to the mirror to convince myself that I am here, in this body. The last time I came here with you and Aisha, you caught me checking my face in the mirror and teased me about my vanity. I spent the whole afternoon struggling to picture my own face, imagining I wore the skin of everyone I came across. My own face has always felt unreliable. I never see the person I expect.

The pool is empty except for a few older women doing calisthenics in the shallow end. In the far lane, a Black woman in a burkini swims laps with such powerful strokes that she could be training for the Olympics. Aisha. Together, you could have put the American relay swim team to shame.

I slip into the pool and make my way over to the slow lane. So far Aisha hasn't noticed me. The water envelops me up to the shoulders, and relief washes through me. With the water supporting my weight, I can almost pretend that my physical self does not exist. This is the constant wish I've harbored since the day the bleeding started: that I could exist outside myself, that I could disappear the wrongness in me. When I was a kid, I never wanted to leave the pool. I used to throw tantrums at the end of open swim. I told you it was because I loved swimming, because I wanted to feel like a dolphin, because I wanted to pretend for another five minutes to be a mermaid. Looking back, it wasn't that I wanted my body to feel magical; I wanted it to feel transparent.

I enter the lane, treading water. Aisha is at the other end of the pool. When she reaches the wall, she takes an extra breath and carves her body down into the water, rolling and pushing off the wall to continue her stroke. She cuts through the pool, perfectly coordinated, so at home in her body that she seems to be a part of the water itself.

I haven't seen Aisha in five years, since before you died. I roll onto my back and fake that I know how to swim the backstroke to buy myself time, splashing and flailing. It's hopeless. Aisha passes me without recognizing me, a knife of contentment and elegance, and between one stroke and another I have convinced myself that this was a terrible idea. I turn over and swim faster, trying to reach the other side before Aisha realizes it's me. I clamber up the ladder on the side of the pool and shake the water from my ears. My breasts are a weight on my chest again, still swollen and painful from the IUD, and the rest of my body has returned. Every step across the wet pool tile heaves my chest up and down, and a despair rises in me that I can't explain, that alarm bell that has been going off in me every day since I began to change, that agonizing feeling that this body does not belong to me but to all the people who insist on how I should exist inside of it, that unshakable twinge that tells me that something, perhaps everything, is very, very wrong.

"As-salaamu alaykum!"

Pool water sluices out from between my toes and forms chlorinated puddles at the pool's edge. I turn, and my wet soles print dark moons on the cement. Suddenly the floor has become very interesting.

"Wa alaykum as-salaam." I clamp my throat around the shaking in my voice, trying not to let Aisha know that wearing this swimsuit makes me feel like I want to die.

"I haven't seen you in years." Aisha adjusts the hood of her burkini, loosening water from her ears. "Masha'Allah, you look just like your mother. Are you still painting? I haven't seen you at the masjid since your teta stopped going. And whatever happened with that job at Columbia that Reem was applying for?"

Normally I'd stiffen at any mention of Reem, but this time the muscles in the center of my belly relax. This last in the wave of questions saves me from having to mention that the only canvases I paint now are the sides of abandoned buildings, or from trying to explain why I don't feel comfortable entering a masjid from either the men's or the women's entrance, why I feel uncomfortable as soon as I clasp my arms across my chest for salah.

"Reem ended up finding a consulting job up in Boston. She hasn't had time to visit since she started."

A group of young boys not yet in their teens begins to splash one another. They rock the water back and forth between them, and the pool overflows. Pool water, that unnatural shade of crystalline blue, swirls around our ankles, then the creases at the base of our calves. It is a flood, and the *whum-whum* of water droplets thrums in our ears.

I follow Aisha out of the pool and into the locker room, wrapping my arms around myself and avoiding all eye contact. The pool water has smudged the ink on my stomach, and a wet gray line snakes down the inside of my thigh. I glance at my face in the mirror.

"How is your teta doing?"

"Hamdullah. Still in remission." I turn my body away from the women blow-drying their hair and reapplying mascara.

"Alhamdulillah." Aisha gathers her clothes, a towel, and a travel shampoo from her locker. "You should bring her to jum'ah. It would be good for both of you."

"Sometime, insha'Allah."

But Aisha knows as well as I do what I mean by that. She turns to me with a tenderness I am not expecting. "What happened to your mother shouldn't separate you from God. You know that, right?"

After you died, I tried to pray, but I wasn't sure what I was praying for. When I was a child, I believed God would set everything right. When I found out about the Nakba, I was sure that one day my friend Ahmad's grandmother would be able to return to her house in Palestine. I waited for the day our teachers would explain the theft of the land we lived on, the way our textbooks spoke about Indigenous people like they no longer existed and all the books we read were written by dead white men. I was sure that the school bullies would be punished, that the police would stop pulling over my Black friends' parents late at night, and that my classmates with undocumented aunties or grandparents would one day be able to stop worrying they'd be taken away. *Allah is the remover of obstacles.* But after the fire, after your burial, after the police dismissed the threats you'd received—by then I'd understood for a long time who had built this system, and for whom, and I'd long since let go of my ideas of justice.

I dart in and out of a shower and yank my binder over my head in a bathroom stall. Looking down at my chest and being able to move my arms without jostling anything, I feel relief for the first time since I entered the Y. My body feels less like an ill-fitting sweater and more like skin. My head clears, the perpetual lump in my throat dissolves, and my movements become less clumsy. I pull on my jeans one leg at a time, wiggling damp toes in my socks. I am alive again.

I come out to find Aisha adjusting a lilac hijab. I sit down on the bench beside her as she pins her scarf in place. She's wearing her favorite accessory today, a thin silver barrette with a rhinestone bird that the two of you found together on a trip to Casablanca years ago.

"Listen, Aisha—" I hesitate. "What can you tell me about *Geronticus simurghus?*"

"Oh, Lord." Aisha's smile crumples. "So she left you her notes after all."

It's not the first time they've cut funding to Aisha's bird sanctuary in Forest Hills, but it looks like it'll be the last. The sanctuary has been open for eight years and saved—Aisha tells me with pride on the R out to Queens—more than five hundred birds in its years of service to the avian public, an impressive number given its size, tiny budget, and skeleton crew of Aisha and two assistants.

I haven't been to Forest Hills since I was a kid, visiting a colleague of yours who lived in what seemed to me at the time a gigantic mansion on a tree-lined street. I have a similar impression now, walking through a stone arch away from the traffic and into a quiet, lush neighborhood of neo-Tudor houses with stucco faces and timber trim. Aisha walks beside me with sure strides of her bright yellow Pumas. We stop at her favorite teahouse for a ginger-and-turmeric tea along the way, where Julio Iglesias is singing on the radio. While we wait, Aisha tells me about the time the owner's daughter brought her a stunned mourning dove with a sprained wing, how she carried the bird like a newborn at her chest, swaddled in her mother's daisy tea towel.

Tea in hand, Aisha leads me down a few more blocks, and then we turn onto a smaller street, a quiet residential block with more substantial lawn space than I've seen anywhere in Brooklyn. We pass a gigantic elm, and behind it sits a large split-level house with wide bay windows. Gardenia bushes encircle the front porch in glossy jade leaves. A squat owl box sits atop a pole in the front yard, just the kind of goodhearted eyesore you would have helped Aisha install.

Inside, the house is a clean, white-walled space with worn hardwood floors. The air is filled with squawking and the trills of passerine birds. Plants in terra-cotta planters dominate the space, spider ivy cascading in clusters and young figs arranged in miniature groves. The large front windows flood the space with light. The house is set up like a veterinary office, with the open main space—once a palatial foyer, dining, and living area—divided into enclosures by mesh wire, the floor beneath them covered with old newspapers to protect the wood. Smaller birds are housed in large, airy cages suspended from the ceiling. A metal cart serves as a staging area by the door, with buckets of food and water, two pairs of thick gloves, and a half-filled notepad scribbled in purple ink. I spot a dozen species before I have time to blink: a turkey vulture with a wrapped leg, a barn owl with one wing in a splint, a one-eyed hawk with its bandages still on, an ivory egret.

At the edge of my vision, a third set of hands trails along the mesh. When you mouth the names of species, your words arise from within my own skull, as though your thoughts, even after death, are my own: *Phalacrocorax auritus—double-breasted cormorant; Megascops asio—eastern screech owl; Falco peregrinus—peregrine falcon; Ardea alba—great egret; Corvus brachyrhynchos—American crow.*

"Let's go back to the office." Aisha has not seen you. She coos at the birds and checks her notes for who's been fed and who's gotten their medicine. "It's gonna be tough when the funding runs out and I have to let my assistants go. This city isn't just hard on its human population, but on its avian communities, too. I guess it's too late to make people see that."

We make our way to the back of the house and into an office. Two eighties-style metal filing cabinets serve as supports for a heavy wooden plank, a makeshift table for Aisha's laptop and a stack of files and medical charts for each of the birds. A milk glass vase holds three white gardenia blossoms, plucked from the bush outside. A speckling of dirt has fallen onto Aisha's keyboard, and she clucks her tongue and rummages in her bag for a wet wipe to smooth it away. Aisha prepares for everything.

"What you might not know from your mom's notes," Aisha says, sitting down at the computer, "is that she managed to tag one of the birds in Lower Manhattan before the rest of the building was demolished." Aisha opens a database and scrolls through, tapping the mousepad with purple nails that match her hijab.

"That was five years ago. The tags must be useless."

"Some species of cockatoos live in captivity almost as long as humans. Even in the wild, an albatross can live to be almost as old as I am." Aisha looks up from the puddle of tea in her paper cup and raises an eyebrow. "Wanna hear a weird story?

"A few years back, I shared the tag numbers with some of our sister sanctuaries on a whim. I heard nothing for a while. Then last fall, early one morning I get a call from a sanctuary outside Detroit. That time of year, migratory species come south through the Mississippi Flyway from Canada or the Arctic circle. The sanctuary picked up a large white bird with iridescent contour feathers, dazed, probably concussed. The sanctuary thought it was some kind of egret or cormorant at first, or a juvenile ibis with unusual coloring. But you don't normally find those north of the Carolinas. Then—take a look." Aisha points to two entries in two separate spreadsheets. "The numbers match your mom's tag. What it was doing in Michigan—that's anybody's guess."

The ornithologist who first identified *Geronticus simurghus,* Benjamin Young, studied in New York City in the twenties, though records of him, like most Black students and scholars in the first part of the twentieth century, are scarce. Legend has it that he spotted *G. simurghus* while on a trip in upstate New York as a research assistant. He claimed to have discovered a new species following an unusual migratory pattern, heading westward rather than north-south. He tracked them for a week, observing their size, markings, and habits. Eventually he concluded that they were members of the *Geronticus* genus, which contains only two other members: the Northern bald ibis or waldrapp, found around the Mediterranean Sea and once thought to be a member of the same genus as the hudhud, and the Southern bald ibis, found only in subtropical southern Africa. Young hypothesized that the species had undergone divergent evolution, possibly due to its unusual migratory route across the Atlantic, a feat shared only with a few birds such as the blackpoll warbler and the Arctic tern. The length of this migration is what inspired Young to name the bird *simurghus*. According to his writings, Young had studied Persian during his undergraduate years and had a copy of Attar's twelfth-century Sufi poem *Mantiq ut-Tayr, The Conference of the Birds,* with him in the field. In the poem, thirty birds, led by the hudhud, embark on an epic search for the mythical bird called the Simorgh, who is to be their king. When Young returned to New York, his colleagues didn't believe his claims, accusing him of inventing the new species. Young defended his findings for years, but over time, *G. simurghus* dropped into obscurity and legend. Everyone seemed to have forgotten about Young's mysterious bird—everyone but you.

I pull my chair closer to Aisha's. "Was it *simurghus*?"

"It was never formally identified," she says. "The poor thing started to go wild at sunset, screeching and throwing itself against the fence. They have a bigger place over there, with mesh enclosures that back up to the woods. A couple hours after it was brought in, somebody found the wire twisted open. The bird had wrenched the enclosure open and taken off into the forest."

I slump in my chair. "So where does that leave us?"

"Not with much." Aisha shuts the laptop. "It had low body fat, so it could have been migrating long distance. But it wasn't the right time of year for that, and anyway it should have been flying south, not west." Aisha rubs her eyes. The sun has shifted in the front windows, casting a slice of citrus light under the door. The afternoon here is so peaceful that it's hard to imagine this place will be closed soon. But that's the thing about money, isn't it, that it's a slippery, shifting thing. Money can be the difference between sleeping in a bed or a bus station, can help build a home for thirty different kinds of birds, can pay rent and electricity and ease your grandmother's anxiety so she stops rationing her medication. But it's not that simple, is it, when the money has to come from some-where, or someone, with power.

Aisha lays a hand on my arm. "Sometimes we have to say Alhamdulillah and move on."

I wait for Aisha to feed the birds as the sun slides down the windows of the house. I draw the curtains. Aisha moves between the cages, her face dappled by the shadows cast by a lemon tree. The fringed end of her lavender scarf swings between her shoulder blades as she adjusts a water bottle. A trio of sparrows dips past the window and into the elm outside. I bend down to fill a bowl with seeds, and a pigeon with a bandaged leg hops over and nudges my hand. My mind is quiet; the pigeon is soft. I allow my thoughts and my shame to slide away. Maybe it's true that we become what we love most, that we exalt the nameless by losing ourselves in it.

SIX / LAILA

THIS LONG WINTER IS dragging into spring. Khalto Tala has promised to take me one of these days to see the countryside beyond
the city, but just when the crocuses poked their chins from the
ground, another snowstorm covered the roads, and Khalti decided
the weather wasn't fit for traveling. I'm starting to see how people
go years without ever leaving this island. Life moves quickly here,
and a day is gone before the coffee grows cold.

I miss you tonight. My life here is dull, so dull that it's hardly
worth mentioning. I wake before dawn to help Khalto Tala with the
chores, eat breakfast if I'm lucky and it's not too late in the month,
then go to school for a few hours before I join Khalti at the linen
shop. I don't know what I expected of New York, but it wasn't the
sore back I've gotten from bending over garments in Mr. Awad's shop
or the cough from the haze I'm always fighting. Sometimes, on summer nights, the auntie on the floor below us who owns a gramophone

puts it on in the window that faces the courtyard, and all the other families open their windows and listen. She likes to play "Amrika Ya Helwa," and I like this Arabic version of "America the Beautiful" best. My father is usually reading one of the Syrian papers printed in the city. In the evenings he pores over reports on the activities of the Gibran Society, articles on how the Holy Week was celebrated in Damascus, and news of which Syrian boys have won scholarships to Colgate or Harvard. All of this is sandwiched between crossword puzzles, advertisements for Syrian-owned rug, radio, and travel companies, and abbreviated reports of crime affecting the community. The latest of these headlines thrilled us all with shock and fear— ARSON SQUAD STARTS INVESTIGATING INTO BURNING OF BOSTON CHURCH (that's the St. George Syrian Orthodox Church; the fact that our church here in New York bears the same name surely added to the commotion). My father alternates his nightly reading between the English-language *Syrian World* and the Arabic *Al-Hoda,* whose articles often have conflicting opinions. One night my father will go on and on about the importance of abandoning Arabic and tradition in favor of assimilation, and the next he'll be wagging his finger at us and complaining that Issa and I always talk to him in English. My mother likes to support my father on this last point, since she rarely leaves the neighborhood, and her English isn't as good.

I should have known when we boarded the ship for Amrika that things weren't going to be the way my father had promised. The first three weeks at sea without you were some of the hardest of my life. I expected you around every corner, entertaining the wildest of fantasies: that you'd stowed away, that we would receive word in New York that you were coming to join us, that the ship would turn around and I would steal away to your mother's garden. Sometimes, even now, I sit watching the girls hang laundry in case I glimpse you in a crowd.

You're probably married by now. Don't be surprised that I know,

B, my mother told me everything. I remember the night well because it was still early spring then aboard the ship to Amrika, and the sea was stormy. It was my habit to go up to the deck after dark, once everyone was asleep, and let the terror of the waves tossing the ship drown out my thoughts. Besides, the air in steerage was rank with spoiled food and sweaty men.

On this night, the waves were particularly bad, and no one could sleep. My parents started to speak of home and of our neighbors. My mother's exact words were: *Soon,* ███████ *will be a married woman.* She told me your mother had found a good husband for you before we left. And why not? ████████ has a successful silk business, he can give you a good life. I should be happy. I should wish you well.

Over a meal of tinned fish and hard bread, my parents began to murmur about my own future, ignoring the stench of seasickness and the roar of the engines to dream of better things: that first glimpse of the statue that stood watch over New York Harbor, college for my brother, a job embroidering linens for me at the store where Khalto Tala had found work. The constant rocking of the ship made my stomach ache. I laid back on my cot and pretended to sleep, but my mother went on dreaming a husband for me. She told my father about the man who would come along one day, a beautiful milk-skinned American who always had his shoes shined and his hair parted. He would be a doctor or a banker. My mother would rub my face with turmeric and rose water to lighten my skin, she said, and make me look like a beautiful dark-eyed French girl. My future husband sounded so alien to me that I felt nauseated at the thought of lying beneath him. My parents spoke as though Amrika, with her fair-haired men and her torch, would cast a spell and transform us all into charmed, unrecognizable creatures.

After the storm had eased and everyone had settled into sleep, I escaped and climbed the ladder to the deck. I emerged to a cotton fog and the sting of salt. Above me, the mast disappeared into the starless gray night.

A boy was standing at the starboard rail, his head cocked toward something in the water. Now and then, he tugged on the worn coat draped around his shoulders. His linen pants had long ago grown too short for his legs, revealing the tendons on the backs of his ankles and his old leather sandals. He seemed totally unaware of my presence. As the mist drifted over the deck of the ship, I began to question whether he was there at all.

When he spoke, I jumped. "They're following us," he said, as though he were continuing a conversation we'd been having.

I crept closer until I was beside him at the rail. He kept his gaze on something off the side of the boat. He sported a fuzz of mustache over his lip, and the black hair at his temples merged into the soft down of boyhood on his cheekbones. He continued speaking as though he were irritated at having to repeat himself, telling me the birds had been following us for a day now. Before I could ask what he meant, a shape unfolded itself from the mist beside the boat, then a second. Two small birds, white-bellied with gray-brown backs and a crescent of charcoal under their eyes, adjusted their wings to buoy themselves on the night breeze. The boy explained that they were storm petrels, identifiable from the black markings under their eyes. He thought they were lost or wounded to have followed us so far, maybe blown to us by the storm winds. Their legs were thin as dandelion stems. It dawned on me that this boy must have made this voyage before, and I told him so.

He turned to me. On the side of his face that had been hidden, his iris was flecked with scar tissue, as though he'd been burned. He'd been turned away once before, he said. The doctors had mistaken eye damage from the glare off the water for trichoma. There was something mysterious about him that I couldn't quite decipher, so I asked him what his parents' names were, and what village he was from. He hesitated at first, then flicked his eyes to the ghosts beside the ship's rail as though he hadn't heard me. He told me his parents were waiting for him. I assumed he meant in New York and didn't press the matter. He couldn't have been much older than me, his voice not yet dropped, his eyes still with that big-eyed look of childhood.

Before I could say anything else, my brother's voice called to me from the fog, and the boy slipped away. Issa strode toward me across the deck, his hands in the pockets of his overcoat. Fog pooled in his elbows and glazed the stiff wool with droplets. He held up an object, breathless and grinning.

Issa has always managed to retain a boyish wonder in things and people, no matter how my parents tell him it's inappropriate for a boy his age, a firstborn son on the verge of manhood, to be so delighted by a flower or by sunlight on the water in the afternoon. I'd always been taught that men were wise and firm and never wondered at anything. Yet my parents have not succeeded in dissuading him from coaxing dry patches of earth to bear violets or from imitating the whistled languages of insects.

Issa bent his shoulders toward me and opened his hand. Inside was a linen pouch, little thicker than cheesecloth, secured with a drawstring. Shaking out its contents into his hand, he told me he'd met a man on the ship from Cairo, a botanist bringing a collection of seeds to Amrika, where he hoped to build a greenhouse and conserve rare plants. He took a single brown seed between his thumb and forefinger and held it up before a squinted eye. The botanist had said these seeds came all the way from Ethiopia, from a tree that grew in the mountains. After college, my brother said, perhaps he could work for him.

He spoke with such confidence that his dreams seemed close enough to reach out and touch. In that moment, under the milky moonlight, Issa's stiff overcoat reminded me of the men I'd grown up with, the fathers and jiddos who met over coffee to discuss politics, while at home their wives discussed who had sons in need of wives. With a snap of the fingers, our futures would diverge one day, and I would have to watch my brother walk through doors that would remain forever shut to me.

"Have you told Baba you're going to be a botanist now?" I said, more harshly than I should have.

The petrels glided through the mist some distance from the boat, ever silent, eyeing us with detached curiosity. Issa put the seeds back into their linen pouch and slid his hands back into his pockets, lowering his face toward the water. I regretted what I had said just then. My brother had still not noticed the birds. I considered calling out my future, too, to the witness of those phantoms, but I didn't want to lie, and I couldn't think of a single plausible future I wanted to name.

On the day we arrived in New York, the sky and sea were the dull gray of a kitchen knife. Though it was spring, the wind raked our necks with ice. Fog had become a constant companion in the mornings, and my parents grumbled of their fears that the ship would pass by the statue and her torch without seeing her. But as the men were gathering on deck to begin the morning's lookout for land, a flock of white egrets soared overhead. As they passed, the sea cracked and the fog parted, and the birds cut the mist before them like dogs through a pasture of goats.

After that, the winds were with us, and before long, a crowd gathered on the deck. An anxious silence settled over us. Issa took my hand and tucked it into the pocket of his overcoat. A strip of fog on the horizon darkened, and soon a silhouette with an outstretched hand appeared across the water. The families around me held their breaths. Her arm emerged, and her torch, then her patinaed face with its uplifted chin.

For a moment no one said anything. I shut my eyes and thought of you, as though your memory could prevent Amrika's enchantment of forgetting from falling on me like a sheet of rain. I'd expected cheers to erupt the moment we entered the harbor, but instead a quiet weeping began to spread across the masses on the deck. The sobbing grew until everyone around me, save Issa, was weeping. The cries of joy became zagharit, as though this were a wedding and the guest of honor had arrived at last. Men took off their red tarboushes and threw them into the sea. Women lifted their hands to heaven and praised God for his mercy. But nausea rose in me, and I slipped my hand into my pocket and closed my fingers around your hidden wing.

I untangled my other hand from Issa's and turned back. Gazing out toward the place we'd left behind, the ocean was wider than any desert. In the white foam of the ship's wake, the discarded tarboushes of my countrymen bobbed up and down behind us like flakes of rust.

As the ship pulled into the harbor, Ellis Island's arched portals became visible, its four copper-domed spires and its red brick. We waited as immigration officials boarded us at the harbor to process the first- and second-class passengers; then we in steerage were ferried to Ellis for processing. Everyone tumbled off the ship, speaking their own tongues, and pulled their baggage up the stairs into a great open hall. I would have given anything to see a familiar face just then, but when I saw the crush of people and the gruff way the American officials spoke to the passengers, I was glad you weren't there. My mother crossed herself and muttered a prayer.

As the other passengers fanned out to sit on the long rows of wooden benches, translators were located. My parents could speak no more than the few words of English Khalto Tala had tried to teach us, and Issa's lessons proved to be in vain, so we were brought to a man by the name of Hamawi with a curled mustache and a caramel for Issa and me.

"Alhamdulillah!" my mother said when the man addressed my father in Arabic. Finding someone from Hama, someone who might even know my father's business partners or friends, seemed a bewildering miracle. Mr. Hamawi asked us our names, where we were from, and how much money we'd brought with us. There were throngs of people all around us, mostly young men with steamer trunks dressed in their only suits, still blinking. After a time, we were ferried into a long series of rail-edged lines, like cattle, until we reached a large desk where a man sat with a buttonhook and a piece of chalk. The examination was quick: the doctor shone a light into our sore eyes, looked us over, and, marking our coats with chalk, pronounced us healthy, despite my fears of meeting the same fate as the boy on the ship.

Then Mr. Hamawi informed us that in America it was best to have names that the Americans could pronounce. My name was all right, he said, but my brother's was too uncommon to take with him. Poised with his pen above the paper that would change everything, Mr. Hamawi made suggestions, settling on Joseph, though Joseph was not at all a translation of Issa. And so Issa became Joseph. Our family name, too, would have to be adjusted for transliteration into English. His pen crackled across the paper, and just like that it was as though our family name had never existed, and the fist of Amrika's enchantments began to close around us.

As my brother and I picked up our family's steamer trunk, I caught a glimpse of a boy in a too-large overcoat, one eye flecked with scars.

"Ya sabi!" He didn't hear me, and before I could drop my end of the steamer trunk, my mother pulled me into line in front of her. A man crouched before us with a camera raised to his eyes. There was an explosion of light, and my mother told me I was a real Amrikiyah now, the kind of girl who has her picture taken.

The boy was gone again. We joined the throng of arrivals in their tweed jackets and Sunday hats and rushed toward the wooden post beyond the registry booth, where relatives were waiting.

A woman moved toward us through the crowd. She was a good

head taller than my father, so tall that she made my mother look like a child. She walked with shoulders curved forward as though protecting a flame from the wind. There was a light in her eyes, the same mischievous light that sometimes came over Issa's face when he discovered something beautiful that he couldn't explain.

"Ta'burni," the woman cried out in a deep voice, and all the other families fell silent. *You bury me.* It was the highest declaration of love I'd ever heard.

I hadn't seen Khalto Tala since I was small. Her warmth barreled toward us across the room, pushing aside wooden benches and towering over bespectacled men. Little wing, you'll believe me when I tell you that people can't help but be drawn to Khalto Tala. Rather than dressing in the plain woolen dresses and slippers my mother had always worn, Khalto Tala was dressed in her Sunday best, but with new twists: she had exchanged the shawl over her hair for a jaunty felt hat girded by a silver ribbon. Her plaid dress was cinched at the waist, a look that gave her a breezy, Parisian air. As she rushed toward us, the square heels of her black patent leather shoes click-clacked against the red tile floor. She had framed her smile with bold red lipstick. There was something different about her, even compared with the sophisticated ladies going in and out of St. Georges Hotel in Beirut. Khalto Tala had blossomed.

I should stop here for tonight, little wing—Khalti will be putting out the candle as soon as her mending is done. I haven't done her justice in these pages. Sometimes I think back to the day we lost our names and wonder if she, too, had to give up her name to that piece of paper for the silver ribbon in her hat, and whether she feels it's been a fair trade.

Little wing,

Another day is over at school and at the linen shop, and I am lying here, exhausted by the spring chill and by my chores. It's been weeks since I last wrote anything in this journal, I have so little to tell. Sometimes I wish I could show you my drawings. There are so many new birds here, B. Even after a heavy snow, I spot cardinals like lost red mittens on my way to school. Now the orange-breasted robins are coming back, too. I started sketching them for you—as though I'd ever have the courage to mail a single page—but then I discovered I liked drawing the birds for their own sake. Khalto Tala has been promising to get me a paint set soon, if we can pull together the money with some extra piecework. She even said she'd help me send one of my drawings to a contest here in the city in honor of somebody named Audubon who also used to paint birds. Khalti heard about it from one of the women in the local chapter of the United Ladies Syrian Society, which she says should keep my mother from scolding me about the contest fee.

The island of Manhattan is more a chain of cliffs and canyons than a city, which makes it perfect for spotting birds. The rock doves wander everywhere, perched on the sides of buildings, fluttering in great spirals over the parks, adorning the laps of statues and the stoops of brownstones. I thought they'd be too shy to approach the busier streets, but they strut right down the Great White Way with its neon, its dancers on their way to rehearsal, its Arrow Collars ads in lights. Strings of weary newsboys lift their chins from their hands to shoo them away from their perches atop stacks of papers. The first time I caught sight of the 6th Avenue elevated, I spotted an American lady in a fur coat tossing the last bite of a sandwich to a group of pigeons on the sidewalk, who squawked and clawed over it. I gaped at everything in those early days: the bolt of birds that appeared from the gutters and the rooftops to devour even the smallest crumb, the wooden-sided car that pulled up for the woman in her fur and pearls, the maze of blue veins beneath the pale bone of her wrist, as though she were held together by the skin on a cup of curd.

Everything about this city has been so different than I imagined it would be. When the ferry from Ellis Island landed at Battery Park at last, I spent the fifteen-minute walk—my brother and I hauling our steamer trunk between us—waiting to see the elegant house I'd dreamed of, with its sculpted staircase and great wrought iron railings. Khalti told us we weren't far from Wall Street, but though I tried to picture well-to-do blond men on their way to the Stock Exchange who would lift their gray hats to my mother and me, we didn't see them. In fact, as we continued uptown, the buildings became more tightly packed and the cobblestones less even. On one corner, a line of men curled around the block in worn coats and hats with chewed brims, waiting for bread. We passed bakeries with signs in Hebrew and Russian, and then my ears caught flashes of Arabic from the crowds: Washington Street, the place Khalto Tala announced was home. The road was packed with pushcarts and vendors selling vegetables, halawa, tea, roasted watermelon seeds, tin pots, religious statuettes, and an assortment of household goods. Men sat outside restaurants with names like Lebanon and Byblos smoking arghile, mustaches oiled and hair slicked, their shirts damp from the day's work. We passed an empty lot where a building had been torn down; its neighbor's blank brick facade bore a hand-painted advertisement for a cola whose name I couldn't make out. Soon we came upon rows of houses crammed like wood shavings in a tinderbox, the alleys between them strung with lines of yellowed laundry. There was only milky daylight the day we arrived; the haze of smog tends to temper the sun. Children played on the steps of the buildings and in the alleyways, some searching the garbage for glass bottles or bits of discarded food, kicking aside scrawny cats. Farther in the shadows of these alleys were plywood huts, some decorated with lithographs with grimy frames, some insulated with newsprint, and Khalto Tala told me these huts house the families who lost their jobs and got evicted. The stink of smoke and car exhaust filled the air, the gutters were stained with soot, and the drains were stuffed with the rusted corpses of cockroaches.

My first impression of our building was of suffocating closeness. Khalto Tala led us into hallways where children hid behind their mothers' skirts and women hummed over their sewing machines. Our apartment—shared with Khalto Tala—was little more than half the size of our house in Syria. The walls of the narrow bedroom were covered with faded orange wallpaper, pressing in on the bunk bed and the mattress on the floor, and the cold kitchen was barely large enough to fit a wood stove and a metal wash bucket.

My mother set about making the apartment a home, *tsk*ing those first few days that Khalti had sacrificed her femininity to this squalid place. Since the very moment we moved in here, my father started to talk about finding a job and moving us somewhere else. He still had something of his youthful charm, and it didn't take him long to become fast friends with a man from Zahle who lived next door. He worked at a factory and represented the union. After coffee and tawleh one evening, this man offered to try to get him a job at the factory where he worked. Someone else had gone home to his own country, he said. *This life is not for everyone,* my father's friend said, and these days my father has taken to saying this, too. When my father comes home from the factory in his denim overalls and wool cap, he says he enjoys a hard day's work. He got a good job making machine parts for printing presses, one of the few manufacturing jobs you can find in New York these days. My mother told me the man before him had been paid three times my father's wages, but I doubt it would have mattered to him. He's proud to feel useful.

Within a few weeks, I started walking from school in the afternoons straight to the linen shop on Rector Street where Khalto Tala found a small job for me. She works in the back room embroidering ladies' negligees or doing lacework for tablecloths, and I help her, bending over the dented table and wiping sweat from my eyelashes until it's time to go home. It's not glamorous, but it has its bright moments. There's a dry goods shop next door, so every now and then, when Khalto Tala goes outside for a cigarette break to rub her sore hands, she gives me a coin for a bit of chocolate or some taffy. In the beginning, when we had a few moments to ourselves, she would pull out a book and teach me to read. I'm a quick study, she says, not just with English but with everything. Over the past year I started bringing books home from school to read to her and chatting away with the shopkeeper next door. It's gotten so that I dread the moment Mr. Awad calls us back into the shop and away from my stories. Khalto Tala brags to my mother about my English, but has sworn me to secrecy about her smoking.

You'd like Khalto Tala, little wing, I'm sure of it. Did I already tell you that? She lets me draw my own patterns on the lace now, bringing them to life with careful stitching. I think the drawing helps. We told Mr. Awad they were Khalti's at first, since I was only supposed to be tracing her patterns, but he likes them. I get bolder each week, outlining sparrows and robins and the petrels I saw at sea. Well-to-do ladies who have heard about my designs from a friend or seen them on a cousin's curtains drop into the store from uptown now, wanting their own. Mr. Awad pays Khalto Tala by the piece, so it's more money for the family. My parents have already talked about pulling me out of school after this year to get a full-time job if we can't make rent. Khalto Tala is the only one who's resisting this plan, with the excuse that she can't fit another body in that cramped workroom for more than a few hours a day.

It was Khalti who gave me this notebook, once I'd started reading on my own, though it took me almost a year to get up the confidence to start writing. She took me into the bedroom we shared and, even with the peeling orange wallpaper, it was like we were celebrating Christmas, the way the notebook was wrapped in brown paper and tied with twine. She had set it in a wooden box from the bilad, the kind inlaid with geometric designs in mother-of-pearl and secured with a tin clasp. In the box, below the package of the notebook, lay a magnificent set of colored pencils. Never had I owned anything so fine. "You have talent, Leiloul," she said to me then, "and I want to help you make the most of it."

I placed your wing in the box with the pencils and set it beneath my cot. Out on the street, they were lighting the gas lamps, and the pigeons were alighting for the evening on the roof-top across the courtyard. I still haven't seen any bird keeper, though there must be one. I imagined God taking the form of a starling to alight on the carts of the men selling tea and ice cream. That was the night I began to draw.

SEVEN / ██████

IN THE YEARS SINCE your death, the city has been drawing birds the way an open wound draws flies. The latest to arrive are the goldfinches, which appear the day they dig up the empty lot beside the last remaining tenement of Little Syria. It begins as a flashing cloud of yellow gold that draws bystanders and cameramen for the evening news. Then the tornado of birds shuts the Irish pub on the ground floor of St. George's Church for the better part of an afternoon. Nothing gets through the swarm of beaks. A news van arrives and sends a reporter into the yellow cloud: she goes in, disappears, and comes out screaming, her pink sheath dress shredded at the shoulders, her face tallied with scratches. The stunt is not repeated.

The storm of goldfinches rages until well after sunset, transforming two and a half blocks of Washington Street into a cacophony of chirping and whirring, a shimmering plague. The birds appear as though they've dug themselves out of the earth, and one by one they start to disappear the same way, landing dazed on the pavement, blinking, and vanishing into the empty side lots or through the doors of buildings. Some of the people who came to watch had grandparents or great-grandparents who lived in the tenements, and the ones who can still remember the neighborhood as it used to be elbow one another and say the birds are part of the brick and the brownstone, that there will be no stray feathers for the supers of the neighboring buildings to find. Still, for a few hours after the storm subsides, a bird hunt is conducted, and the staff of the hotels and bars grumble that next time they'll just get someone to drive their car through the cloud and clear up the mess.

By about nine at night, the last of the birds have disappeared. Aisha and I scour the blocks for injured birds, but we find none, so Aisha heads back out to Queens empty-handed. The crowds drawn by the noise have long since dispersed.

I approach the mound of rubble that is now the empty lot. The construction company has put up a fence around it, advertising a future high-rise apartment complex, blue glass in the sunlight of an imagined morning. I slip through without so much as a scrape. Inside, the machines have gouged the building's blank face, clawing away my graffitied hudhud, leaving only a deep wound where I'd set down golden paint.

"No. No." I fumble around on the ground, seizing chunks of brick and testing them in the holes left in the side of the building. A couple of pieces are still painted, but I can't match the colors. I run back to the fence and squeeze my way through to the street, then stalk over to the windows of the community house and peer inside. The construction company has gutted the inside of the building from top to bottom, leaving only the remnants of a staircase in the corner and preparing for the demolition that will take place in a couple weeks. They will be replacing this building with an overpriced pub or a restaurant for the good old boys, the chalkboards advertising bourbon drinks and artisanal charcuteries. Though the church is protected, the two lots that house the tenement and the community house have been bought, and soon something unfamiliar will stand in their place.

I am tired. I am bleeding again, and my body feels heavy and bloated, my chest so sore that I want to rip off my binder and feel the night air on my skin. I lay myself down on the step in front of the boarded-up door. The clang of a construction site rings out into the night. A block away, a street sweeper makes its rounds. I touch the film of coolness on the sidewalk and hear the voices of the workers who laid the cobblestones beneath; below that, I hear the whispers of the enslaved people who were forced to clear the land to build the walls for which Wall Street is named. I used to think remembering could be a kind of resistance, but I'm not sure it's enough. For years, I forced myself to pore over my memories of you, to do as much remembering as I could stand. I hang on to a handful of moments that don't hurt: the fountains in Central Park in the summer, the curve of your back over your work table, sitting with our feet on the fire escape under the moon. There aren't many stars in this city, but you told me a full moon can show you your own shadow. I know the fire wasn't my fault, and the collapse of the fire escape was a freak accident, but the ghosts of things are circular enchantments. You cling to every iron ladder in the city now, slipping off every platform into the night.

Something buzzes past my face. I reach up to swat it away, and the last goldfinch escapes into the building's broken window. A red silk fisherman's knot is tied around the chained door handles, swinging in the night breeze.

Oud music drifts toward me from the street. I get up and dust myself off, then follow the sound. Manhattan is hushed, listening. Away from the streetlights, my body is invisible. The plucking of the oud's strings turns the corner from Washington onto Albany, and so do I.

A boy strolls toward the Hudson River esplanade playing a bowl-bodied oud. A rope of red silk, identical to the one tied to the sealed doors of the community house, is fastened to one of the tuning pegs. The falconer's knot on the end sets the rope swinging like a pendant. Sami once told me this knot was used to tether birds of prey to their perches, two knots of the same type beside each other, because birds in captivity often untie their bonds and free themselves. The oud player passes under a streetlamp. He is humming a maqam to the darkness.

"Sami."

The oud player and his music stop. Samer Shaaban turns to me, the red knot brushing his thigh. He is as fragile and invincible as a cord of spider's silk. The goldfinch is perched on the neck of his oud, its head cocked as though listening. Sami laughs, and the goldfinch flutters off on the ribbon of his voice.

"Girl," he says, grinning, "where have you been?"

I've avoided Sami for six months, long enough to forget how persuasive he is. He convinces me to hang out for a few hours, so we take the 4 back to his place in Crown Heights. With nothing to say and Sami smiling so broad it's like he's never been happier to see anyone, I try to remember that this is how he treats all his friends. Still I blabber on about your notes, and Laila Z's last painting, and the bird Sabah and Aisha don't believe exists. By the time I finish the story, we've arrived at Utica, and we wind our way off the platform and past the cops posted at either exit. Aboveground, teenagers huddle in clusters up and down Eastern Parkway, and the faint smell of weed permeates the street. Carrying his oud in its soft black case on his back, Sami leads me past open-late laundromats, tiny liquor stores with their clerks behind bulletproof plastic, and half a dozen barber shops. His apartment sits atop a Trinidadian braiding salon; the owner's husband is outside chatting with their neighbors when we arrive. Sami gives him a fist bump and they exchange a few words before he unlocks the door to the staircase that leads up to his apartment. It's a studio, populated by a fold-up futon, a refrigerator that looks like it's from the seventies, and a coffee table that doubles as Sami's workspace. The table is scattered with bits of dyed rope, scraps of linen, and braided silk. Sami straightens the blanket on the futon, which serves as a couch, and gets me a soda from the fridge. It's his last can; he's probably been saving it for visitors. He lights a fat candle on the corner of the table.

I sink down onto the futon. "I like your new place."

Sami laughs. "Don't say that. Every time I get to like a place, they raise the rent. Maybe liking it is bad luck." He flops down next to me and picks up a light-brown length of braided linen, not yet dyed. He ties a simple overhand knot like a meditation. Then, as though remembering something, he gets up, favoring his left leg, and opens the window to drink the night air. An ashtray filled with the butts of hand-rolled cigarettes and the stubs of incense sits on the sill beside him.

I roll my soda can between my palms, grateful for a bit of distance. I can still see Sami catching his toe in the gap between the subway car and the platform, gashing his knee on the concrete to the white, bloodless bone. I sterilized it, bandaged it, changed the gauze on the way home when it bled through.

"You never got that checked out, did you?"

"Unbelievable, considering how many places are dying to give you a job with health insurance, right?" Sami tugs at the keratinized scar, a purple circle of tight, shiny skin. "Could've healed worse."

I pick up an oysterman's stopper knot tied on a length of white rope. "The reporters said an illegal breeder had a shipment of finches escape on Washington Street. You believe that?"

"Not for a second. But it's their job to explain things."

"You say that like it doesn't piss you off, but I can see your ashtray from here."

Sami laughs into the knot in his hands, a good-natured belly laugh. This is what I love most about him: he is always laughing, especially at himself. "Have pity on me, I'm a Pisces. Virgo season has me all neurotic."

We both laugh. My chest hurts because this is just how it used to be, Sami and me, holed up in whatever rent-stabilized apartment he'd managed, miraculously, to snag a sublet in, sharing a cigarette even though neither of us smoked because it took the edge off our hurt.

I hold up one of his silk knots. "Is that why you're holding a bondage convention up in here?"

Sami shrieks with laughter and wipes away a tear. He's grown a short, dark beard. I never saw him bearded when we used to hang out. He's wearing a vibrant purple T-shirt sporting one of his own designs, an illustration of a peony that looks like the love child of O'Keeffe and Leyendecker. These six months have given him a couple gray hairs, but he looks younger than ever, sitting on that windowsill with a bit of rope beside him, sparking a lighter against a cigarette.

"You look good."

Sami doesn't hear me. "I use the knots to mark where things happened. Marking a thing is a kind of witnessing. The past is already bound to the ground where it took place. I'm just making the bond visible." Sami leans out to check for people on the sidewalk, then ashes out the window. "Plus, knots are sacred. Traditionally, we called Pisces 'the cord' instead of the fish, and Alpha Piscium was called al-Uqdah, the knot. So according to Arab astrology, I was literally born for this."

I laugh. The candlelight is warm, the kind of light you could fall asleep in. "Kind of woo-woo, but I can get behind that."

Sami cants his hips and lowers his chin to his chest, and the earring in his right ear sparkles in the candlelight. "You know me. I love woo-woo." He takes a drag of his cigarette and grins at me again, a childlike grin that tells me he is glad that I am here, and I feel guilty for wishing I were somewhere else. I take a swig of my soda and set it on the floor. Beside me is a pile of sketchbooks, the top one open to a portrait in progress of Hajjeh Shaaban. Sami is drawing from a photo taken just before her death, eight months after we lost you.

"Of course," Sami is saying, "the knots don't actually matter. The whole point of binding things is to draw attention to them, to keep them alive."

"About that." I want to get up and join Sami at the window. I bounce my leg up and down instead. "Everyone's telling me the birds are a dead end."

"It's not your fault. Laila Z was talented, sure, but you'll never be able to prove that what she saw and what your mom saw were the same thing." He puts out his cigarette on the windowsill and settles back into the futon.

"I know this painting exists. It has to."

Sami raises his eyebrows, an Arab *no*.

His disbelief burns. "Maybe we don't have to prove it. It would be enough for me just to know." I blink in the candlelight. "If I could find Laila—"

Sami snorts. "With a seance? Laila disappeared after they demolished her building. Her last act of resistance was facing down a wrecking ball. Girl was made of iron."

"We don't know for sure that she's died." I wring my hands to keep from picking my cuticles. "What if she just got tired of the spotlight? Moved away from New York?"

"Don't you think somebody would have heard from her?" Sami says. "That she would've gone on painting?"

I bristle. "Look, I'm just saying we don't have all the information. I'm not giving up until I know for sure."

"Suit yourself." Sami sighs and runs a hand through his curls. "I'm supposed to meet a friend at this party in Bed-Stuy in an hour. We do it every couple weeks. You should come."

The room feels stifling. I get up and go to the window. The street is deserted except for the black trash bags on the curb and a lean rat darting between them. The breeze strokes my face. To the night, I am a body without a past or a future, a pillar that bends light. The night doesn't know my name.

Sami lays his hand on my arm, and I flinch at the lightning of it.

"Hey," he says in a softer tone. "It's just a couple birds."

On the nights when I've been dancing—which aren't many—I've always loved the girls I couldn't be: the ones with arms open, those sneaker-dancing, thunderstorms-in-their-blood girls whose soft wisdom was a flood. Sami and I roll up to the bar in Bed-Stuy, an unassuming building next to a masjid and a grocery store, blue neon buzzing in the window. Inside, televisions play music videos full of pastels and neon, and people in bright leather jackets, trucker caps, bangles, and mesh, glitter and hair piled atop their heads, fill the space. Someone slides past me in a purple mesh tank top and glitter eyeshadow. Couples make out in the back booths, sipping vodka or soda or some kind of blue concoction dreamed up by the bar staff.

When I turn back to the bar to look for Sami, he's already down at the end greeting a Black femme in overalls, a black-and-white keffiyeh, and chunky black boots, box braids piled up atop a fresh undercut. The place is too packed to get by, so I squeeze by a couple at the bar and wave an awkward hello over Sami's shoulder.

"This is Qamar," Sami yells over the music. "Qamar's doing their PhD thesis in art history."

"Defending next week," Qamar yells back. "You a friend of Shaaban's?"

I nod and nudge Sami to the side so I can rest my elbow on the bar. I yell back my name and wish the noise of the bar would swallow it.

The bartender hands Qamar a beer, and they sip the head off the top before lifting it from the bar. Their nails are painted a vibrant shade of magenta that throbs under the blacklight, and they wear a gold crescent moon choker at their neck to match their name. I cannot imagine loving one's own name enough to wear it as an adornment. Sami gets us each a beer, and the three of us retreat to the back to sip our drinks and people-watch.

"Yara? Malik?" Sami asks.

"Yara had to work. Pretty sure we lost Malik to that guy in their building." Qamar sips their beer and raises their eyebrows at Sami.

Sami rolls his eyes. "You know what, fuck it. Tonight we celebrate you."

I raise my drink. "To your defense next week."

Qamar laughs. "Don't jinx me," they protest, but we toast anyway.

I lean over to make myself heard over the DJ. "I love your keffiyeh."

"It was my mom's." Qamar smiles and touches the scarf's white tassels. "From Ramallah."

Sami claps me on the back before I can respond. "She's an artist," he tells Qamar. "A painter."

I almost choke on my drink. "Not really. I just went to art school." An awkward pause. "What's your thesis on?"

"My grandfather was an ornithologist," Qamar says, "and a birder, back in the twenties and thirties. I'm completing his work."

I freeze. Before I can open my mouth, the DJ turns the music up, and Missy Elliott comes on. Sami grabs my arm. "Reem! She would love this. Would she pick up if we called her?"

"She's up in Boston at her new job. You know, being the responsible kid." I drain my beer. Qamar takes out their phone and scrolls through their messages.

Sami pulls me onto the dance floor, and I don't protest, though I want to. I've become just like the white boys at middle-school dances: the boys by the wall, earthbound boys, wing-severed boys with stiff bodies. There is nothing behind the door in my chest that should uncage the kind of feminine softness I should have, the kind you told me would settle into my chest and my hips. It never did.

"I don't dance," I yell to Sami above the music.

"Dancing is a myth," Sami says.

Sami dips his chest and lifts his hands, and he is not dancing, but trying to fly. He is testing his body in the wind, feeling the weight and breadth of it. My heart is a new bird throwing itself against the space he is taking up. There are no long-legged white girls around us, no pale, over-cologned boys snicker-flirting with the bartender. Instead, all around us, there are brown and Black bodies marked with glow paint and tattoos. There are micro-minis and leather short-shorts and calf-length dresses in pleated faux silk atop unshaven legs. There are bodies with breasts, with thighs, with scars, with canes; wearing high heels, wearing high tops; large bodies, small bodies, bodies that twirl and shake and fill the room. This is not dancing, but a becoming of winged creatures.

The DJ turns the music down, and the room stills to listen. Even over the bass beat, the sound of the isha' adhan next door is loud enough to make itself heard. The DJ has lowered the music out of respect, so that the call to prayer becomes part of the music. The room continues to dance as though this is simply another rhythm to move one's body to. Once, a friend of yours from Marrakesh played us a recording of the adhan from the streets of the old medina. She said it reminded her that, no matter what she was worrying about, life was fleeting, and one day none of the fears that plagued her would matter at all. I always liked that about the adhan: that a sound could both remind me that I was going to die and comfort me with the reminder that I was still alive, that it could remind me of the ways my ancestors touched their foreheads to the earth. That a single sound could tap that ancient place in my bones and make it sing like a plucked string.

The last time I went to the masjid with you is as alive as though it's still happening. It is Ashura, and I am fasting. It is a hot day. I put on my abaya, wrap my hijab, walk with you up the stairs to the women's room. I take off my sandals and set them in the cubby, and inside, the carpet meets my hungry toes. The women burst into the room like eagles, faces bright, their abayat emerald and night-black and pomegranate. Half of the women who greet me look like Teta, like the woman I am supposed to one day become. As-salaamu alaykum, we say to one another as women arrange themselves in rows for prayer, wa alaykum as-salaam. We recite and bow our heads and turn to our angels on either side. Then the day is gone, and we break our fast behind closed doors where teenage girls whip off their hijabs and laugh, sequester themselves from their mothers, tell dirty jokes, oil their fingers with turmeric chicken. Bismillah, we say, and eat until we are full. In those days, as out of place as I felt in the world, I would have dared anyone to tell me we were anything less than our own feast.

I haven't prayed since the day they slid you into the earth. Your grave faces a copse of pines that separates the cemetery from the homes of rich families who don't want to see the dead and the grieving. We buried not a person but a continent that day. We're made from clay, after all, aren't we, and underground springs and threads of copper run in our veins. When this country asks me where I'm from, they aren't asking for the city on my birth certificate, but whose earth is in my blood.

Then the adhan is over, and I am swimming in the music. I paint the space around me with my body. I think of the last time I used my hands to make something beautiful. As long as my body was not for myself, I stopped allowing myself the luxury of wanting. But here in this space that smells of sweat and sage and cigarette smoke, anything seems possible, even desire. Sami curves his back, his knees, his neck. He is beautiful, and I am still in love with him, and this is not a mistake.

I bend and untangle and step out of my body, lightening myself into this swollen room where boys like me are arcing and vaulting our unruly bodies, shaking the wet newness from our wings.

EIGHT / LAILA

B, I THINK KHALTO Tala might be like me.

It's been nearly a month since I last wrote anything in this journal, but I can't keep my thoughts in my head today. The dawn was cold, one of those chilly April mornings that feels like winter is setting in again. I woke up at dawn to find Khalto Tala missing from our narrow bed. I kicked off the wool blanket and wrapped one of her embroidered shawls around my shoulders, the asymmetrical one—the scissor had slipped off the bias, and Mr. Awad rejected it, so Khalti took it home—and exposed one of my arms to the chill as I shuffled out into the hallway. A few of our neighbors were already awake, humming at the windows into the courtyard between the eastern and western wings of the building. Women tugged on the lines to hang their laundry for the day, and the predawn breeze swayed towels, sheets, and children's underthings. Imm Faysal next door opened her window to move the stale air, and a faint argument drifted out from the bedroom. On the street, Lower Manhattan was waking. Boys put on their caps and left for their jobs delivering newspapers or selling fruit by pushcart; shop owners walked to the market on Washington Street; neighbors greeted one another from their stoops. Beyond our neighborhood, the horns of Fords and Hillmans pierced the blue shadows as Midtown stretched and grumbled.

I made my way down the hallway in a pair of my mother's slippers and took the narrow staircase to the roof. To be a bird, I remember thinking, to be a bird and see the streets from above the iron canyons, to look toward the place where I was born and see the first ray of sun falling across the island of Manhattan. Our building is five stories high, and dawn is the only time I have to myself before Issa goes off to school and the demands of the day begin.

I'd never explored the tar-papered roof before. That morning, when I pushed open the door, I was greeted by the ceaseless cooing of pigeons. Grit and pebbles dug into the thin soles of my slippers as I propped the door open with a rock, then walked toward the edge of the roof. As my eyes adjusted, shapes emerged from the shadows around me: the silver tubes of exhaust chimneys and the discarded blankets of the people who sometimes sleep up here on warm nights.

Farther off sat several enormous wooden crates. A lanky figure moved between the boxes, hunched but brisk, a canvas bag in one hand. I crept closer. A key squeaked into a lock, and the bars of one of the cages creaked open. The figure tossed seeds from the canvas bag inside, and as she straightened, the first caress of morning light kissed Khalto Tala's yellow work apron.

I called out to her, and she jumped. From inside the row of wooden coops came the fluttering of hundreds of wings. The boxes were dovecotes, at least four wide coops of plywood and mesh chicken wire. As Khalto Tala jumped back, out the pigeons went in a sea of clucking complaints, a fury of gray and white wings, and took to the muddy skies above Washington Street. What a sight! Khalto Tala cried out and covered her face with her arms as the wall of feathers tumbled past her, but soon she was laughing. She brushed her hands on her apron. Seeds lay spilled on the papered rooftop, picked at by the few remaining pigeons.

It turned out the pigeons weren't Khalto Tala's at all. A woman in a white lace kerchief emerged from behind the dovecotes, laughing into a fistful of her apron. She was darker than Khalti, with sharp black eyes and bolts of silver at her temples. I recognized her as the widow Haddad, one of our neighbors who works in a haberdashery, cinching ribbons around the brims of cloches. She lost her husband in the Great War before I was born, and though she has no children, she's never remarried, opting to live alone ever since. My mother talks about her sometimes when she scrubs my face in the summer with turmeric and lemon, for which I've always felt too ashamed to speak to her.

"Tell me, ya bint," the widow Haddad said, and her accent was of Jabel, from the mountains. "Have you any experience with racing doves?"

Khalto Tala laughed and told her to let me be, but I joined the widow Haddad at the roof's edge. She took a rag and a bucket of water and began to scrub the perches, soiled with the birds' white waste, and motioned for me to look inside the coops. One pigeon had declined to fly out with the others. He cocked his white head at me and searched me with bright, curious eyes. A cape of black feathers gave way to mottled brown-and-white wings, and a ruff of iridescent feathers crowned his neck, the black flashing pink and purple as he moved his head to get a better look. He seemed a strange sort of bird, but I liked him. I held out my hand, and the pigeon dipped his beak into my palm as though expecting a treat.

The widow Haddad told me to be gentle with the bird, whose name was Khan. She shook a mound of seeds into my hand and went on scrubbing the perches, telling me how, after she came to

Amrika after the war, the bird was the only friend she had. The Haddad family has bred pigeons for generations. Their birds are strong flyers, she told me, fast and brave. Khan was the start of her flock in Amrika.

"You'll find birds much more agreeable than people," the widow Haddad said.

Khalto Tala brushed her hands on her apron and agreed.

Below us, the street markets were coming to life. Carts of peanuts and carrots were set outside of grocery shops, wool dresses had been hung above the doors of dress shops, and women walked the cobblestones with their market baskets. I held out my hand, and Khan pecked carefully into my palm, taking the seed first with his tongue and then with his beak, as if he were trying to be gentle.

When I glanced back at Khalto Tala, she was no longer paying attention. She and the widow Haddad stood side by side, not touching, but standing close enough to hear each other breathing. Khalto Tala handed a rag to the widow Haddad, and that's when I saw it—the brush of Khalti's fingers on the back of the older woman's hand, her pinky clasping Khalti's. They were slow to pull away, each woman humming the same tune.

My mother has a particular candle she burns each night during her evening prayers, after the washing up and mending is done. She brought it with her in our steamer trunk when we left the village, wrapping it up in her tattered socks to conceal it in case the other passengers or the inspectors had sticky hands. It was given to her before we left by a neighbor, one of the oldest women I know of, so old that my mother dressed the bodies of five of her sons and three of her grandchildren who died in the uprisings of my parents' youth. Now long since widowed, this ancient woman used to walk herself to church every Sunday without fail. My mother never told me the story of the candle, but I'm clever enough, little wing, to understand that the more mourning a person has done, the more they pray. Or so I used to think. When we first arrived here, my mother lit the candle each night like this woman's gift was the only thing still nursing her faith.

Tonight, my mother's holy candle stands unlit.

The day began without incident. Khalto Tala sent me over to Mr. Shaheen's dry goods store when it was still dark to pick up a new wick for the oil lamp we used in the back of the shop. We had long ago lost the luxury of buying chocolate or taffy at break time. I was only sent over now when we ran out of paper or ribbon to wrap the packages, or if I was to pick something up for my mother before the shop closed. The steam was rising from the subway grates, bringing with it the smell of train brakes and urine, a smell that will probably always remind me of this city. It began to rain, the clouds threatening a downpour. The shop's sticky heat and the icy drizzle had uncoiled my braids, and I shivered as I returned from Mr. Shaheen's with the wick. I passed a subway entrance and fantasized of all the places I've heard about from Khalto Tala that I would have rather escaped to in that moment: a jazz show in Harlem, watching a woman in a dapper suit performing at Coney Island, riding a steam-powered merry-go-round in Central Park.

I shuffled back into the workroom out of the wet, which was when all the trouble started. I had just started sewing Chantilly lace trim onto the straps of a camisole when Khalto Tala came into the workroom and said there was a woman there to see me.

At first I didn't believe her. I cracked open the door to peek out onto the floor of the shop, though, and sure enough, there was a white woman standing there, sighing and checking her yellow hair in a pocket mirror. I'd seen her a few times before, usually stepping out of her Rolls-Royce in a ribbon-trimmed hat to peruse the negligee in the shop's window display. Once, I'd spotted her disappearing into one of the photography shops on Rector where wealthy American women had pictures taken wearing our grandparents' thobes, dripping with gaudy costume jewelry the photographers found in the pawn shops. She was out of place here on the shop floor, shifting from foot to foot.

I turned to Khalto Tala, who nudged me out. I may be nearly grown now, but I'm still my mother's scrawny daughter, and I have a habit of walking so quietly that no one sees me until I startle them. As I approached, the woman didn't notice. She slid off one of her gloves to run her fingers over the lace sparrows I'd embroidered on a shawl and cooed with satisfaction. Mr. Awad, who was never far away, strode over quick as lightning to tell her about the excellence of the design she'd been admiring, that all our merchandise was made by the finest Syrian craftsmen, that the silk was imported from the Holy Land. The Americans seemed to like us better when we mentioned the Messiah.

I coughed, and at last the woman turned to appraise me. My face was grimy with sweat. She frowned. She gave me the same look as the other women who frequented the store, the look that made me feel like a baby mouse found in a kitchen cupboard: unusual, but not something she wanted to touch.

The woman's name, as it turned out, was Mrs. Theodore, a "patron of the arts," she called herself. Khalto Tala translated for me: Mrs. Theodore had donated the prize money to the art competition I'd entered.

Little wing, I won. She had to say it twice before I believed her—in fact, it wasn't until she told me she'd agreed to spend the afternoon with the winner that I understood she had come to give me my award. From the look on her face, I wasn't entirely what she'd been expecting.

Mrs. Theodore handed me a certificate with my name on it and put her gloves back on as though she were ready to leave. Khalto Tala pushed me toward her.

"Congratulations," Mrs. Theodore said, "you should be very proud." She motioned for me to follow.

Mrs. Theodore's black Rolls-Royce was parked outside. A man in a suit and white gloves opened the rear passenger door for us. I hesitated, and Mrs. Theodore beckoned me inside. "Hurry up now, girl," she scolded. I slid myself into the leather seat, my face hot.

Soon we were zooming away uptown. Mrs. Theodore batted dust from the hem of her dress. "Now I remember why I stopped coming down here," she said, dabbing her handkerchief at a fleck of soot. "Don't you people sweep your steps?"

Mrs. Theodore made a noise between a scoff and a chuckle, and the polite smile froze on my face. Had it been a joke? The space shrank to a tight, airless box. I dropped my eyes to the smooth leather of the back seat with its wooden armrests and silver door handles. I was afraid to touch anything. I tried to smooth the wrinkles in my gray skirt, tucking my ankles into the hem to hide the scuffs on my plain leather shoes. I began to fear Mrs. Theodore would spot the dirt and the stains on my clothes and decide she didn't want me soiling the leather. I had only ever learned to find my way around Little Syria and Battery Park; I wouldn't know how to get home from anywhere else.

Mrs. Theodore pulled off her gloves and thumped them in her lap. Her smile reappeared, brisk. She adjusted her hair in a pocket mirror, and I had the strange sense that I was standing just out of frame in a movie about this woman's life. I admitted to myself that she was very beautiful, and she had the childlike air of a person who believes themselves to be likable and just. She told me she had big plans for our afternoon together, that I would see *real culture*, though I wasn't sure what she meant by that, and that I would see the most beautiful bird art there was.

I told her I liked to draw birds very much, and that one day I wanted to be a painter. Mrs. Theodore gave a faltering smile and then burst out laughing as though I'd told her I wanted to go to the moon. "What an odd little girl," she said with her hand to her mouth. When she spoke, her crisp English made me feel like I'd walked out onto a frozen pond, waiting to fall.

Mrs. Theodore leaned forward to open the glass partition, gave the driver a name, and then shut it with a click. Soon our car pulled up to a curb in a section of Midtown I had never seen, a wide plaza filled with pale businessmen in dark suits. The driver opened the door for us. I tumbled out after Mrs. Theodore as she fluffed her hair and adjusted her fur collar.

I followed Mrs. Theodore through a set of glass doors trimmed in black marble. Inside was a low-ceilinged hall with sleek wooden paneling and sculpted lamps. The room felt close, but the warm light kept it from feeling stifling. Americans in rich attire, mostly men, were seated in rows, watching another man at the front of the room gesture to a large print on a wooden stand. A woman arranged the page on the stand with gloved hands as he spoke.

Mrs. Theodore took a seat and motioned for me to stand beside her on the nearest aisle. From this distance, I could make out the rust-colored feathers of the red-tailed hawk in the print, the stripes on its tail feathers minutely etched.

Apparently Mrs. Theodore, too, had a passion for birds as well as for art. She described to me the technique of copperplate etching, where a picture is drawn onto a sheet of copper with a metal tool and used to print many copies. Audubon, in whose honor the competition I'd won had been held, had hand-painted his prints with watercolor after etching them. To tell you the truth, little wing, I'd never seen anything so fine in all my life. But though I itched to move and get a better look, Mrs. Theodore wouldn't stop talking. She droned on about the life of the artist, from his birth in the French colony of Haiti to his death here in Manhattan. She seemed to think this was an end worthy of admiration in itself. She told me some of Audubon's birds, like the dodo, were extinct by now. I asked Mrs. Theodore why the birds' necks and backs were twisted into impossible silhouettes. Mrs. Theodore blinked and said, "He did shoot them, dear."

Bidders began to raise their hands. Soon the print was whisked off the auction stand, sold to a fat man in a bowler hat who only raised his finger and never spoke. As the auction continued, he outbid Mrs. Theodore every time—first on the red-tailed hawk, then the great blue heron with its chest whiskers bright as fresh cream, and finally the emerald-feathered Carolina parakeet—until Mrs. Theodore huffed and told me he represented a collector who never showed his face in these auctions, a certain eccentric millionaire known in the art world only as Mr. H.

After the auction was over, Mrs. Theodore, still grumbling, led me back outside to her car. I was looking out the window when out of the corner of my eye I noticed her studying me.

"So, dear," she said, patting my head and smoothing my hair, "did you enjoy Audubon's birds?"

I nodded. I could not figure out why she had touched me, though she'd made it seem so natural. Mrs. Theodore told me we would make one more stop before the driver took me home. When we arrived at the public library, there were newspaper photographers waiting for us. Mrs. Theodore got out of the car smiling and waving, but I shrank back. Mrs. Theodore pulled me from the car, a bit sharply but without malice, and whispered to me by way of encouragement, "Silly thing, they're here for the winner. For you."

After I'd held up my certificate and the photographers had taken our picture, I followed Mrs. Theodore into the library. A large glass case sat in the foyer on display, and Mrs. Theodore stopped before it and motioned for me to join her.

I was struck by the size of the book before I realized what it was. It was as big as our kitchen table at home, thick as a stone block. The elephantine book was seated on a massive stand, open to a print of two birds on a branch, the background a drab gray lake. The bird on the upper branch was brown and mottled, standing on one leg with the other drawn up beneath her. The other bird regarded her from a lower branch, his back to the viewer and his gray-blue tail feathers, fine as hair, draped from his back. He had a curious face, with a white streak beneath his golden eye and a cream-colored crown extending from the top of his head like a fan.

I recognized the style immediately—it was the same painter we'd seen at the auction house. I was struck not only by the unusual look of the bird but by the quality of the print, which was much more luminous and detailed up close. I set my hand on the glass and squinted at the shimmering watercolor, the etching of each individual feather. I traced each one on the glass with the tip of my finger and felt, for the first time, the possibility of beauty stretch out before me like a field of fire. What lines might my own hands make, I thought then, and what colors; and it was as though the whole world was laid before me to be recorded, fast slipping away into the past, and I had already wasted so much time, because there wasn't time in this life for all that I wanted to make.

One of the library's curators had pulled Mrs. Theodore away to greet her. Where she had stood there was now a slim Black man with a tweed driving cap in his hands, a rose-colored bow tie at his neck. He wore a fine coat with pearl buttons and polished shoes, and I felt that he must be someone very important. He held a notebook in his hand, in which he was scribbling while gazing at the painted bird.

"The yellow-crowned night heron today," he said, then looked down at me and smiled. "They turn the pages every four days. Last week was the red-breasted snipe. Come back tomorrow, and you'll see the American bittern."

The man introduced himself as Benjamin, but when he shut his notebook, it was embossed *Dr. Young*. He explained that he was an ornithologist, a researcher who studied birds. He spent weeks in the field gathering information about all kinds of wild birds, their behaviors and habitats. He told me the world is full of creatures we don't dare dream of; even birds who cross oceans to overwinter in South America and fly over the world's tallest mountains.

"And *your* favorite bird," I asked him. "What is it?"

He grinned and handed me his card. On the back was the same yellow-crowned night heron from the book. "I wouldn't have missed this one," he said, "as you can imagine."

When Benjamin had left and Mrs. Theodore was finished, we got back into her Rolls-Royce, and she rubbed the skin between her eyebrows and sighed. The car felt stuffy and uncomfortable, as though Mrs. Theodore's patience was running thin and she might at any moment pull the car over and make me walk home.

But then she smiled and raised a finger to her lips in a conspiratorial way. She said I must be hungry, and I said that I was. She pulled out a package of chocolates, not fancy like I had been expecting, but the kind Khalti and I might buy to share on our break at the linen shop. Mrs. Theodore tugged off her gloves and giggled, snapping off a piece of chocolate for me to share as though we were two schoolgirls. "I can hardly stand all that fuss without something sweet," Mrs. Theodore said. "The way I see it, chocolate should be a girl's God-given right. You people do eat chocolate, don't you?"

Something in her voice made me feel as though I should apologize, though for what I wasn't sure. The chocolate was milky-sweet, though, and I felt then that maybe I'd misjudged Mrs. Theodore. "Yes, ma'am."

She gazed at me in the way I'd seen her gaze at the mannequins in Mr. Awad's shop. She licked her fingers and tucked a lock of black hair behind my ear. In that moment I regretted my reticence to being touched and that I'd been afraid of her. I wished we had a whole string of afternoons to spend together, like sisters, lying in some grassy place we could reach with her car and eating chocolate in the warm midday.

"You're just as cute as a bug's ear, aren't you?" Mrs. Theodore lifted my chin with a pink finger. "A little lighter, and you would have really been beautiful."

I burned and jerked my face away. Mrs. Theodore did not give me any more chocolate, and I did not speak for the rest of the car ride. I fingered my colored pencils in my pocket and stuffed down that furious urge to apologize for something I couldn't name. I still felt the eyes of the bidders from the auction house on the dirty hem of my dress. My family hasn't had a plugged nickel to our names since we arrived in this city, but no one had ever made me feel dirty. What beautiful things are left in the world for people like us, B? The birds that led us into the west and the night were no less beautiful than Audubon's herons or cranes. But Amrika's enchantment has erased any trace of those birds from my mother's stories. Sitting in Mrs. Theodore's Rolls-Royce after the taste of the chocolate had gone, I tongued the grit of my mother's turmeric between my teeth.

When the car pulled up in front of our building, my mother was standing in the doorway talking to a man who worked at my father's factory, his cap in his hands. It was the union representative who'd helped him get the job.

I stepped out of Mrs. Theodore's car. The door closed behind me, and the car sped away. Looking back as it disappeared around the corner of Rector, it was easy to imagine it had never been there at all. I looked down. I had dented my certificate with my thumbs.

My mother turned to me as though I had materialized out of the air. My father's friend beside her was smeared with oil and something that I took, at first, for beet juice.

There had been an accident.

Issa was still at school, so my mother and I rushed over on foot to my father's factory. That afternoon was the first time I saw real fear in my mother's eyes. I imagined my father's mangled body, the smell of blood. Though my mother was once a dresser of the dead,

I had never imagined what I would say to a dying man. A sea of union workers greeted us at the factory doors. The union man led us to a great machine with teeth as large as my head. A figure was crumpled up there, one hand in the belly of the iron wheel.

My mother fell to her knees beside my father. Half-delirious with pain, he laid his head against the wheel, now still, as though he were concentrating very hard on something he knew once but had forgotten.

My mother examined my father's crushed hand. A union worker told her a doctor was on the way, but my mother only glared at him and went back to her handiwork. She had seen enough amputations over the years—seen folks' hands crushed by cart wheels or legs gashed by plows. But there was something different about my mother now, some hesitation I'd never noticed.

My mother worked the gears and asked for oil. One of the union men poured a dark liquid on my father's hand, and my mother worked the motor oil into the spaces between my father's ruined fingers. He moaned. One by one the fingers came free—all but one, which had been eaten by the machine and remained, bloodless and gray, in the teeth of the wheel.

The crowd of union workers began to cheer, but my mother and I remained silent as she tied a tourniquet around the severed knuckle and wrapped my father's hand in strips of linen. Without my father's job at the factory, we wouldn't be able to eat, and this would be added to his string of disappointments. My mother rubbed a smear of motor oil from the lapel of his work shirt. Then, setting her hands under each of his arms, she lifted my father from the floor. She moved with slow dignity, ignoring the presence of the union workers. It was almost possible to believe that none of this was really happening, that she could take my father home on her shoulder and all would be well. But something heavy remained in her eyes. I wondered if these were the stones that had lined her belly with each death in the village, with each miscarriage. My mother had coaxed life into the world and led it out again, but perhaps those passages had each left their mark on her as well, as a mountain of even the smallest pebbles becomes an unbearable weight. All these years, I'd seen my mother carry the burdens of grief, birth, death, war, and disfigurement with a superhuman strength. But perhaps my mother could not, in the autumn of her life, bear so heavy a stone.

Later that evening, as my brother and my father slept in the bed beside us, I woke to the sound of my mother crying. It was the first time in years that I'd seen her cry. The night murmurs mostly hid her sobs, and in the dark it was impossible to make out the shuddering of her shoulders.

I called to her in a whisper. At first, she sniffled and said nothing. Then she lifted her head and whispered back, "Hayati, will you rub your mother's back?"

I sat up and laid my hands on her shoulder blades. The muscles of her back had been twisted for so long around her ribs and her shoulders that it was like caressing a thick vine. I pressed the balls of my palms into the plane of her broad back. She didn't cry anymore, only lay silent on the narrow mattress. It occurred to me then that I would not have woken to her crying in the night in our house at home in Syria, now half a world away, and I wondered how many times my father had heard her sobs and pretended, as a mercy, to sleep.

"What did they see, Mama?" I murmured to her. "What was it that came to meet the birds that flew into the west?"

My mother stayed quiet for a moment. I kneaded her back and read in her skin the fate that had awaited her, and her mother before her, and her mother's mother before that. This was a back that had carried the pain of others until it had become impossible for her bones to unbend themselves, like certain saplings will become permanently twisted under the force of windstorms. I thought of Hawa, whether it was this slow bending she had tried to escape with her linen wings, and whether there was any mercy in the world for those who decline to carry the burdens they are assigned to carry. My mother's back and mine were made from the same mold. Our spines were fashioned for bearing and bending and bowing and burying. Our backs had been honed over generations for the thankless labor of women. They had never been made for wings.

My mother turned her face to me over her shoulder. "What came," she said, "was night, with all its names."

NINE / █████

REEM'S PRESENCE ANNOUNCES ITSELF, as always, before I even open my eyes: the tap of warm metal on my nose, the click and buzz of electric wings. I swat the air and come up empty-handed. On the windowsill sits a mechanical starling, my sister's latest invention, courtesy of a lifelong passion for building things and an engineering degree wasted at a consulting job. I call it a starling only because, with its coat of iridescent black paint, the flash of circuitry within its hollow body, and its solar-powered wings, I don't know what else to call it this early in the morning.

Grease pops in the kitchen. The mechanical bird skitters across the sill and zips out into the hallway. The apartment smells of French toast and floral perfume. A giant mountaineering backpack the color of an overbaked sweet potato is sitting on the floor in front of my bed. I shove the thing out of my way, and it thuds to the floor. One of the zippers has come undone, revealing a soldering gun and a massive tool kit.

The thud prompts an immediate response: "Careful with that!"

I groan and amble into the kitchen. Reem is tall and dragonfly-lean, flitting about pouring Arabic coffee with cardamom and flipping toast onto our plates. She's dressed in a gray linen sack dress she somehow pulls off, her toes painted the same plum as her lipstick. She's glossed her thicket of black curls with henna, turning her hair a deep shade of wine. Teta is seated in her easy chair in the living room, laughing at something Reem's said.

"Your sister's home," Teta calls to me from the living room.

I pour myself into a kitchen chair. "To what do we owe your majesty's presence?"

The mechanical bird buzzes into the room and alights on Reem's shoulder. She turns to me, and her face is a perfect replica of yours. She eyes me with that don't-sass-me look she's been perfecting ever since she hit thirty-five, as though I were her child rather than her kid sibling.

"I had a lull in clients and decided to come down for a week or two. Wallah, if there's anything I've learned from consulting, it's that I got way more sleep as an engineer." She hands me a demitasse of Arabic coffee. "We can fit another mattress in there, right?"

I fumble the coffee cup. It spills onto my lap, but I bite back a yelp and manage to catch it before it smashes. "No way. Not gonna happen."

Reem bends over to feed Asmahan a bit of turkey bacon, and Asmahan licks her fingers, twining her tail around one of Reem's legs. "I'm not crashing on the couch. Those days are behind me."

Asmahan lays herself across Reem's feet. Teta calls out, "The air mattress is in the hall closet, habibti. I washed the blue sheets."

I shoot Asmahan a dirty look. "Traitor."

Reem shakes off her hands and pulls her hair into a half-updo atop her head. Her hands could be your hands. As she reaches up, her racerback dress reveals a tattoo at the base of her neck, but she fans out her curls, and I wonder if what I saw was only a trick of the light.

"If you want to blame someone," she says without turning to look at me, "blame your best friend the wandering minstrel, not the cat."

"Sami?" I frown and scratch my belly below the hem of my T-shirt, and my fingernails come away with pen ink underneath. "He called you?"

Reem hesitates. She glances at me from over her shoulder and waves a sponge in my direction. "Forget it. Just get over here and wash."

The sun is strong on the window. Reem is reflected in the glass in brown, plum, and merlot. After she left home and you got divorced, I spent years hating the way our father was still present in my face, hating the nose I'd inherited, the pink of his palms, the freckles that appeared in summer, the five different shades of foundation I'd need to cycle through if I spent an hour outside. In high school, I used to hate visiting him and his new girlfriend, a white woman from New Rochelle who gave me unsolicited advice about my body hair and always claimed to forget that I didn't eat bacon. Reem looks nothing like our dad; she could be your sister rather than mine. She was living two hundred and twelve miles away in Cambridge when you died, yet the minute she walks in the door, she belongs. I will never understand how two people with the same parents can come out so different. Once, in art school, I sketched her while she read a magazine, and I ended up drawing you instead.

"Forget the dishes." I pull my knees to my chest. "I thought you had some big product launch next month."

Reem pulls an empty chair toward her and settles down with one leg up. "The team can prep without me."

That doesn't sound like her. "Can you at least get that alien yam out from in front of my bed?"

"That alien yam has gotten me over the Himalayas, so show some respect. But we have to make space for the mattress anyway." Reem curls around her coffee like a smug cat. "And before you say no—we're going out tonight. No excuses."

I beg Reem and Sami not to take me dancing again, so Sami packs his oud and the three of us get on the 3 from Crown Heights and ride up to 14th Street. Qamar meets us at this noodle place in the West Village that Reem's been craving since she left New York. We end up on Bleecker with our takeout boxes, Sami traipsing ahead of us in his best runway walk until he's got a group of college girls in the Marc Jacobs shop window whispering and staring. Qamar whistles, then joins him, first draping their keffiyeh like a fur stole, then vogueing their way back. Pretty soon we've claimed a stretch of sidewalk for our own personal runway, and even Reem whoops and snaps.

A flock of two dozen grackles follows us overhead, eyeing our takeout boxes. When we stop at an intersection, I bend down to retie my shoelace and touch the ground. I see the city as the birds do: they trace the road that once ran along the shore here through the marshland called Saponickan, its branches carrying travelers up to what is now Harlem. These roads may be paved over, but their travelers are not gone. You used to tell me stories of jinn; all the other Arabs I know believe in ghosts.

We walk, and the grackles circle us. Threads of purple cloud rise up in the east. Qamar has a pair of old-school fabric-covered headphones on that leak high, thin notes of Arabic. When they notice me staring, they show me the ancient Walkman in their pocket.

"You've still got one of these things?" It's heavier and squarer than I remember. Qamar has covered it in stickers and written their name on the front in Sharpie, a kid's handwriting: *Qamar Benjamin Young*.

"My grandpa Ben gave it to me, back in the day. I'm named after him. Wanna take a listen?" They offer me the headphones.

I slip the hard plastic over my head and adjust them. *Ya ta'ir,* Fairouz sings—*O bird—*

Qamar watches me. The grackles stop circling and dart off uptown in shimmering waves. Reem steps off the curb to cross the street and tosses her hair over her shoulder. There is a breeze coming off the Hudson tonight, warm and close with the clean scent of a coming thunderstorm. Tonight is the kind of night to make a person glad to have a body. I think of Reem's mechanical birds with their transparent chests and wish my friends could see through me to the flashing circuit of my heart.

Eventually we find a spot on the stoop of a brownstone to sit down and eat our noodles, which Sami and I wolf down and Reem savors, determined not to get a speck of sauce on her dress. Qamar tugs their headphones down and lets them dangle around their neck while they eat, letting Fairouz's voice drift into the street. When Reem is finished, she sets aside her takeout box and tucks her sandaled feet on the step below her. Sami hands her his tobacco and rolling papers and gets out his oud. As he plays, drunk college kids stumble by down Bleecker, headed for the pirate-themed bar or the Irish bar or the faux-swanky Italian place that still pronounces a hard *g* in *sbagliato.* Reem rolls a cigarette for Sami and one for herself; Qamar doesn't smoke. Sami hands Reem his lighter. She glances over at me. "You mind?"

"Aren't you afraid Teta's gonna find out about your smoking and tattoos?" My voice is harsher than I mean it to be. I get up and take hold of the trunk of a slim gingko in the tree box in front of me, then walk around it, avoiding Reem's eyes.

Reem raises an eyebrow. "There's dog shit in that box."

Sami takes a drag of his cigarette and sets it on the step, then goes back to plucking his oud. Qamar taps the step with their foot. A light comes on in the brownstone across the street from us, and the silhouette of a woman comes to the curtained window, listening.

Sami exhales. "Back to the sibling rivalry."

"Shut up, Shaaban." Reem turns her icy glare on me. "Not all of us have the luxury of doing things our way all the time. Some of us have to respect the way things are done."

I shoot back, "Then you better hope she doesn't see the ink on your neck."

Reem narrows her eyes and takes a drag of her cigarette. "You wouldn't dare."

Sami and Qamar avert their eyes. Reem wasn't there the night the sparrows fell, or the night you slipped off the fire escape, or the string of dreamless nights I spent lying awake in Teta's apartment, drawing fire across my belly in ink. "Why are you here, Reem? Did you expect things to be just like they were before you left? Before you abandoned me to take care of Teta by myself?"

"I had to make a life." Reem is close to shouting.

"And now you're worried about me." Sami has stopped playing and is resting his hands on the strings, his cigarette hanging out of the corner of his mouth, watching. "Because I didn't end up respectable, with a successful boyfriend and a good job? Fuck your guilty conscience."

"Khalas!" The round brightness of Reem's voice bounces down the block. "There is no job, all right? My team lost a deal, and they let me go last week. No health insurance, no unemployment. You want to be the one to tell Teta that?"

"Hey, hey." Sami springs up, takes his oud in one hand, and crushes his cigarette underfoot. He sets his hand on my shoulder. "I didn't invite Reem as an intervention. She saw my knot project on social media and called me. I said I was worried about you. Okay?" He raps his hand against his chest. "There. My fault."

"Noodle." Reem used to call me that when I was a toddler and she, already a teenager, babysat me for our parents. "What the hell is up with you?"

I close my eyes. Fairouz reaches me from Qamar's headphones. *O bird—take me—if just for a minute—and bring me back—*

By the time we arrive back at Teta's apartment, it's late. We take the elevator to the roof, where there's an unused firepit and a few forgotten bags of trash. This could be a nice spot to watch the lights if it were cleaned up. The rooftop faces Manhattan; Queens gives off a soft glow on our right. The subway clatters by somewhere below us and then dissolves into the muffled complaints of the Brooklyn night. Sami rolls another cigarette and dangles his legs over the roof's edge. I want to ask him if he was awake the night the sparrows fell from the sky. I want to ask him if he saw, the next day, like I did, a white-throated sparrow splayed on the windshield of a parked car.

I look up at the stars, inviting vertigo. You used to say you saw the pair of birds gliding in to roost at night, when the moon was full enough to see by. I take the cigarette from Sami; it tastes like last winter, like the couch in Sami's last apartment.

Qamar has their Walkman out again, nodding their head to the music. "Hey." I rummage around in my messenger bag and pull out a sleeve of cassette tapes of Fairouz, Umm Kulthum, and Abdel Halim Hafez. "I found a bunch of these in my room the other day. My player doesn't work anymore, but since yours does, I figure somebody should enjoy them."

Qamar grins. "Oh, cool! Thanks." They go through them one at a time, then laugh when they find a cassette of Arabic kids' music. "Oh my God, 'Ha sisan, shu helween'—I haven't heard that in years. I had this same cassette growing up."

Reem puts out her cigarette. "Mom used to put that on to help me sleep. You, too?"

"After Mom got divorced," I say, "when I couldn't sleep, and she'd be watching cooking shows at two in the morning, I used to stay up and listen to it."

Reem is silhouetted against the orange arc of the Brooklyn Bridge. "I used to call her up at night to check on her. She had to keep it together for you."

"At least she talked to you." A cockroach crawls over the toe of my sneaker, and I let it clamber down the other side. "I always thought that was why she got involved with saving the Washington Street building. To get her mind off things."

Sami has come to stand closer, silent and swift, between me and the eight-story drop.

Qamar lowers their headphones. "Wait, I remember hearing about that. That was your mom? Was she the one who—the fire—?"

"Yeah, that was us."

"Allah yarhama." Qamar's voice is soft now. "She was an ornithologist, too, right? Before she became an activist."

"The activism just kind of—happened." I avert my eyes. "She was trying to document a pair of rare birds in the area when she died. I found her notebooks in Teta's closet."

"Astaghfirullah," Reem says, "you haven't been going through all that, have you? What good can it do after all these years?"

Maybe she's right. Remember the day I picked the lock on the older tenement, the one you were trying to save, the one that's now long since leveled? I crawled onto a ledge five stories up to prove that the birds you were protecting did not exist. It was a Tuesday, late morning, while you were out buying groceries for Teta. The August heat had burned off the clouds, and a damp had settled over Lower Manhattan, slicking the brick. There had been no sightings of the birds for a few days, and most people were saying that either there was no nest or the birds had moved on because of the noise and pollution.

Still, you chose to go on believing, and I envied you. In the end, it wasn't the ornithologists from Boston, or the press, or Sabah or Aisha who were the first ones to tell you you were wrong. I was the first one to doubt you.

I climbed onto the ledge where the nest lay because I was jealous of your ability to believe. Do you know how many years it took me to realize that you were the only thing I believed in? You spent so much time away that summer, your notebook always in hand, sketching or taking notes on the lengths of wings and the potential for eggs in the nest you'd never even seen. You told me the birds were going in and out of a ventilation duct reachable by a crack on the side of the building. No one had been able to get a clear look at it, but you claimed you'd seen the birds flying in and out of that crack, bringing in gingko twigs and bits of insulation.

I don't remember you rescuing me from the ledge, though the pictures made the paper the next day: a hijabi woman gripping a lanky teenager by the forearm on a ledge no wider than a two-by-four. There was a fear in my eyes that I don't remember feeling. What I remember was the warmth in the bottom of the nest, and my hand touching cool softness, and the shame of my disbelief, and your hand on my arm pleading with me not to let go. It wasn't the first or the last time I felt I was perched above the end of all things. But miraculously, you got me back inside and into your arms.

"If she really saw something," I say, "and I can show the world she was right about it, it would be a waste not to try."

Reem turns to me. "She's been gone five years, Noodle. You almost died that night. How many miracles are we permitted in this life?"

I've always put my faith in things that I could touch and hear and see: you clutching me on the ledge, your fingers in the crook of my elbow, the answer to a prayer I'd been too proud to pray. You, reciting to me when I was nine, a single mother broken free of the jaws of a man, brushing back my hair and telling me that surely these are signs for those who have eyes. The first dream I had after the fire swallowed you, after an abyss of forgetting had devoured three years of dreams, was of climbing to the very top of a tree where a gathering of birds was convening, asking them to take me away from this world where the smell of your scarves in my closet was a cut that refused to heal. The birds took me up by my sleeves in their beaks and their talons, lifting me from the tree. I had this dream over and over again for months, always with the same ending: I was no longer a child, and the weight of grief had made me too heavy a burden for the birds to carry. I've accepted this weight, this wanting to disappear. But I've never had faith in anything so much as my hand in that nest, those speckled blue eggs, the heat of life pulsing against me whether I believe in it or not.

When Qamar heads home, I tell Sami and Reem I want to sleep and lock myself in my room with a mirror and a sketchbook I haven't opened since you died. I tug off my shirt and Teta's shapewear and set myself in front of the mirror. I sketch my face, that defensive look, and then I remember why the female Impressionists—Mary Cassatt, Berthe Morisot—so rarely painted other women naked. I don't want my breasts or my body on the page. I'm drawn, like Laila Z, to observe, to find the truth of things, but my truth isn't inscribed on my body. It lives somewhere deeper, somewhere steadier, some-where the body becomes irrelevant. Nothing must be changed for this to be true. If I am in a state of becoming, it has no endpoint. I imagine replacing the memories of everyone I've ever spoken to with the impression that they have only ever seen me as a being clothed in light. In the early part of the twentieth century, homophobes and eugenicists joined forces to study what they called inversion, an early term for homosexuality, gender nonconformity, and transness. They believed they could read and police queerness on the body.

Maybe this is why I don't want to make myself legible. I want to erase the meanings that have been ascribed to my breath, to my sweat, to my hair and fat and skin. I trace the green veins in my neck that branch down into my breasts as feathers. I am painting myself as the bird that, to the world outside this room, does not exist. I draw myself clothed in wings and tell myself that even the angels are sexless.

I tug my shirt back on and replace the mirror. A rectangle of cleared dust sits where the pile of your old cassettes once lay on your work table. I am thinking of the Sharpie on Qamar's Walkman when it hits me that Laila, too, once knew a Dr. Young.

TEN / LAILA

Sweetest B,

I haven't written since my father's accident. It's easier to forget the days when you don't mark them, and sometimes, when I lift my pencil, all my unsaid words start to screech like a tea kettle, and I can't bear to say anything at all.

My father hasn't spoken in the forty days since the accident. Sometimes I dream of the machine chewing his words in its iron teeth. He's languished at home these six weeks, unable to work, twirling his cane on the unfinished floor while my mother clips laundry to the sooty line. Children chase one another down the hallways the same as ever, their mothers scrambling after them, the stink of smoke thick in the building. My father is too worn down to complain about all this, to mourn our coming here and say that we lived better when we were in Syria. My mother has held in her panic about our finances by going off by herself during the day when my father falls asleep in his chair. I followed her, once, and found she'd taken to haunting an abandoned apartment in which she'd found a broken rocking chair. I spot her through the window from the roof, across the courtyard, and sometimes, if Khalto Tala lets me go home early from the linen shop, I might even catch her wringing her hands in that empty room and talking to herself.

My mother has resigned herself to my father's injury. She's taken on work as a seamstress, bending her sore back over trousers and wool dresses. The pay isn't near enough, but there are few jobs to be had here for an unlettered woman from the bilad. Probably this is the reason Khalto Tala approached her in the evening last week, after the washing and the cooking were done, and told her she planned to take me along with a group of families from the neighborhood who were driving west to sell provisions—rosaries, laces, trinkets, foods from Syria, things like that. It's not as common now as it once was, but some of the parents or the jiddos in the building did it at one time or another, walking door to door with a heavy kashshi full of goods for sale hanging from a strap around one's neck, and this depression has made us all desperate. Even my mother, who often warns me in hushed tones about the lewd behavior and lost honor of women on the road, bowed her head and gave her blessing. For a month or two, I'll be one less mouth to feed.

If you were here, B, you'd notice the photo I've slipped in on the opposite page. Khalti and I were packing tonight—we leave tomorrow morning for the journey—when she called me into the bedroom to give it to me. My father watched the fire in the kitchen while my mother busied herself with a pot of lentils and rice. From the pocket of her skirt, Khalto Tala pulled out a small piece of cream-colored paper.

I'll admit, my first thought was that it was a photograph of you, not me. I am ashamed to admit that I've been thinking of you less and less these days, when the cockroaches come out in the dark and the bitter-cold nights make me resent the memory of warmth. No boy has ever moved me the way you did that afternoon on the corniche. This is not how I am supposed to feel. The lack of you hurts. You are the knife with which I cut myself.

Khalti got the photo from a friend of a friend whose husband worked as a translator on Ellis Island. It was taken the day our family arrived. I have to admit, B, it doesn't look much like me—not that I ever see myself, except reflected in the window of the linen shop to adjust my stockings or my hat. It occurred to me then, for the first time, that other people were looking at me, perhaps really looking and judging, and I remembered what my mother had said periodically throughout the spring: that soon her friends would come asking about me for their sons.

I asked Khalto Tala if she thought I should get married. She took a long, hard look at me, the kind of look she used to give before launching into one of her stories about the forests of Canada or the silver claim she'd once staked there, one of the many adventures she'd had before she'd settled down in New York. After a moment she said, "There are lots of ways to pin a woman down, Leiloul, but most of them involve a man."

After that, I gathered my pencils and my notebook into the wooden box inlaid with mother-of-pearl that Khalto Tala had brought with her from the bilad. I've been keeping your wing there for months, well hidden. Khalti gave me the box "for precious objects," she said once, and it's become my single private space in this cramped apartment. Aside from a few old dresses, this box will be all I bring with me on the road.

My only regret about tomorrow is I won't be able to say goodbye to Dr. Young. I've escaped a handful of afternoons of work over the last two months to take the subway uptown to the public library on the days when they turn the pages in Audubon's book. Khalti sometimes gives me a bit of money to see a movie with a friend from school. I can't go too often or people will start to talk.

But Dr. Young is always there, and we talk a little about winged creatures, and he puts names to the new birds I've seen around the city since I've last met with him.

I ran into him at the library one other time, with my mother, as he was coming out and we were walking past on our way to the post office. He tipped his hat to her, and she nodded, and though I wanted to tell my mother who he was, my stomach went cold, and all I managed was a meek hello. For the rest of the afternoon I felt like crying without knowing why. It wasn't until later that I realized that I couldn't picture Dr. Young walking into Mr. Awad's store—how could I, when Mr. Awad warns us to always check for the back of a cloche hat or a curl of yellow hair before we step out to dress a mannequin, so that the American women won't see our dirty hands? The white Americans might be ajanib, but my parents say we're white, too, or we must be something close to it if we are both Christians, and I think they really believe that if we keep our noses in our work, a day will come when we'll earn more than their disdain. In the meantime, my mother whispers about the widow Haddad and scrubs my face with turmeric, and my father warns me against dating like the American girls, saying, *Do you know how hard we worked to get you here?* Neither of them know what Mrs. Theodore taught me about my color in the back of that Rolls-Royce. In that moment with my mother and Dr. Young, little wing, when I felt the cold drip of fear in my stomach, I realized that an infinite number of moments had instilled in me a reflex as potent and inescapable as a sneeze. It was like seeing the shape of something large coming toward you in the dark.

In the kitchen, my mother is feeding the wood stove with old newspapers. Cats prowl the alley beneath us, snarling over rotten vegetables and rats. My father has his face to the flames. On the windowsill beside me sits my mother's candle, now lit, and an open copy of a field guide to the birds of the state of New York. Khalti found it lying beside a dumpster one day, its cover missing and its spine deformed, and took it home for us to use to practice our English. I'd learned from this book that the passenger pigeon was once one of the most common birds in North America, maybe in the world, but that the arrival of European settlers, their destruction of the forests, and their hunting caused the species to die out just a couple of decades before we arrived. The passenger pigeon was beautiful, with a powdery blue-gray back and a rosy breast. Now the city is everywhere, and this bird is nowhere, and though I'm glad to see the mountains and forests and cities of this country, I don't yet know if I want to call it home.

Little wing,

We left for Toledo today under a pink-and-gold dawn. Our band gathered over the course of an hour, shouting to children or parents from inside the kitchens, laughing with one another on the stoops. People walked by us to their groceries or their factory jobs and wished us well. Most of our traveling group were women trying to make a bit of extra money for their struggling families, along with a few younger men who might have wanted a bit of adventure for themselves or were making their way west anyway and preferred the company of their own neighbors to that of strangers. Khalto Tala and the widow Haddad had just let the pigeons out for the day, and they circled over our heads. It would be the last time Khalto Tala would let her pigeons out of their coops for months.

I arrived downstairs ahead of Khalto Tala to a pair of pickup trucks blocking the road and shouting coming from all directions. A bag of spices had fallen off one of the truck beds and was lying partially spilled in the street, and a round-faced woman in a smudged apron and a rust-colored skirt was shouting at the man who had dropped it, who was making indignant excuses. "Kul hawa!" she shouted, which shut him up, and followed it with a string of reprimands for his carelessness. I stepped in between them and gathered the top of the bag to cinch it shut, but the auntie was angry, and rightly so, since the money from what he spilled could have fed her family for a week.

The argument went back and forth for a few minutes, until the woman told him to go tile the sea, and he sulked off to join the other men drinking the last of their coffee on a nearby stoop. "Tfeh," she said by way of dismissal. I helped her hoist the sack back onto the bed of the truck. "None of these old gray mountains will move themselves," she grumbled in Arabic, then wiped the dust off her hands and kissed me on both cheeks. "Maryam Ibrahim. Our papers say Abraham, though, so I suppose you can take your pick." She set two bags of rosaries into my arms and said, "If a customer asks you, these were made in the Holy Land."

I fought my way toward the lead truck through the flurry of packing. The pigeons had found their way to the spilled spices and flour, and were now pecking at the cobblestones around us. Then there was a ripple in the sea of birds, and the pigeons shot up into the sky, protesting.

There he was with a crate of dry goods from Abu Hamdeh's shop: the boy from the boat, his overcoat folded across one thin arm, the sleeves of his linen shirt rolled up to the elbow.

"The boy of the storm petrels," I said.

"The dresser of dead birds. Ilyas." He held out his hand for me to shake.

"Laila."

He pressed his hand to his heart and tipped his hat to me, and then he disappeared into the truck behind us. Before I could follow, Khalto Tala took me by the arm and ushered me into the lead truck with her. It seemed to me the perfect opportunity to ask her about Ilyas, which was how I found out that he worked in Abu Hamdeh's shop—and that he had no family in New York at all.

Toward the end of the block, a pushcart selling ice cream stopped in the street, and our truck honked. I leaned out the window to look back one last time at our building. I didn't catch sight of either of my parents. I knew my mother didn't approve of my going with Khalto Tala, but I was disappointed no one had come down to wish us goodbye.

"Tousalou bi salameh!"

Just then, a lean figure in a driving cap came running up the sidewalk. Panting, Issa reached up and took hold of the truck window. He took my hand and squeezed it, wished me a safe arrival again, and then my brother was gone. The truck lurched forward. Issa had pressed a seed into my hand, one of the seeds he'd been given by the botanist on the boat, the ones that could grow into a huge tree in the soil of their native mountains. I thought of the rocky dirt I'd run my hands through in the park and wondered whether a seed like that could produce anything in the difficult American earth.

I spotted my first oriole in Pennsylvania today, through a grove of silver birches in the foothills of the Appalachians. We had already made our way through the rocky north of the state, over cliffs and mountains where quarries had been cut into the hillsides. The oriole was little more than a streak of orange through the blur of the trees. May has been warm so far, so the osage orange and apple trees were scarved in their finery, their leaves full and blossoms weighting their branches. We passed the time on the road telling stories and singing songs, and Maryam chattered on to Khalto Tala and me about her village in Syria. She hadn't been out of the house in months, since before her husband passed away in an accident at the same factory where my father used to work. They had been hoping to start a family, she said, but had never been able to conceive. She even picked out a name long ago in case it was a girl: Sawsan, after her teta. But Maryam blamed her body for not being able to handle the stress of coming here, blamed herself for not eating enough or sleeping enough. Her grief had stopped her cycles for months since the accident, and she told us that maybe it was her body's way of recognizing that she would never be a mother. She spoke like a woman whose words had been dammed up inside the lake of her mouth. Her cousins had urged her to get out of the house, so she decided to sell imported items on the road—cracked wheat and olives, a few odds and ends. Maryam reminded me of all the women who had come to my mother over the years for advice on what herbs balanced hormones or regulated cycles, how they'd hung on her every word of caution. I realized now why she had been so revered in the bilad.

We stopped to rest our legs in a clearing by the road where picnic tables had been set up. This stretch followed a railroad cutting through the Pennsylvania farmland, and at the crest of the hill, you could hear the train whistle echoing around the bend in the valley below, as though there were both a train and its ghost. The patchwork farms stretched out beneath us, cones of tobacco gathered and dried last fall hanging in the doors of barns, the Pennsylvania Deutsch farmers riding their plows behind their horses to prepare their fields for corn and summer squash. We were headed to Toledo, a city near the shores of Lake Erie, I'd been told, where there were glass factories and a large community of Syrians who ran dry-goods shops and restaurants. We could sell our wares, restock, and be given beds for a few nights before moving west.

I found a shady spot under the trees and was sketching my oriole when footsteps approached through the grass. Ilyas sat down beside me. I went on sketching, adding the orange in spurts of my pencil.

"You don't have to say why you lied to me," I said to him. "But if you're going to go on doing it, I'd rather not be your friend." I hope I sounded as sure as this seems on paper.

Ilyas turned his whole body to face me. He admitted he'd lied to me on the ship, that his parents weren't waiting for him in New

York. He had made the crossing alone, twice, and been lucky the second time. He hadn't heard from his parents in almost a decade, he told me, and he didn't know where they were or if they were living or dead.

Ilyas got up and brushed himself off. "It's nobody's business but mine, and I don't want to talk about it," he said. "But I'd still like to be your friend."

I got up and followed Ilyas to the railroad tracks. The rest of the group was beginning to pack away their blankets into the trucks and toss their apple cores into the woods for the squirrels. Ilyas infuriated me in that moment with his turned back, his defiant stare, the way he pretended he needed to retie his boot rather than look at me and wait for my answer. I turned in a huff and fixated on a coil of steam rising up in the distance from an approaching train, and in that moment it seemed to me that all the people Ilyas and I were missing were on that train headed away from us into the green Appalachians, and soon the both of us would be left alone with our wounds whether we talked about them or not.

I opened my tin of colored pencils and showed him your wing. He picked it up and held it in both hands. He had an artist's hands. I didn't tell him it was yours, little wing, though I did tell him it was made by somebody very dear to me, back home.

Today seemed like it would never end, taking the trucks around all afternoon selling to the folks on the outskirts of the city. The women in our group split off from the men to sell to the wives of the farmers. The wives are more likely to buy linens, lingerie, and rosaries from other women—they feel more comfortable inviting us into their homes. The uncles say that people who live outside the cities depend most on people like us, who come to them and save them the trek into town, or at least they used to before the automobiles and the railroads came and changed things. Twenty years ago, they say, going door to door with your boxes and notions was a booming business. People still return to it when they get desperate, of course, as the past few years have made us all. But I feel ashamed for it sometimes because of the way people look at you and the things my mother said about women on the road. Sometimes I don't feel respected by anybody but the other folks I came here with. The Americans never offer you water, let alone something to eat, never mind that you've been on your feet all day and your face is dirty with the soot from the trucks or the factories or God knows where you've passed through. The Americans don't usually want us in their houses long. Maryam always bemoans the lack of hospitality here, wagging her finger. She's right. My mother used to come out with trays of coffee and bread for the men who worked in the fields near our house. No one I know would let a person leave his door hungry.

The brothers hosting us were kind, even if a lot of us were down on our luck with our first day of selling. They own a grocery store in downtown Toledo. It seems everybody knows somebody here, a cousin living in the North End who runs a movie theater or an uncle a trolley ride away whose wife makes the most delicious kunafeh. It turns out that even here in the North End, which is full of Syrians, there are lots of things we brought with us from New York that you can't get in Toledo: olives, burghul, za'atar, good olive oil, the things from the bilad that people miss. I asked Maryam why we don't sell Syrian bread as we were driving toward the house this evening, but the others laughed at me. "Who do you think these women are?" Maryam said between guffaws. "They bake their own bread, and sell it, too!"

Now my belly is full of shish barak and I'm too full to sleep. The daughter of one of the Khoury brothers made the meatballs for the shish barak, and her mother made the yogurt sauce, and I have to say, from the first bite it was better than my mother's, though I'd never tell her that. Or maybe it was something that happened in the kitchen. Ilyas and I cleaned up after dinner, which I wasn't expecting because I thought Ilyas would disappear into the sitting room to talk with the other men. The women tried to shoo him out, but he said he didn't want to listen to all the politics, and besides, the faucet was leaky, and he offered to tighten it. It seemed a little suspicious to me, and a little strange to the other women, too, but no one said anything, aside from a few clucked tongues.

Someone must have put a second pot of coffee on and forgotten about it. As Ilyas was finishing with the faucet, there was a sizzle, and the pot of coffee overflowed onto the gas. Something must have sparked, because in half a second the dark foam was burning, and then the flame caught the grease Maryam had yet to scrub off the stovetop, and pretty soon the range was on fire. I grabbed a rag, soaked it in cold water, and tossed it over the burner to smother it. Ilyas tossed white powder over the remaining grease—bicarbonate of soda, he told me later. We tamped out the fire until the air was smoke and dust, scrambling over each other in a flurry. At some point I realized our hands were touching. Ilyas had placed his hand on mine on the edge of the stove while he leaned over to mop up the powder.

In the moment we became aware of it, something about the touch changed. I felt his breath in the length of his arm, the tiny olive wood cross batting the bone in his chest with each movement of his hand. He didn't look at me, but I knew that he had noticed, and a full second passed before I closed my hand over the rag and pulled away.

ELEVEN / ▓▓▓▓▓

THE DAY AISHA'S FUNDING runs out, Sami, Reem, and I go up to Queens to help her move her equipment out of the old house in Forest Hills. She's been winding down her patients for weeks, so the cages are empty. We load chicken wire and potted plants into the back of her station wagon. As Aisha locks the door of the house, the birds fill the sky as though drawn to our sighing. They've been arriving every day from nowhere: orioles roosting on fire escapes, stray jays clinging to box air conditioners, dozens of ravens walking the shop awnings. People harbor different theories about what's bringing the birds to New York. They congregate like white blood cells to a wound, drawn to arson and eviction notices, to a pig's head hurled at a masjid door, to the murder of a Black trans woman deadnamed in a police report or the white man who set fire to a woman's blouse on Fifth Avenue for wearing hijab.

One thing everyone's agreed on since the goldfinches arrived:

never before has New York been so full of birds. A neighborhood petition's been started to get someone to come in and clean up their droppings, which are everywhere. A week ago, some of the gentrifiers blamed a pair of brothers, whose family had been in the neighborhood almost eighty years after moving from Barbados, who've got a pigeon coop on the roof of their building. But it isn't only pigeons that are filling the streets. Hordes of sparrows block traffic, circling the Brooklyn Public Library and soiling the gilded entrance. Snowy owls arrive out of season and roost in the rooftop gardens of brand-new apartment buildings, spoiling evening soirees with their swooping and screeching.

In the station wagon on the drive to Yorkville, Sami and I crowd the windows with our faces, trying to count the wings. Blackbirds and wrens flank our car, and we glide toward Aisha's apartment in silence. We unload the crates and the cages, the mesh and the bandages, the empty filing cabinets and the boxes of records. When we've deposited everything into Aisha's storage unit in the basement of the building, she locks the door and we head back upstairs for one last cup of coffee. The lotto numbers come on the radio. We sit around the table, and I think of all the things I'd do with half a million dollars: I'd cover all of Teta's co-pays, rent and electricity, health insurance for Reem and Sami and me, funding to keep Aisha's sanctuary going. Growing up, those of us who had to put a hyphen before "American" got scoffed at for sending money home to cousins in the old country or supporting aging parents here on green cards. But you used to shake your head and tell me how, back home, nobody put their parents into nursing homes or let their kin go hungry. The same thing lives on among Sami's queer and trans friends of color, he tells me, crowdfunding for medical care and housing online, or in the group chats he tells me about where friends help one another escape abusive relationships or housing crises with safety planning and couches to sleep on. We take care of one another because no one else will, he says. But every time is a gamble.

Aisha won't let us help her unpack, but we insist on washing our cups for her. As we exchange cheek kisses, a scarlet tanager perches on her fire escape like the curve of a shut tulip.

After, Sami gets a text from Qamar, and we meet up with them at the basketball court in Carl Schurz Park. We exchange salaams. An afternoon drizzle has started, the kind that often precedes summer afternoon downpours, so we've got the court to ourselves. I'm anxious to ask Qamar about their relationship to the Dr. Benjamin Young Laila once knew, but before I find the words, Qamar challenges us to a pickup game, two on two.

I haven't played in years, and as they check me the ball, I remember why. If my body disappears in water, it's twice as awkward on the court. The binder makes it hard to get a full breath; even playing a half-court game, I quickly find myself struggling to fill my lungs, straining to yawn. Qamar notices but says nothing, and I notice them noticing. My friends move slower to accommodate me, but my chest is heavy, my legs leaden. My skin feels like a shoe three sizes too small. I begin to dissociate from my body. I grow heavier, sleepier, far away. Qamar makes a basket, and we return to the top of the key, panting. They say nothing, but they give me an extra moment to breathe before we start up again, which I'm both embarrassed by and grateful for.

"When I really need to think something out," Qamar says to me, wiping the sweat from their eyes, "I gotta move."

I try to tell myself I'm just not like that, but I remember my days on the monkey bars as a kid, and every cell in my body is screaming at me. I tune it out and rush to snag the ball from Sami, but he dribbles around me. I'm off-balance. I skid knee-first into the blacktop.

I swear and roll myself over. I've ripped a gash in my jeans and stained the torn edges with dark blood. Reem, ever the Girl Scout, pulls out a stack of spare napkins and blots at the wound.

I limp over to the side of the court. "Sorry. I'm not very coordinated."

Qamar and Sami each give me an arm, and together we make our way under a tree. "I shouldn't have faked you out like that," Sami says.

Qamar pulls a Band-Aid from their pocket and hands it to me. "Come on, you got a few good baskets. The rain's picking up now, anyway."

Everyone gets quiet. It's now or never, but I don't know where to begin: with my mother's search for a bird that's not supposed to exist, with Laila's painting of it, or with my hunch that the same Dr. Young that Laila used to meet at the library is Qamar's grandfather.

While I chew the inside of my cheek, Qamar says, "I think I know a friend of yours."

"Really? Who?"

"Sabah and her father. They go to my masjid, the little one on Flatbush and Bergen."

A flash of color, like a stray umbrella, and the scarlet tanager from Aisha's window alights on a branch above us.

"Oh. Yeah. She and my mom were friends for like, fifteen years." I look around for you, but either my voice doesn't conjure you or the pain in my knee is too distracting for me to notice.

"That's not the only reason I know her." Qamar rubs the soreness from their calves. "Part of my thesis was on American bird art from the first half of the twentieth century. My grandfather was an ornithologist who did field studies on a certain species of rare bird. It was only ever documented by one other person. Well, supposedly. I'm trying to complete his work."

"Benjamin Young *was* your grandfather!"

Qamar smiles. "Sabah said you might be familiar."

When I lift Reem's napkins off my kneecap to bandage it, I'm trembling. I've bled through without noticing. "Your grandfather wasn't the only one who documented *Geronticus simurghus*."

Qamar shakes their head. "But I can't prove that. I've scoured his records. He often wrote to an artist named Laila who supposedly made an illustration of the bird, but as far as I can tell, the work is lost, or missing. I've got nothing more than a doodle in the margins."

The rain has stopped, giving way to hesitant sunshine. "So we've got nothing."

"Nothing."

When we leave the park, the scarlet tanager shakes out its navy wings and cocks its head after us like we're mad to walk back into the thick of the city, like it is waiting for something to happen.

At home, Teta complains that her plants aren't getting any sun. The neighbor upstairs has hung a blanket over her window to block the birds from accidentally flying into her apartment, and the fabric is waving in the breeze, its shadow blocking the sun from getting to Teta's plants on the fire escape. She asks us to help her take the plants to the roof, where they'll get more sunshine and the cherry tomatoes she's planted won't wither in the shade.

Reem and I carry the plants inside one by one in their pots. Teta insists on coming with us up to the roof, so I take her by the arm and Reem takes the plants up on your brass coffee tray, and we all make our way upstairs together into the milky haze.

We set the plants on the roof according to Teta's direction. She changes her mind several times, until we've got the pots lined up in a constellation of greenery near the old firepit, and then Teta instructs us to get the watering can and plant food and bring them up to tend to her seedlings. I bring up a kitchen chair for her, and Teta plops herself down in the sun, wiping her brow and keeping her back straight as though the rooftop were the throne room of a personal palace. I set to folding the fertilizer into the potting soil while Reem follows me with the watering can. I try not to think about you. I used to water your thyme for you when it was humid and your arthritis was acting up; do you remember?

Before you died, I learned about death from Jiddo, whom I was never close with but whose death taught me that someday even our family will be gone. After that I held each of your hugs just a second longer, even when I would have rather been doing something else, because someday you'd be gone and I would wish I could go back to those moments. But now you are gone, and your absence hurts too much for me to think about those hugs, those games, those afternoons watering your plants. It's been five years, and time hasn't healed any wounds. You are all I think about some days, and yet I can't bear to remember the way things used to be.

Teta smiles and folds her hands in her lap. "You are sisters. You should spend more time together. Masha'Allah, Reem, you look just like your mother when she was your age."

Reem kisses Teta's hands and slips a sprig of purple basil flowers between her fingers. They are the perfect picture of womanhood. You are standing on the roof not far away, lifting your face to the sun, which makes your hijab into a golden halo. You crouch down to lift a leaf to your nose without casting a shadow. I wipe the sweat off my brow with my forearm.

Teta is stroking Reem's hair. You used to brush my hair and tell me it would be beautiful like hers one day, how the most beautiful women had hair to their ankles. I used to dream about it; it was one of those body dreams that seem so vivid you can't imagine they'll vanish. Reem has grown her hair to her waist. I asked her once if she ever thought about cutting it, but she told me it was something the women in our family had always done, that she had never considered doing anything else.

"It must have been hard growing up an only child," Reem says.

"It was almost that I had a brother." Teta isn't looking at either of us, but into the soil of the flowerpot I am holding as though she could dig up the kazbara's roots with her eyes. "I ran to the midwife's house, but she was with Imm Shams, she had a baby the same night. The midwife's daughter came, my friend. My mother, she bled, but she lived. My brother—my brother. Allah yarhamu."

I look up, startled. I have heard this story before, but not from Teta. There's a moment of quiet before anyone speaks. I glance at Reem, but her face gives nothing away. I study Teta's face, her hands, the lines on her forehead. Time hides the people we might have been if things were different.

Reem clears her throat. "Last time I was up here, Noodle was graduating high school. Pretty sure there's a photo of us on the roof, probably hanging around Teta's closet in a shoebox. We should dig it up."

I grimace into my flowerpot. "Let's not."

Reem laughs. "You were the cutest little dork in that big gown. There was this one shot, you were so awkward. You looked like a total dude."

I bury my hands in a pot of yellow cherry tomatoes. "Still my awkward self. Sorry."

"If you put on a dress once in a while, habibti, you will see the boys come running, eh?" Teta gets up from her chair and bends to tug off my hair tie. She uses her hands to let my long hair roll down over my back, then thumbs my chin to make me smile. "You are a beautiful girl. You never let us see."

I catch your eye, standing close by her side. And I do smile back, that false smile that I am supposed to make because now, as then, there is no room for me on this rooftop, and neither Teta nor Reem know the difference, because I have not smiled a real smile since the day the crows came to mourn their dead, and even my family no longer remembers the smile I lost.

Back in the apartment, golden light is sifting through the holes in the threadbare blanket hanging from the window, and the owl is back at the sill. Teta settles into her chair, Reem sinks into the couch beside Asmahan to read, and everything outside of me is as it should be. Teta's bedroom door is half open, and inside, her shoeboxes of photographs are piled on chairs and on the floor, her rack of old clothes, piles of socks meticulously folded, her closet with its forty years of memories. Teta's invited me in on occasion, but she's always careful about what she wants me to see. Entering her room has always felt like intruding on her private inner world. Lately, she's been falling asleep in the living room chair, so I rarely find her sitting on her bed or looking at the photographs of you and me that she keeps tucked into her bedroom mirror.

Teta doesn't like to tell stories quite the way they happened. If I'm lucky, I'll catch her in an unguarded moment when she's willing to tell me the story the way it felt to her, or to tell me a fable instead of a memory. I never imagined I could know someone so well and yet know so little about them. You used to tell me about growing up with Teta, about when she was young, but by the time you died, there were still so many things I wasn't ready to hear. Until Reem arrived here, Teta was all I had left. It sometimes feels as though she holds universes of history I'll never be allowed to know, as though it's improper for us to ever really know each other, and sometimes our silences are more than I can stand.

Reem gets up and goes into the kitchen to start dinner. I sit down on the couch beside Teta. "You never told me you had a baby brother," I say.

"Habibti, he was gone before he was here. What is done is buried." Teta shifts her weight in her chair, and I lean over to adjust the heating pad at her back. She turns her face to the window where the owl waits. It would be easy to fall back into our usual pattern, stirring a cup of tea or chuckling at Asmahan licking the water from the rim of a plastic cup, letting the drone of the television put us to sleep. But when my gaze drifts to the shoeboxes lining the walls of Teta's room, I think of the robin's eggs and wonder what hidden things Teta has been telling me all along that I've never bothered to hear.

I curve my chest over my folded hands and smell the faint scent of my own blood. My body is tired, my belly swollen after three weeks of bleeding. You would probably tell me I should have spoken more sharply to the doctor, or maybe tell me to go to the hospital. You were a lion when I had appendicitis, when the nurses were late with my pain medication or when I threw up from the anesthesia. You learned this from Teta. When Jiddo was in the hospital, Teta never left his side. She slept sitting up in a hospital chair for three weeks before he was sent home with palliative care. But I never saw in Teta's eyes that wild love, the desperation of impending loss. That was the way I felt when you died, the way Sami felt when we found his mother lying in the garden with a flower in her open hand. Teta mourned Jiddo, but not like that. I had never considered that there might have been someone else, a first love, a haunting of which I knew nothing.

"You said there was someone else." I hesitate. "Before Jiddo."

She gives me a long look, as though I have broken our rule of silences. "Not all love is the same, habibti."

"But there was someone."

Teta fumbles with the remote to turn on the television, but I know she's heard me. "Whoever they were, you loved them. Right?"

Teta looks up at me with a sharpness I am not expecting. "I loved them both the best I could," she says, "but less than they deserved." Then she lifts her curled hand to her mouth and inhales. "There is nothing to say. An opened scar doesn't heal."

"But Teta—"

"Give us a moment." Her voice is sharper now. I have gone too far. "Please."

In the kitchen, Reem hums to herself. Asmahan chases one of Reem's mechanical birds across the tile floor, batting it like a translucent cockroach. You are seated at the table again, watching Reem's back this time as she shakes garlic in hot oil. I close Teta's bedroom door.

I can't sleep, so when the tapping comes at my window, I look over and see the owl that has been coming every day to visit Teta, the same owl that led me up the stairs and into the darkness of the community house in Lower Manhattan. As soon as I crack open the window, it flees, and the sound of the oud appears.

"Hey." On the street, Sami is calling to me. "Get down here. Yalla."

I step over Reem and Asmahan asleep on the air mattress and slip out of the apartment. Outside, the night is warm for September. The fist of summer has yet to open. Sami is a spirit made of starglow and smoke, strumming his oud in the middle of the street.

His mood is heavier than other nights. He leads me without speaking, his music guiding us. When I look back, the single owl at my window has become dozens. We amass a cape of a hundred owls gliding behind us like a procession for the dead. I don't speak for fear of unraveling this enchantment. We continue down Atlantic in the middle of the empty street, and the white bellies of the owls are brighter than the streetlights.

We walk for what feels like hours, but time has no meaning. We march on in silence until we enter the Brooklyn-Queens borderlands, and the arrow of zodiacal light appears on the horizon. We enter a neighborhood where the streets slope downward into lowlands, and in this triangular neighborhood near Ozone Park we find pools of stagnant water in the streets and empty lots. No one's awake. We pass twisted rust-lined fences with the owls at our back until we stop at a house that's sat empty for some time. The owls follow us until we reach its front steps, where they stop, too. They perch everywhere, maintaining their silence, on the uneven roofs of the houses, the side mirrors of rusted cars, and the iron scrolls of stoop railings.

In the vacant lot beside the house, sunken into the earth at least three or four feet, there was once a garden that now sits untended and overgrown. What were once plots of moonflowers have become a carpet of white buds and bells. There in the sunken garden are more owls than I can count, as though they've arrived for a great council of which we know nothing. Night-blooming cereus once planted here has now grown wild, exploding in luminous bursts over broken glass and rusted metal. As the owls keep watch over the carpet of bone and pearl, I think to myself, Who is to say this city doesn't hold greater mysteries than we ever imagined?

Sami stops his playing. He walks to the edge of the lot until pale blossoms overflow the toes of his sneakers. He stands silhouetted against the lot as though over a pool of milk, poised to dive.

"This was where it happened," Sami says.

After you died, Sami and I were inseparable. It was his mother who took care of me when I couldn't face the mirror of my grief in Teta's eyes. Imm Sami was a kindhearted woman who never had to ask me if I was all right. She would feed me and sing me songs to cheer me up, and let me stay for days and nights without asking questions. She must have taken in half the city over the years. Sami brought home needy friends like strays, kids with cruel parents or no parents, undocumented kids, gay kids, bullied kids, kids missing months of dreams. It was a heart attack that took her in the end, here at the house where they lived in this triangle between Brooklyn and Queens without drainage or subway stops, while she was weeding her garden. It was a death that could have taken anyone on an afternoon when no one was around to call an ambulance, leaving Sami and me nothing to blame but our own clay bodies.

Sami turns and looks at me. I take his hand. We move heavy through the field of white flowers until we are surrounded by them. The vines are up to our knees in places, and the lot is thick with the fragrance of them. We stretch our bodies without letting go of each other's hands; we exorcise our grief. We twine and bend while the owls look on. I am reflected in Sami's eyes. I am not a girl in that moment, or a boy, but a person-shaped beam of light, and we see each other as we are, as energy that has willed itself into these bodies because the desire to dance is the first kind of longing.

When Sami pulls me to him and wraps his arms around me, we are brothers. He is weeping. The birds around us, who know what it is to grieve, hide us under their wings.

"Why do you play the oud in the street?" My feet tangle themselves in a moon-white patch of morning glory, wet with dew.

"So she can hear me," Sami says, and I know exactly what he means.

After we get home and Sami goes to bed, I lock myself in the bathroom with a set of clippers. Since you died, my life is full of illusions and unbroken spells. A few years ago, I had the opportunity to go to Beirut with a friend, with the promise of a possible trip to Damascus. I hadn't been back to Syria since I was there with you when I was five years old. I remember Teta wore dark sunglasses and carried an umbrella the entire trip because she'd gotten Lyme from a tick picked up in Central Park, though the cousins just thought she was being vain.

I opted not to go to Beirut. I refused to admit it, but Damascus was the last place I wanted to go. It was as though as long as I didn't go back, I could pretend that you would be there waiting for me, having a coffee on my auntie's patio and bouncing her baby on your knee. Going back to Damascus meant facing your absence, dispelling the illusion.

Facing myself in the mirror is like that. If I never cut my hair, if I don't acknowledge that I've never allowed anyone to really know me, I can pretend that a perfect road awaits me. I can pretend there's some medicine that will magically allow me to see myself. But going down that road might mean discovering that there is no magic strong enough to bring me into harmony. Breaking the illusion means acknowledging the parts of myself that will never be visible.

I raise the clippers to my skull and carve an undercut around the sides of my head, two arrows of gray skin. Hiding beneath fantasies has not brought you back, has not protected Aisha's sanctuary, has not stopped the birds from arriving. As I cut, I can see my father's face in my own. If I turn to just the right angle, I can see my first awful blueprint of masculinity.

I have never known men to be gentle. Once, when we went on a family road trip to Pennsylvania, we passed through mining country, then vast fields of high corn and yellow tobacco gathered into neat rows of hand-tied cones. Our car got stuck behind a line of horse-drawn buggies bearing a single reflective triangle for caution, and you pulled off into a gas station in the middle of nowhere to look at a map. The foothills of the Appalachians were flooded, the scarred terraces of old quarries slurried with mud, and the mesh netting lining the sides of the highways bulged with water-loose rock. The music had turned to country long ago. Night was falling. We were lost.

A gray pickup truck entered the gas station lot and parked at the pump in front of us. On the bumper was a sticker in Arabic: كافر. Kafir, meaning unbeliever or, sometimes, atheist. I'd been warned about the people who think it specifically means non-Muslim. I knew enough to know it was aimed at people like us.

Two white men got out of the pickup, one in camouflage with a military-style crew cut and the other in a neon-orange hunting jacket. Camo jacket stepped to the bed of his truck and leaned on the bumper. They stared at us. You hesitated, your hand on the ignition, and I whispered, *Let's go, let's go.* That moment lasts forever in my memory, though I already knew, from the way my teachers told me I looked like my father as though it were a compliment, that it wasn't me they wanted to intimidate.

Even now, I sometimes run over in my mind all the men who catcall me the moment I step out my door, the men who corner me on subway platforms, the man who reached under my dress at a parade once and slipped his finger beneath my underwear. I think of my father complaining to my mother that the dishes weren't washed, or of the time they fought over something stupid and he called her a camel to shut her up. I grew up with dozens of boys who would one day become the same kind of man. Sometimes the world is one long chain of men from whose anger there is no protection, an obstacle course I run to stay safe.

I don't want to look in the mirror and see my father's face.

Yet as black hair falls to the floor, there you are instead—in my nose, in my jaw, in my brow. There is Jiddo. After a moment, when I blink and part my lips, there is Teta, too.

There's a knock on the bathroom door. Sami is standing there with a pair of scissors. He cuts my bangs without speaking, then takes the clippers and fixes the back of my head. We are still damp with exertion and the humid night, tendrils of cereus vines still tangled in our shoelaces. Sami smells like owl feathers and the empty lot near Ozone Park. He stands so close to me that the two of us are staked together like two unruly vines of myrtle. Dancing with Sami in the field of cereus, I felt the same thing I felt in the club in Bushwick: that sense not of shedding my body, as I almost did on the basketball court, but of growing into it the way a vine unfurls itself to inhabit a broken fence. I rub the soft, bony places on the back of my skull. The remnants of moonflower leaves are laced into the black rings of hair on the floor. I have been the ghost of myself, but this has never been about waiting to be raptured out of my own body. If I am a fox-hearted boy, then so be it. Call me king of the foxes, king of untamable, unreadable things.

Sami and I emerge from the bathroom at dawn, just as Teta is fixing herself a cup of tea and settling into her easy chair. She motions me over, and I pull away from Sami and come.

"You remind me of someone I used to know." Teta runs her hands over my fade and through the short curls on top.

I bow my head under her hands. "I couldn't do it anymore, Teta."

"My storm of the storms." She tips the top of my head toward her and kisses it. "You never had to try."

TWELVE / LAILA

ILYAS AND I DIDN'T ride in the same truck from Toledo to Detroit, and I didn't see much of him today until we were in the south end of Dearborn, under the smokestacks, when I helped serve coffee to the men after dinner. Well, that's not entirely true—we did stop once on the ride into Detroit, along the western shore of Lake Erie. We'd passed so many miles of picturesque white cedars and maples that everyone began to complain; why didn't we stretch our legs, they said. And it was beautiful, the lake so big below it might have been an inland sea. Someone pointed out a group of loons, and Ilyas spotted the one set apart from the others, a rare, red-throated bird.

After that, I didn't see him for hours. We split up when we got close to Detroit, parked the trucks and went off on foot. I went with Maryam, stopping when she took hold of my elbow. She gets out of breath sometimes when we walk too long; she blames it on her poor diet and these last long months of mourning in her apartment. She sat down on the steps of the last house on the last long block, a neat little two-level house with cream siding and a wooden porch. We'd barely made any sales by then, and the afternoon was dragging on under a drizzly spring sky, and I was thinking of all the things I could buy with a bit of pocket money. By now I know the things to say to try to make a sale: *You got a daughter, ma'am?* Or *Maybe you got a friend who needs somethin'?* But today, the women who opened their doors just weren't interested.

When I rang the bell and the knob turned, I knew right away this last woman, in this last house, was going to be more of the same. She was dressed in a prim pearl-buttoned blouse with a long skirt, holding a satin clutch as though she were about to leave with her husband for an evening out. In desperation, I glanced around for something I could use to make a sale. A jeweled enamel of a swan was pinned to her blouse, so I asked the woman if she liked birds and pulled out a scarf I had embroidered under Khalto Tala's direction. It was decorated with hand-stitched cranes, their necks bowed and wings spread. The woman seemed delighted. She bought the scarf and asked me if I had any other items with birds. I didn't have anything else with me, so I thought quick and tore out a page from my notebook. I had sketched a pigeon with my field watercolors, his ruff of iridescent feathers puffed, his eyes curious.

The woman was disappointed, naturally, the pigeon not being the most regal of birds. I started to tell her what I loved about the pigeon, how noble a bird he is, how underrated, how anyone may conclude the same for himself. She seemed impressed with my English and didn't chase me from her porch, so I went on about how he is a clean bird, always preening himself, and how he regards a person with an intelligent expression very near human. He is a kind and gentle creature, the pigeon, never as aggressive as a grackle, for example, who will even attack people for food or territory, nor as temperamental as the goose. The pigeon has a quiet, hardy dignity about him, visible to those who are willing to look.

As I spoke, something shifted in me. The feeling rose that this woman, if she were to deem the pigeon unworthy, would also be judging me, and Khalto Tala, and the widow Haddad. It was an absurd thing, but there it was. A second sense came on its heels, something I had never felt before and which frightened me: the sense that I could not convince this American woman, whose judgments dictated my livelihood, of the value of things and people I cared a great deal about.

When I had run out of words, I stood on the porch, red-faced, as though I were about to burst into tears. The woman must have taken pity on me, or at least wanted to get me off her porch. She took the drawing from my hand and replaced it with a folded two-dollar bill that smelled of her clean linen pockets. I took it and turned back to Maryam, who regarded me from the steps of the house, and I was still standing there when the woman closed the door.

That was how we came to Detroit, or entered the sprawl of it, anyway, before we arrived at Abu Majed's house. Abu Majed is the aging uncle of one of the boys in our group who offered us a place to stay in Dearborn. He says he came from Highland Park nearly two decades ago to work at the Rouge, after Ford announced the five-dollar workday. His son Majed is grown now, and Abu Majed's grandchildren were outside scrubbing the family car when we arrived. We coughed when we got out of the trucks—the air smelled so bad I couldn't imagine hanging laundry out to dry—but the children seemed used to it. The steel particles in the air settle on the cars, though, and they have to scrub and scrub to get the stuff off, or it will eat the paint.

Abu Majed and his family seem to love it here. The men all walk to work at the Rouge, and the neighborhood is full of Syrians and a smattering of folks from other places—Italy, mainly, and a couple of Polish families. A lot of the Syrian families in the south end are Muslim, more so than back in New York; they even built a masjid in

Highland Park, before most of the community moved out to Dearborn, and they're working on building another here. We walked the neighborhood after dinner with Abu Majed's grandchildren, and they called out their hellos in English to all the neighbors sitting on their porches. It's easy to forget where you are, here, so much seems to revolve around the Rouge. You walk down Dix and find everything you could want: three different Arab restaurants, two Arab grocers, three coffee houses, a halal butcher, and lots of other businesses owned by immigrants—a theater, a laundry, a five-and-dime shop. Everybody knows one another here, or seems to. Just like back in New York, the shopkeepers here give credit to their neighbors, even the ones they know can't pay these days with so many people out of work.

But there's a point, too, when you cross the T-bridge and this neighborhood ends, and I know—because we drove through it—that these two Dearborns don't much go together. Walking around the rest of Dearborn, ringing the doorbells of the white families with big houses, you get the sense you're being watched, or maybe that you're not wanted, or something a little like both. *Buy somethin', buy somethin',* you say, and some of them just stare at you and close the door in your face.

The Black families in Detroit are kinder; one couple even let Maryam and I sit out a downpour on their porch. Abu Majed says the Arabs and the Black folks get the harder jobs at the plant, like at the foundry or the stamping factory, because we work hard and tend to stay, even if a drill sends up sparks and scars you, even if the rest of the men on the line call you names. Factory work is hard, Abu Majed says; you have to make your quota if you don't want to be out on the street, and you can't talk to the other workers on company time. But Abu Majed takes a kind of pride in that, I think, and he says it's not just cars he's helped make, but America herself.

Abu Majed and his family insisted we stay the rest of the weekend, since today was Saturday, and they want us to stay for Sunday dinner tomorrow. We stayed up late—or rather, the men stayed up late after dinner, talking. Ilyas was speaking to Abu Majed about the union at the Rouge when I came out to bring the coffee, so absorbed that he hardly thanked me. They talked about the union well into the night, until the women scolded them and stopped refilling their cups so they'd run out of steam. Abu Majed was the last to give up his monologue, clutching his demitasse in his lap, his gray shirt still stained here and there with the faint brown of automotive grease. He reached his hand upward to emphasize a point. He had rolled up his left sleeve, and where the fabric met his skin, you could see the red bumps of a rash starting around a dark stain of motor oil. He rolled it down as soon as it appeared, but I began to wonder at what he had endured that remained unspoken, and Abu Majed, too, knew that we were imagining this, and knew that we were pitying him. I understood my outburst about the pigeons then, and understood why our neighbors played "Amrika Ya Helwa" on the gramophone from across the courtyard, and understood, too, why my parents always listened, even my father, who had long since stopped reading *Al-Hoda* in the evenings.

Yesterday was Sunday, and Abu Majed's children piled the table high with mezze for Sunday dinner, not just hummus and Syrian bread and muhammara and baba ghanoush but chicken liver in pomegranate molasses, bowls of tabbouleh with cilantro and purslane, two dozen skewers of kofta, and stuffed grape leaves. After we ate our fill and toasted our hosts, someone brought out an oud, and another a rabab. The young men, who once again refused to go to sleep, began to trade stories of their time in America or back home, but the elders grew tired of this nonsense and began to tell their own fantastical stories.

Khalto Tala joined the circle and began to speak. She told us about her days prospecting for silver in Canada before my parents brought Issa and me to join her in Little Syria. Silver had been discovered in Ontario, she said, and lots of people had traveled west from New York to pursue it. There were thought to be large veins of silver out there, the kind a person could live out his life on, rich enough to send money home. But it wasn't that simple. Khalto Tala had arrived in the tiny boomtown of Cobalt almost thirty years before, in her young and wild days, with nothing but a canvas bag and a pair of gloves and boots. A few months later, she cut her losses and headed back to New York after an encounter with a mother black bear and her cubs, which Khalti took as an omen that it was time to return. I pictured her facing down the mother bear with a calm in her eyes that I could never hope to possess, inscribing in the space between them not terror but wonder and portent.

After, I dreamed of you. Astaghfirullah, I have not stopped dreaming of you since the day we left Beirut. Sometimes you come to me in a white linen dress, and other times you come to me wearing nothing but the sea along the corniche, pulling yourself up on the rocks by your purpled elbows. Tonight you came to me as a bird, and I could not tell the difference between you and the holiest of lost things.

I haven't been able to get back to sleep, not after that. I got your wing out from my tin of pencils and set it on the windowsill, where the moonlight has soaked into it like milk. I take good care of it and keep it hidden always. The feathers are still smooth; none have fallen out from your stitching. I counted each one and tried, as I do every night, to stitch you into my memory. I can't remember you without writing you down. I am afraid to forget you, afraid that in my darker moments I wish bad things on you in the hopes that, one day, we might cross paths again and you won't love another.

As dawn approached, I brought my paints to the window and began a watercolor of a red-throated loon. I painted until the pale green light was in the sky, when Maryam rose with a hand to her belly. She watched me paint in silence for a few minutes. She says

I have real talent, that I could sell my pages and be an artist, God willing. When she left to wash up, I took a pin from my hair and pinned the page to the wall so I could step back and look at it, imagine it hanging in a gallery or in the foyer of the public library. The room began to wake then, and I hurried away to the bathroom to ensure I'd have enough hot water to wash my face. I only realized later, after we'd left Dearborn, that the red-throated loon was still pinned to the wall beside the window where I'd left it, a fine layer of soot darkening the corners.

B,

The further north and west we go, the less spring seems to have advanced, and there is still stormy weather. While New York enjoys mild days and chilly nights and purple crocuses, Michigan is still struggling to break from winter's grip. Maryam wasn't feeling well since we arrived in Detroit, and earlier today, as we headed for Chicago and the shores of Lake Michigan, she blamed the water and the food and the jostling of the trucks, ignoring the remedies Khalto Tala suggested for her hard, swollen belly.

We were only an afternoon's drive from Chicago, but the spring storms that had threatened all morning broke violently about two hours outside of Detroit, in a desolate stretch of road through flat farmland where not a single house could be seen for miles. The rain turned the road to mud in places, and first one truck became stuck, then the other. When the second truck mired a wheel in the mud, Ilyas got out to check on it. The tire was flat. Khalto Tala murmured to Maryam in the back seat while I hopped out to help lift the sunken wheel from the mud. There was no changing the tire in this weather. The rain picked up and lashed us, and after a few minutes of sliding in the mud, Khalto Tala came out of the truck, frantic.

"Maryam's fainted dead away," she cried.

Someone spotted an old barn not far off, and so we carried Maryam to the barn, where at least it was dry and warm. It looked as though the barn had once belonged to a farm that had been abandoned long ago, the only structure around for miles.

Maryam was delirious. Khalto Tala listened for her heart, then laid a hand on her belly, which was stiff as a stone. She asked Maryam when she had last had her cycles. I felt Maryam's swollen belly, hard and higher than I'd realized. Khalto Tala told me her fears: that Maryam could be pregnant after all and not have known it.

We did our best to make her comfortable, bringing blankets and linens from the trucks to keep Maryam warm. We propped her up in a corner of the barn and kept her wrapped up, one woman rubbing her feet while another brought her water and stroked her forehead.

If it was a baby, it was coming too soon. Ilyas, seeing that I was troubled, knelt beside me and reached for my hand. "Tell me what to do." He squeezed my hand. "I'm not afraid."

The labor was long. Maryam's contractions lasted well into the night as the rain lashed the sides of the barn. She was in a good deal of pain, and as her contractions continued, the linens beneath her became soaked with blood. We didn't have the equipment for a transfusion, so I sent the younger boys—who were pacing the barn and whispering to themselves—to go out and try to free at least one of the trucks so that someone could go for a doctor.

But Maryam was losing blood by the minute. I forced myself to see Maryam's face rather than your mother's, Ilyas's hands rather than your own. Even so, the night was as deep, and the blood smelled of the same iron.

The baby's head slid out first. I caught the smooth dome in my hands. But Maryam wasn't responding. Khalto Tala batted her cheek, cradling the younger woman's face in her hands. "Maryam!" Khalto Tala blew air into Maryam's mouth. A shudder went through all of us, and just like that Maryam was gone, and I was holding a red-faced baby in my arms.

Later, those who were there said they saw a second shape jolt up from the amniotic sac, that a white-throated sparrow bit through the umbilical cord and wriggled free to bolt for the rafters. As it beat its wings, the tip of a feather touched the newborn's cheek, and where it had touched her it left a purple birthmark, like a drop of hibiscus tea. The bird shook itself in the air and shot upward, shattering a high window. It was gone. Through the jagged glass, we peered up at the clearing sky.

B,

The day we buried Maryam was unusually cold, and frost was thawing along the shores of Lake Michigan. Abu Majed and his family came from Dearborn to lower her into the ground, and the old man held her infant to his chest as we chanted prayers and set down flowers. Beyond St. Joseph's lighthouse, Lake Michigan reflected the milky gray of the sky. Maryam told me not three days before she died that steamers left every day from here for Chicago, bringing fresh fruit and picnickers in the summer. Folks called St. Joseph the Coney Island of Michigan. Maryam said she took that ferry once, years ago.

Our time in Chicago was short, and we stayed inside most days, within the bubble of a terrible quiet. We stayed with a woman named Imm Ibtisam and her daughter, whose sliver of a house was sandwiched between a bar and a soup kitchen. The lake had a cold beauty to it, and the city, too, but when we took our wares out, we drove to the countryside. There was a tension in that city I hadn't felt anywhere else, a feeling that, should you walk down the wrong street, you might anger someone—Imm Ibtisam warned us of the way the police treated strikers here, as well as of the streets controlled by shadows referred to only by whispered family names. A man had been shot in broad daylight on Outer Lake Shore Drive, she told us, down by the old grounds of the '33 World's Fair, and hardly anyone had been surprised.

We left for Minneapolis yesterday. The nights are still cold and damp here, and since we left Dearborn, it has seemed like nothing is going right. People close their doors in our faces, calling us swarthy and suspicious. This week I've slept with the baby on my chest every night. Ilyas and I take turns giving her bottles of milk, singing to her, and carrying her in a sling Khalto Tala fashioned out of a shawl. We've named her Sawsan, as Maryam wanted, and Ilyas and I, perhaps by virtue of delivering the baby, have become her temporary caretakers, since as far as I know Maryam had no other family in New York. She's a good baby, quiet and observant, with downy, pink cheeks and a patch of chestnut hair. I am eternally amazed at the smell of her, at her softness, at her newness.

Yesterday afternoon in the truck, chilled to the bone in a passing drizzle, I traced the swirl of her hair. She was sleeping on Ilyas's chest, a line of drool marring his work shirt. I must have mentioned to him that we had never baptized her, and Ilyas had blinked and pretended not to hear. He seemed not to want to talk about it, which unnerved me. Khalto Tala, on the other hand, opened her bag of holy items and took out a vial of holy water. "You blessed this yourself," I said. We sold the last of the holy water we brought with us some time ago, and we haven't come across a priest in weeks.

"Ya binti," Khalto Tala said, "it's no less sacred. There's more holiness in each bone of our bodies than we imagine."

Ilyas kept his face to the window and stroked Sawsan's back. A cloud of swallows kept pace with the truck between the road and the sun, casting a curtain of shadows across his face. The birds that have followed us northwest are our only companions these days, shivering with us through the nights. I dream about them as I once dreamed about God in the form of a sparrow, and you become the most beautiful of the flock. I've been plagued lately by the strange feeling that the past is not so far away, that things that happened a long time ago are, in some corner of my mind, still happening. Or maybe it's only you happening to me, over and over again.

Minneapolis lies on the banks of the Mississippi River, across from its twin, St. Paul. The Twin Cities are made up mostly of low brick buildings and factories, of smokestacks and grain mills, of broad avenues shaded by ash trees planted by the Civilian Conservation Corps. All the agricultural production of the Midwest seems to pass through Minneapolis, where grain gets milled into flour or brewed into beer and bottled. Factory jobs like that are coveted these days. A good-sized Syrian population has settled here, too, drawn by the work, and after decades of toiling for someone else, lots of families have opened their own dry-goods stores and bakeries. They gather their children in the parks on Sunday afternoons, their daughters in white, platters of ma'lubeh and mezze spread on the picnic tables.

But the chilly spring here has kept away the picnickers. Ilyas was icy to me yesterday, speaking in short words and ignoring me to feed Sawsan. After we made our door-to-door rounds and the sun began to set, we drove the trucks to the house of a cousin of one of our group, Abu Muhammad, and piled into his foyer, shivering and hugging our arms. We had a small supper and, after exchanging news of family in New York, the families dropped off to sleep. I changed Sawsan and prepared her blanket, but Khalto Tala took her from me, telling me I deserved some rest.

Outside, Ilyas sat on the front porch in his shirtsleeves. He hardly seemed to respond to my presence. I was tired of his stony air, so I asked him why he'd been so upset when I'd suggested we baptize Sawsan that morning. He told me he wasn't upset, but that he didn't see why it mattered.

"So if she were your child," I said, "you wouldn't want to give her the gift of faith?"

A bat fluttered by over our heads. "Faith isn't a gift you can give," Ilyas said. "It's something we find for ourselves." He stretched his legs, then got up and started toward the blue truck. I followed him.

We drove through downtown Minneapolis toward St. Paul. The night was cold again, and the barges on the Mississippi rippled the water as we crossed the bridge. We passed the court and the boardinghouses and left downtown for St. Paul's neat rows of single-family homes and grassy lawns. As we drove, the streetlamps glittered over the angles of his jaw and the river of arteries in his neck.

Eventually we came to a stop in front of a plank-sided barn. Ilyas got out of the truck and swung open the old wooden door. Inside, the barn was filled with a rustling and a soft chatter. Ilyas lit a carbide lamp, and the shapes in the dark resolved themselves into wire cages, then into birds. He said that our host, Abu Muhammad, also owned this property, where he raised birds for sale. After dinner, when the men had talked amongst themselves, he'd invited Ilyas to have a look. I held my tongue about whether he'd be pleased we'd come in the middle of the night.

Ilyas took a ring of keys from inside the barn, and we tramped our way through the field at the back of the property, toward the marshlands. A fence ran along the edge of the water. When we reached a padlocked gate, Ilyas used a silver key to open it. "This area is protected," Ilyas said, "so nobody comes trespassing and bothers them."

"Them?"

Ilyas led me through the dark, cautioning me of thorn bushes that overlay the path. When we emerged into a clearing with a pool of water, Ilyas crouched down and waited, and I followed suit. We waited in the shadows for what seemed like hours, the moon arcing over the still water. I shivered. And then, just as I was about to tell Ilyas that I was getting a cramp in my calves, a

shape came gliding over the pool, a steely body with a slim neck and a large head, ending in a heavy bill. The bird landed by the water's edge, and as it shook its head, the moonlight glistened on the water droplets on its yellow plumage, a pale golden stripe running from between the eyes to the back of its head. It moved as slow as a ghost, setting one leg in the water and then the other, so that only the flash of its crest made it visible in the darkness.

Ilyas told me it was a yellow-crowned night heron, rare in this part of the country. This one had been coming here for years, protected by Abu Muhammad's care.

"We're lucky," Ilyas said. "It's a good omen."

"This is what you have faith in?"

Ilyas turned to me in the dark. "I have faith in things that are beautiful and good," he said, "and don't tell other people what they need to do to be loved."

"You are beautiful and good," I said.

When I leaned in to kiss him, Ilyas stiffened. He tasted of thyme and smelled of musk and earth. I liked kissing him. When he curved his body into mine, I slid my hands up his chest, and that's how I discovered it.

I froze, and Ilyas jerked back.

I whispered, *Your chest—*

Yes, he said.

You're a man?

Yes.

I looked at Ilyas and saw a boy, exhausted and afraid. He held his breath. The night heron glided to the opposite bank of the little pond, slicing the water with its legs. The moon passed behind a cloud, and for a moment the heron's yellow crown was the only light.

"This is who you are," I said.

"I've been nothing but honest with you about that."

"But when you were born—you weren't called Ilyas."

"My parents abandoned me," Ilyas said. "I don't give a damn what they called me. Is that what matters to you, what they saw when they looked between my legs?"

I took his hands. The night heron swiveled its head at the movement and lifted itself, its wings two silent sails.

THIRTEEN / ██████

Sabah leaves for Detroit on Thursday morning, so Sami arrives at Teta's apartment on Friday, his arms laden with blue bags of flour. Sami bounces down the stairs to the street, and I follow, tugging on a knit cap to keep Abu Sabah from freaking out about my haircut. I check Teta's mailbox on the way out. A note from Aisha is folded neatly inside: *Didn't see you at jum'ah last week. Come with me tomorrow?* She must have dropped it off last night. The tea-stained paper smells like gardenia blossoms. Reem is rummaging around in my bedroom for an old hijab she can use to go to jum'ah later at the Islamic center. Abu Sabah will be there, and Sabah's cousins. There will be questions about me from the aunties, of course, as they sit cross-legged in the women's room upstairs and read Qur'an, and about Teta, too, whose back hurts her too much to come. They will cluck their tongues at my absence, wonder why there isn't a boy in my life yet, tell Reem about their sons in business school. I replace Aisha's note and bang the metal box shut.

Sami is waiting for me on the sidewalk. Hoyt Street is usually pretty quiet in the early hours, but Atlantic Avenue's dawn silence is almost unsettling. The sidewalk is littered with stray napkins and cigarette butts among the black circles of old gum. A white woman on her phone strolls down the other side of the street, and two teenagers hurry by us making weekend plans in Spanish. I'm struck by the feeling that I know none of my neighbors. Folks come and go so often now it seems pointless to get to know them. When Teta was in the boldness of her middle age, everyone on a block knew each other and asked after each other's children. In Yorkville, before it all burned around us, before I moved in with Teta, you used to stop into the Yemeni bakery around the corner for fresh bread and ask how the owner's son was doing. You used to wave hello to the sisters down the hall, Russian immigrants in their nineties whose husbands had long since passed away, who would invite us in for tea and round sugar-dusted cookies. The woman who owned the laundromat down the block, whom you'd known for twenty years, kept my baby pictures in her wallet.

When I touch my palm to the brick of a building, the street is flooded with the sound of hoofbeats on cobblestones, the creaking of wooden carriages, the honking of old automobiles. Men argue in Teta's Arabic, now the dated dialect of grandparents and great-grandparents and the long dead, while lovers clasp their pinky fingers in alleyways and children answer their mothers in a language only one of them can understand. This place remembers all its strangers.

We arrive at Sabah's shop before it opens. Her father is already there, counting out the register and signing for a shipment of dates. He waves us in from behind the front windows, rising up on his tiptoes to make himself seen over the crowded displays of ouds and tawleh boards and tasbih. When we open the door, the bell chimes and the silver medallions stamped with Ayat al-Kursi tinkle and swing on their silk cords. Abu Sabah asks after Teta and after Sami's health, pours blessings like salve on both our dead, and invites us each to try the puffed chickpeas he just got in. We dip our hands into the basket on the counter, dusting our fingers with turmeric. Abu Sabah disappears into the kitchen and returns with three cups of black tea and a tray of Turkish delights. We eat; Sami recounts the white couple who suspected one of his silk knots was a bomb and laughs; Abu Sabah tells us the Colombian family who lives next door just had a baby. I'd forgotten the ways in which this shop, this neighborhood, can still be a womb.

When we're finished with our tea, Abu Sabah shoos us into the kitchen, and Sami and I tie aprons around our waists. Sami needn't have bought flour: Sabah has set out everything we'll need on the table, with instructions for how many batches of bitlawah, ka'ak, and ma'amoul we'll need to make. I start by measuring out the semolina for the ma'amoul, and Sami crushes pistachios according to my directions.

"This is the most domestic I've ever seen you," Sami says, suppressing laughter.

"You don't make much of a domestic goddess yourself." And just like that we're back half a decade ago, cracking jokes at 3 a.m. on the 4 train toward Utica, drunk on sleeplessness and youth, and neither you nor Imm Sami are dead yet, and I can still imagine that my strangeness might reverse itself, and there is still a place in the world for joy.

We spend the morning making date and pistachio ma'amoul, then move on to batches of bitlawah. When the shop opens for the day, we deliver towel-covered trays of cookies to Abu Sabah, who stuffs them into boxes for hungry customers who haven't yet had breakfast. Then we retreat to the kitchen again, our private world, the vein of memory we've opened.

Halfway into a batch of bitlawah, Sami tips a bag of flour over.

He tells me not to step in the mess and kneels down at my feet to clean it up with a damp rag. For a moment I am standing over him. He is close enough to curve his wrist around the back of my knee. There is not enough air in the room. His crown of black curls bounces when he stretches his arm to cup the flour with the rag, scraping it toward him with his hair dangling in his eyes. You showed me a frillback pigeon once, a bird descended from the rock dove but bred for the ornamental curly feathers on its wings, a mane of ringlets soft as mohair wool. The frillback was your proof that the beauty of ordinary things often goes unappreciated right under our noses. Sami turns his face upward to look at me. There is something new in his eyes. His T-shirt, cream-colored with narrow robin's egg stripes, hangs from his shoulder blades, revealing his collarbones. His arms are subtly muscled, his Adam's apple a marble of bone he has swallowed. When I imagine kissing him, I see myself lifting him, surrounding him, taking his head in my hands, my thumb on his jaw. I imagine his face pressed between my legs. I am never female in these fantasies; I am a hurricane. Sami's chest rises and falls, and I realize that, with nothing in the way, he can hug his loved ones closer to his heart. My two desires—the desire for him and the desire to be him—disappear into the hollow of his throat.

Sami rises with the flour in the bowl of his hand and tosses it into the trash. We put the bitlawah in the oven and listen to Abu Sabah greet a neighbor in Arabic who's come to pick up some burghul and ful. Sami leans back on the table and wipes his brow. A rounded vein runs the length of his forearm.

"Aisha Baraka asked me to go to jum'ah with her today." I draw a circle in the flour on the cutting board.

"You going?"

"Nah. I'm hiding out here until it's over."

"Girl. Who are you hiding from?"

Sami means well. He means to include me in that sisterhood of femmes, a sacred circle to which Reem belongs. But it's a place I've never been at home.

"Please don't call me that."

Sami looks at me as though seeing me for the first time. "Okay."

"I don't go to jum'ah because I don't know which door to use," I say, and it sounds so much more helpless than I planned.

"Listen," Sami says, "you don't have to go to the masjid to talk to God."

For the first time there is pity in his eyes. I cross my arms high over my chest, hiding nothing but desperate for something to do with my hands. The slip of paint on brick has been my only form of prayer for longer than I can remember. In this moment, I want to be tugged out of my own flesh like a soft crab. In Attar's epic poem, the beloved confounds the one who seeks the divine, tests their faith, leads them beyond everything, even their own earthly bodies.

We finish the baking, reassure Abu Sabah that we'll be back tomorrow, and then head to Crown Heights so Sami can change his flour-splashed T-shirt. His neighborhood has changed, too, as the Bajans and Trinidadians have been pushed out of the rowhouses south of Eastern Parkway that many of their families have owned for generations. On the subway, Sami nods off and tilts toward my shoulder, and even through my shirt, I burn at the touch of him. Something about the intimacy of this touch makes the riders around us snap to attention, frowning and staring at my short hair, my flattened chest, my baggy clothes. A teenage boy lifts his cell phone and starts to film us, whispering commentary to his camera. I meet his eyes with a glare, but he doesn't look away, as though I am an animal he is observing. I have seen that stare before, seen other lovers drop each other's hands to escape it. Yesterday, a man on the subway asked me if I was a boy or a girl, then ran his eyes the length of my body, and I felt less than human. I wrap my arm around Sami's shoulders.

When we arrive at Sami's place, he strips off his top. I avert my eyes.

"That shirt looks good on you." My voice is uneven.

Sami laughs. "I could see you in stripes. Here, try it on." He tosses it to me. I slip it on over my own shirt. It's much too big on me, but the over-washed fabric is soft and thin. "Cute," he says, pointing up and down.

"Thanks." Something in the pit of my ribs swells to bursting. The shirt smells like Sami, damp with his sweat. But when I look down—that implacable lump. The urge to rip off the shirt and throw it across the room is a physical need as solid as breathing, as real as the desire to peel off every inch of my skin.

I slip off the tee and fold it on the bed. Sami has already slid on a different shirt, a linen tunic with long sleeves that he rolls up to the elbows. He makes adjustments in the mirror. I use his body to block my own and examine my profile from behind him, my hair now shorter than his. An angular face and strong jaw have appeared where they were once hidden behind my long hair. Unable to see my body, I am hit with the unexpected relief of my sharp, angular profile, as though my brain has always been hungry for exactly this and is having its ravenous fill.

When I look away from the mirror, Sami is gazing at me with his hands folded. "You look like you've had that haircut forever."

Reem is at the house when Sami and I arrive, up on the roof having a smoke. She's dragged a couple of cushions up here to make a little seating, and to my surprise Qamar is giving her a light.

"Hey." Qamar slips their lighter into their pocket and hands me a cup of fresh orange juice, squeezed by the juice cart we passed on Atlantic, one of the ones that sells plastic baggies of sliced mango in the summer. They smile and adjust the headphones around their neck. "We ran into each other at jum'ah. I took the afternoon off."

"These are delicious, thanks." I sit down on a cushion and lift the plastic lid from the orange juice. The first sip is honey-sweet and electric cold. "So your family goes there, too?"

"My mom started going there a few years ago," Qamar says, and I remember asking you, years ago, why people referred to the other masjid in Brooklyn as the Yemeni masjid, or the Bangladeshi one, or the Pakistani one. That was when I learned that being a light- to medium-skinned Levantine meant that you were privileged at pretty much any masjid, blessed with the luxury of walking in and expecting everyone to look like you. "There was a while there when I didn't go. But the new imam is pretty cool, so the past few months I've started to come more often."

We are all silent for a moment. Reem starts up a conversation she must have been having with Qamar before we arrived, about Qamar's thesis project.

"Technically it isn't finished yet," Qamar says. "My grandfather never actually got to publish his discovery of *G. simurghus*. The reviewers assigned to his papers kept citing that there were no other documented sightings, that it must have been something else. He couldn't find anyone who believed him—except an obscure bird artist from Lower Manhattan. The problem is that no one's found anything with enough detail to make an identification, especially this painting that's supposed to be out there, somewhere, hiding in someone's attic. I've put feelers out to every collector and foundation in the city, but nothing's turned up."

"So if you found it," Sami says, fiddling with a braided knot he's pulled out of his pocket, "you'd have enough documentation that you could get his notes published."

"Theoretically." Qamar gets up and walks to the edge of the roof. They're fidgety, like they can't talk without movement. "My grandpa Ben was the first person I came out to. He struggled with my pronouns, but he tried. When he passed away, he willed his field notes to me, all his notebooks and letters. Even this was his—

it's an early translation of a Sufi poem he read in school. He studied Persian. He was cool like that." They motion to a pillow, where they've set down a small yellowed book with a worn leather slipcover, so old that the spine has long since cracked. It lies open on the pillow, the pages ruffled by the breeze. I look over and read from Attar's *The Conference of the Birds*:

> *If you can contain the whole,*
> *why trouble yourself with the parts?. . .*
> *Desire all, be all, become all.*
> *Choose everything.*
> *Choose everything.*

I say to Qamar, "I know what you mean."

Qamar laughs to themself. "I chose my name because it was one of his favorite words in Arabic." They hold up the moon charm on their necklace with their thumb. "The moon itself has no gender."

Reem puts out her cigarette into a dish and ties up her hair into a bun. "Abu Sabah wanted to know why you didn't come to jum'ah after you got done baking."

I busy myself with Qamar's book. "You know how hot it is back there? We were disgusting and sweaty."

Reem huffs and settles into one of the cushions. "You know how people talk."

The first time you ever said those words to me, I was in my junior year of high school. You liked that particular friend of mine, the one who walked me home every day after drama club, which is why I didn't think you'd be looking when I kissed her goodbye on the lips. I remember what bothered you wasn't that I had kissed a girl like that, but that I'd done it in broad daylight when someone we knew might have seen. *Me, I don't care, habibti,* you'd said, *you love who you love. But what will I do? People will talk.* That was the moment I saw the net that held me, the mesh of aunties and uncles and cousins and the family back in the bilad, how none of my actions, my joys, or my shames were solely my own. When I told my friend I couldn't kiss her in public again, she accused me of being a coward. She was white. I have always suspected it was easier for her to say this.

An adhan alarm goes off on Reem's phone for maghreb. She used to turn them on for Ramadan, when she would try to pray more regularly, and then a few months later she'd visit and they'd be turned off. This time, Reem disappears downstairs and comes back a few minutes later with Teta's old sajajid and sets them out on the rooftop. Sami declines, but Qamar and Reem move to the corner of the rooftop to pray. With Reem's hair in a bun, the tattoo on her neck is clearly visible. This is why she only ever ties her hair half-up, I think to myself—because people will talk, and not just about her. Reem and Qamar wrap their hijabs and deliberate about who will lead the prayer. A third prayer rug sits rolled up on one of the cushions like an invitation.

Unlike you, I always wanted explanations for the way God built a bird's wing. I wanted to understand the machinery of flight. First I collected feathers, lining them up by length on my bedroom dresser. Then came the day I found a whole wing ripped from a jay by a stray cat, all the contour feathers intact. I brought it home and washed it in your tub after you'd gone to bed, letting the grime run down the drain as though making ghusl before prayer. I placed it next to the husks of robin's eggs and the turkey feather, fat and marbled, laid on one of Teta's doilies like a spare quill. It was weeks before you discovered it by its smell. You must have stuffed it in a garbage bag to keep the rats and the raccoons away, but when I came home from school and couldn't find it, I imagined you'd opened the window and tossed the wing onto the street, where it would have fluttered down like a maple key. I spent an hour searching the sidewalk just in case, thinking I might come upon it behind a trash can or in one of the boxed-in maples in front of our building, that maybe someone's dog had picked it up and spat it out a few buildings down. I never found it. You told me to trust you, that it had been rotting, that I would find more beautiful treasures. But I have never been good at trusting what I cannot see.

I take the rolled-up rug and lay it out apart from Reem's and Qamar's. I clasp my forearms across my chest. I asked Sami not to call me girl, but if you were here, if I told you the thing I am too afraid to say, I fear that you would see masquerade and think to yourself that masquerade's got limits—say, the border of another boy's body on mine, or the place where my forehead touches the covered earth.

Qamar's voice reciting verses brushes the night as the lights come on in the apartments across the street. When I kneel with my forehead to the ground, I paint in my mind, each stroke a feather or the sheen on an eye. I push back and stand and recite, then kneel again. I point one finger on my thigh into the east. When I close my eyes, the shape I have painted in my mind is before me clear as the lump of waxing moon: the white-throated sparrow, the first to fall on Brooklyn.

Sami once told me the moment he first believed, really believed of his own volition. He said it was a kind of knowing no one could take away. It happened a few years back, after the rooftop of a nightclub collapsed. His friend was inside when it happened, wearing an evil eye bracelet Sami had picked up for her in Cairo the year before. She was almost crushed, but one of her hands was sticking up when the rescuers came. The flashlight hit the blue of the bracelet's little eyes, and they pulled seven people out with her. She's got a couple kids now, last Sami told me.

I make dua for Teta, for Sami, for Reem, for Qamar. The light is fading. Vega, the falling eagle, hangs overhead. Once, I asked Teta about the spring that the French shelled Damascus, Aleppo, Hama, and Homs after the United Nations had finally recognized

Syria as an independent nation. She told me she spent the days sequestered away inside her mother's house tracking the movements of the white storks that migrated north to Turkey to breed in the summer, returning from their overwintering south of the Sahara. She marked the number of storks she sighted with hidden pencil marks on her windowsill and wondered to herself how the world must look to them. Imagining the world from up there was what got her through that long loneliness.

The stork migration was upset that year by the shelling, and only a few storks passed over Teta's house. Once, a shell blast brought down the pale body of a stork with its pink beak and black-tipped wings. It plummeted in a line before being turned like a branch by the wind. Its wings caught the air and opened, wider than a man was tall, and its body disappeared into the orchard. This was long before my mother was born, yet Teta insisted that stork was the reason that, years later, my mother would come to the States armed with a degree in ornithology from a French university, an irony she never failed to comment on. One event can change everything, Teta told me, so that one small miracle placed underfoot can tumble us onto an unexpected path, and isn't that, she'd said to me then, the hand of God?

Saturday morning is hot and humid, a false summer in the middle of autumn. Everything is so damp that the cardboard packages in the mailbox are wet to the touch, flexible as fabric. When Sami and I arrive at Sabah's father's shop to make the pastries for the day, Abu Sabah is stomping out the remains of a fire, cursing. The front windows are shattered. The impact of a brick or a stone has broken the neck of an oud and shattered a tawleh box inlaid with mother-of-pearl that Abu Sabah brought back with him from Syria more than twenty years ago. The fire was set in the window displays, evidently, a rag or something soaked in alcohol thrown inside, and the wood is blackened by flame. The white foam of a fire extinguisher is scattered inside the display case like chemical snow. Abu Sabah leans against the doorjamb with his arm over his wet face.

"Abu Sabah! What happened?" Sami and I hurry up to him, and Abu Sabah collapses against Sami, shaking with rage.

"They burned my shop," he says. "I was coming up the block to open and I saw it. I've lived on this block for forty years. I've lived in New York more than half my life. I was here when the towers fell. Who would do a thing like this?"

Sami and I exchange quiet glances. In all the years I've known him, I have never seen Abu Sabah look older than he does in this moment, his gray flannel work shirt pushed up to the elbows, his hands blackened and cut by the broken display window, his glasses askew on his face. He is an old man lost in his own city. I've heard him talk about the decades before the new millennium, when a light-skinned Arab might get by laughing like a good sport at his own name. But I don't remember those days, or better—I figured out pretty quick that the light skin my father gave me didn't magically mean I wouldn't get called a terrorist by my classmates. You made sure I never believed the lie that I'd earned the extra privileges that came with being light, and I learned from listening to you and Aisha that none of this shit was new. I was young when I learned these lessons; Abu Sabah wasn't.

"Let me put something on your hands," Sami says, and we try to take Abu Sabah inside, but he is adamant and refuses to leave the broken displays. He takes an elbow to the broken glass and knocks a few pieces inside, then reaches in to try to salvage what he can. There isn't much to be saved: a few small jewelry boxes; a few evil eye charms to ward off jealousy and ill will; the silver medallion of Ayat al-Kursi, the same verse of the Qur'an you and Teta always hung in our apartments to protect a home.

Sami's phone buzzes in his pocket. "Reem. Calm down—what? Anjad?" He looks up at me. "The masjid burned last night, too."

"What?" I set down the rag I'm using to collect slivers of glass from the floor. Sami and I tell Abu Sabah we'll be right back and jog down to Flatbush, slowing to a walk near the Barclays Center to catch our breath. Even from here, we can see the crowd gathered out front, murmuring. A lot of them are our neighbors, Abu Sabah's friends and customers, Sabah's cousins, aunties I remember from iftars and weddings. A lot of them are other Arabs from Lebanon or Yemen or Libya, older folks, some of the same people who come to Abu Sabah for spices and pickled olives and cracked wheat and, every now and then, news of home. Their faces are stricken. This is worse than Abu Sabah's shop, not only because the impact is legible on the faces of everyone around us, but because as we near the door it becomes obvious that not only was the door bashed in and the lock broken, but the attackers set a fire in the stairwell leading to the women's section. Qamar and Reem are already there when we reach the door, carrying out the charred remnants of a couch.

"Let me help you with that." I lift up one corner and help them set it down on the curb. "What happened?"

"The fire downstairs put itself out before it did much damage," Qamar says, wiping their forehead with their sleeve. Their face is tired, and sweat beads at their hairline. The sirens of fire trucks wail in the distance.

"But the sharmout smashed the upstairs window and threw something inside." Reem wipes soot from her cheek. She's got her hair half-up again, just enough to cover her tattoo. "Luckily it landed right on the couch. Thank God for flame-retardant fabric."

"The ceiling will have to be repainted," Qamar adds, "but the smoke damage isn't too bad."

"Fuck." Nothing I could say would be appropriate. I don't know what to do with my hands. I touch the burnt cover on the arm of the couch and am greeted with a rush of despair. "Fuck."

The crowd breaks into task forces—one group to greet the

firefighters, another the reporters who are sure to follow, another to get sponges and rags to scrub the stairwell, another to go upstairs and assess the damage. Two light-skinned women volunteer to deal with the police. Meanwhile, members of another nearby masjid, a historic community of Black Muslims, have already heard the commotion and arrived with brooms and bottles of water, and soon there are others, Bangladeshi Muslims from a masjid in Flatbush, four college kids from the pride center in Bed-Stuy who saw what happened on social media, members of the synagogue a few blocks away. Reem wipes her hands on her pants and slips back into the building after Qamar, stepping over the twisted remains of the lock. The ringlets covering the ink at the back of her neck are damp with sweat.

Sami puts his hand on my arm. "We'd better check on Abu Sabah."

When we get back to the shop, the police are leaving and Abu Sabah is outside talking to a small group of neighbors who have gathered on the sidewalk. Something in him has broken. He is quietly cursing the last seventeen years he's spent in this city, the American ban on people who come from the place where he was born, the fires that crop up again and again like weeds because people like Abu Sabah, people like us, are not welcome. His neighbors nod, their faces pensive or sorrowful or terrified. Some of them, though not all, once had the luxury to believe things would be different.

"We should at least call Sabah and let her know you're all right," I say to Abu Sabah when he's gone quiet. "Between this and the masjid, it'll be on the news."

This gets Abu Sabah inside, and we dial the number for him. Sami and I slink off into the kitchen to give him privacy, though we can hear him sobbing from the next room. The orange cat comes in and curls up in my lap at the table, watching my eyes for an explanation.

Abu Sabah appears in the doorway a few minutes later. "Sabah for you."

When I come to the phone, Sabah's voice wavers, but she's calm. "I was waiting for it. Hoped it wouldn't happen, but I was waiting anyway." There's a pause on the line. "Listen. The artist whose studio I came to visit, the glassblower? Laila Z was one of her influences. Laila was here, in Dearborn. This artist has one of her aquatints, a rare one—the yellow-crowned night heron. Some of the people who met her when she came through here in the thirties are still alive. They said she was here for a while—something must have delayed her. She shipped a bunch of prints back to New York when she left. If the records we have are accurate, and a private collector really did commission a complete series from her when she got back to New York, these might have been studies for those later illustrations. A lot of her aquatints were done in Dearborn: her sandhill crane, the cedar waxwing, the indigo bunting, the white ibis. If she painted *simurghus,* well—no one knows where the damn thing is."

The idea that art, or the natural world, could ever be anyone's property has always made me uneasy. A work is shaped not only by the artist, but by everyone who interacts with it; it belongs a little to everyone. This, too, is how a life is made: with the support of many hands. Outside, Abu Sabah is back with his arms through the glass, gathering objects: boxes, miniatures, strings of beads. His blood is on the sharp edges scattered on the sidewalk. The only thing I know of glassblowing is that it's the fire and the air, not your hands, that shapes the glass. The glass can't be shaped without the fire; the heat makes it smooth. I list in my head the ways the natural world consumes itself: lightning, volcanoes, forest fires. Abu Sabah's neighbors have joined in rescuing his precious objects. Word will have spread by now of what's happened at the Islamic center, and the crowd will have grown. Abu Sabah is not crying now, no longer outraged. He steps back into the darkness of the shop, his arms laden with charred treasures, and begins to coax out the burnt foam with a rag. Abu Sabah told me once that when he first moved in here, the basement, now used for storage, had a massive problem with black mold. Everything had to be ripped out and cleaned. Once he laid his hand on the wall downstairs, he said, and his palm came away green-gray, leaving a fuzzy outline of his hand. It was only when his new neighbors offered to help him clean it out that he felt the place was his, and that he belonged to it. Sometimes, after a long day's work, he'll talk about the shopfronts and the neighbors who have come and gone over the years, the cycles of coming and of leaving, the ways in which he is still learning that none of them, himself included, have built any of this alone.

FOURTEEN / LAILA

█████ B,

An unremarkable string of days. We've left Minneapolis for Dearborn, skipping over Chicago on our way back. Khalti says we'll drive back to New York the way we've come, stopping for a week in Dearborn to visit Abu Majed and bring gifts back for our own families. Ilyas and I never seem to know what to say to each other now, though often I will set down my hand on the seat of the truck and find his there, waiting. Sometimes, when we talk, I have the feeling that I know what he's going to say before he says it, as though I am in his body with him.

The closer I get to Ilyas, the more I think of you.

I'm stalling. But if I set down the whole truth here, little wing, maybe I can let you go.

I haven't gone a single day without tasting your lips on the corniche again, sweet and tart like salted licorice. You were so much softer than I expected, your cheek as silken as the inside of my thigh. No one was looking that day when I cut my finger on the back of your earring, or when you dabbed my blood with your handkerchief. Did you ever have a kiss like that again? Did you ~~No one was here~~ No, I don't want to know. You must be married with a handful of children by now, a respectable woman, a mother, a wife. Did you throw away my locket when you married? Was your stained handkerchief inside where I folded it and tucked it tight, so that a part of me would be with you forever?

Forgive me. I used to think of my body as a part of yours, and I never did manage to stop.

B,

If Dearborn has taught me anything, it's that life in a factory town is only calm if the factory and the town get along. There was a tension in the air when we arrived the day before last. The union has been gaining in popularity among the workers at the Rouge, the fathers coming home to their families with pamphlets and ideas mentioned in a murmur around the dinner table. It was the same in Chicago. The factory doesn't like it much, of course, but now things seem to be building to a thunderclap.

There had been a time, five years ago, Abu Majed told us, when workers were laid off and times were hard and people were desperate. People were starving to death every day in Detroit back then, he said. Thousands of protesters marched on the Rouge on one of the coldest days of the winter in March of '32, all the way from Detroit, and nothing much happened until they got to the Dearborn city limits, where things started to escalate. Eventually, both police and security men started shooting into the crowd of marchers. Four workers didn't come home to their families that night, one of them little more than a boy. Abu Majed says it's things like this that show how important the unions are. Tomorrow, the union is planning to hand out pamphlets at shift-change time, advocating for $8 an hour and a six-hour workday. Abu Majed says there's a lot of support for it in the community. In some departments at the Rouge, like the assembly and the foundry and the engine plant, there are lots of Arab workers, many of whom are joining the union. Majed told us tonight that he and some of his fellow workers will be there tomorrow to help pass out the pamphlets at gate four, and a few of the boys, including Ilyas, offered to come along in solidarity. I decided to go, too, and I know it's the right decision because as soon as I said it, I felt a little braver, a little more like Khalti. Khalto Tala will come along, too, of course, though probably she'd been planning on it all along.

We've exhausted the goods we brought to sell on our westward journey, so I've started to paint and sell canvases of birds, first in watercolor and then, when someone's second cousin begged for a painting that would be more resistant to sun bleaching, in oils. I have a secret dream of making prints, so I've started making sketches, hoping one day I can etch them in copper.

Aunties talk, and I should have known word would get around eventually. No surprise, then, that my reputation as a painter preceded me here on our way back. Word spread that the daughter of Abu Issa from New York, of the Zeytouneh family, was painting American birds. That's how everything spreads: everyone wants to know who your people are. When we arrived in Dearborn, friends of Abu Majed were there to buy illustrations for their cousins and their children, some sign that I had been there and that they had supported me. Someone's father requested a painting of a red-tailed hawk of the kind that used to circle his family's duplex in Highland Park every morning; someone else's daughter loved the quaint face of a barn owl she'd spotted gliding over Dix. I hadn't intended to show my work to my community, but people were so sincere in their support that it would have been rude to refuse them. I never let anybody pay much, just enough that I have some pocket money, something to buy milk for Sawsan without troubling Khalto Tala. I don't allow myself the luxury of higher aspirations, not yet.

Ilyas stays close to me while I work, rocking Sawsan on his chest, licking his finger to remove stray specks of paint from my face late at night, rubbing my hunched shoulders after too many hours over a canvas.

Ilyas and I haven't spoken of the yellow-crowned night heron since that night in the marsh, and it's the one work I made on the road that I haven't sold, the only work that I, in fact, have refused to sell. On the ride back to Dearborn, we kept the canvas rolled up in the bed of the truck with the last few sacks of spices and jars of pickled olives, wrapped in spare blankets.

Ilyas broke his silence today. We only have time to talk after everyone else has gone to bed, when we give Sawsan her bottle and burp her by the window before she falls asleep. Khalto Tala usually just eyes us and shakes her head—"like two buttocks in one pair of underwear," she says. Sometimes I lay my head on his shoulder and pretend it's possible for a long future to stretch out just like this, that this is the kind of life a person could choose. Everyone must assume we'll get married when we get back to New York, that we're playing at a family. New York—the thought of coming back to the city is like squeezing myself into a too-small blouse.

Tonight, sitting together by the dark window, Ilyas lifted Sawsan to his face and rubbed her nose with his, telling her what a beautiful black-eyed girl she would be one day. I replaced Sawsan's knitted cap on her head. *Sooner or later we'll return to New York*—I must have said something like that. I don't know why I said it, except that I couldn't get it out of my mind and I couldn't see beyond it. My return to New York with Sawsan and Ilyas seemed an impossibility, as though what I had once considered a normal life couldn't exist with them in it.

Ilyas's face closed like a struck flower. He wrapped an arm around Sawsan's back, and the gesture was so protective it was hard for me to imagine he'd ever give her up. I still remember what he said: "We could make something of this." He kept his voice low so we wouldn't wake anyone, not even Khalti with her sharp ears.

I stuttered a moment, then said something about us playing at a regular life. I regretted it immediately. Ilyas turned to me, wounded. He had not removed his hand from mine, and his fingers were stiff and cool. He asked me, keeping his voice even, if this life weren't real.

It wasn't an argument I meant to have. *We can't get attached,* I whispered back.

Ilyas pressed his lips into a line. "Are you talking about Sawsan," he said, "or are you talking about me?"

That took me aback. We don't know the first thing about caring for an infant, I argued, and Ilyas countered that we've been doing just that, all this time. He was talking about something more than caring for Sawsan.

I asked him if he wanted a family with me.

He paused. He'd been controlling the volume of his voice, but I was afraid that at any moment Abu Majed would wake and enter, and I would blurt out everything. It wasn't so much that I might blurt out *that* particular thing, that night by the water in St. Paul with Ilyas, because the need to say aloud what I felt for him was a need so strong that giving voice to it seemed beyond doubt, but rather that threaded into the fabric of that truth would be another truth: the dark stain of my shame, the same acid shame that rose in my chest when I kissed you on the corniche, and that this time there would be no running from it.

"I've made my choice," Ilyas said. "Now you've got to make yours."

I am ashamed—write it!—but I said nothing then. Nothing! Ilyas took Sawsan up on his shoulder and brought her to bed. I was frozen to the windowsill, afraid that time might run backward like the tide if I moved. I thought of your hands pressing the hand-kerchief to the bead of blood forming on my torn cuticle, the way the tiny dots of blood made wine-colored constellations on your mother's thin cloth. You sucked on my finger to stop the bleeding, and though I flinched, the touch of your saliva didn't sting at all.

The red-winged blackbirds were calling from the trees behind Abu Majed's house this afternoon when we left for the Rouge. We gave Sawsan to Abu Majed's daughter-in-law, Imm Ibtisam, to look after for a few hours. Sawsan was still sleeping swaddled in her blanket, and we hoped we'd be back before she needed to be fed again.

The day was cloudy, but warm. The weather has finally turned. It's almost the end of May now, and here in Michigan that means the leaves are finally on the trees again, and the afternoon sun is pleasant in the worn coveralls Majed's wife gave me; her sister used to work at the Rouge. We gathered men on our walk to the Rouge until we were a small throng. As we approached gate four on the overpass over Miller Road, there was already a group to meet us, swelling like a clot in front of the factory doors. A group of men were posed for a picture for reporters there. A second group approached them, perhaps two dozen or more, maybe company service men by the look of their trench coats and trilby hats.

It happened quickly. One of the trenchcoated men grabbed a union worker, pulled his coat over his head, and then they were pummeling and kicking him. The fight became a brawl. Our group surged forward, the boys throwing punches. I lost Ilyas and Majed and Khalti in the scuffle. The fists seemed to be disconnected from the bodies. I tried to squirm away, only to take blows to my chest, my head, my shoulders. I blocked with my arms the way Khalto Tala had taught me. The crush of men throbbed and shoved. I found out later that one of the union men had been

thrown down a flight of stairs. More men came, maybe because it was shift change and the other workers had seen us up on the overpass.

Khalto Tala pulled Majed from the brawl. The throng of workers writhed like a single aggrieved body. The crowd was too thick to escape, so I rode the current of bodies until, taking a hard blow to my ribs that left me sputtering, I was ejected back the way we'd come. There was a dull heat, a wetness at my waist, numbness. I didn't feel anything at first because of the adrenaline, just shock and a ringing in my ears. Ilyas limped toward me. It was as though he'd materialized out of the ground.

"Where did you learn to fight like that?" I asked Khalto Tala, breathless.

"You learn a few tricks when you're a woman alone on a silver claim," she said. She frowned and pressed a hand to my ribs. It came away bloody.

We limped some distance from the factory before I started to wheeze. The pain was sharp and unrelenting. I collapsed in a patch of grass by the side of the road, not far from Abu Majed's home. The fist had left a red and purple welt across my ribs that oozed pus and blood. Khalto Tala tugged a handkerchief from her pocket and pressed it to the cut. Nauseated with pain, I blinked away sparks of light. I wanted to beg her to stop, but I was afraid of what would happen if she did. I looked up at the sky. The clouds were the cream color of your mother's handkerchief dotted with my blood.

Ilyas's face appeared between the clouds. I reached for him, but lifting my arm brought sharp pain. Even now, writing this in bed hours after, I have to be careful not to stretch as I write. Those first minutes of pain, real pain without the adrenaline to mask it, were sharper than any I'd ever felt. The thought crossed my mind that I'd been shot. I didn't know what it felt like to be shot, but I thought of the Hunger March five years before in this same town,

and the four dead workers, and thought that maybe shot people didn't realize right away that they'd taken a bullet. I began to fear that I was going to slip away any second. Khalto Tala told me later that I kept asking if they'd heard gunshots, but they assured me no one had. Ilyas slipped off his jacket, folded it, and slid it beneath my head. My ribs had become a pulsing ache. The panic subsided.

I opened one eye to Ilyas and managed a smile. "Will I live?"

Ilyas laughed. "Tough little bird. You'll be all right."

Khalto Tala bound my chest in bandages and helped me up. The weather had turned, and the afternoon air threatened rain. I grinned, the stupid grin of the newly terrified. Looking at the greening bruise of my ribs now, in spite of it all, I have to admit I'm a little proud that I'll be able to prove all this to my mother by my scars.

FIFTEEN / ██████

I WAKE UP BEFORE dawn with a sharp pain low in my belly. I'm bleeding heavily now, soaking through an overnight pad every two hours.
I roll my swollen body out of bed. I'll call someone tomorrow, or
next week maybe, after Reem goes home, after we've finished fixing
up Abu Sabah's store. I don't want to get the whole family in an
uproar over nothing.

The ruby-throated hummingbirds appear with the morning
light as though they're a part of my bleeding. First one flits up to
the windowpane in my bedroom, and then it's joined by a second
and a third. The light unfurls in a ribbon across the floor where
Reem lays, drawing a triangle of red light on my comforter, which
Sami has thrown off in the night. The tendon at the back of his
knee is exposed to the light, a boomerang of muscle blanketed in
soft dark hair. A hummingbird flits across his pillow, and he mum-
bles in his sleep. He reminds me of all the brown boys I wanted to

be growing up, the ones who looked like my jiddo when he was young or like the cousins I saw in photographs, lined up on the rooftop of the family home. I changed and swelled and bled, but each year they only grew taller, stronger, more angular. I could never see myself in the haughty white boys I grew up with at my private school, but I could almost locate my face in my cousins', could almost imagine myself a body that existed for no one and nothing but myself.

I wrest my eyes away from Sami. I want nothing more than to curl up on the couch in a ball, so I walk into the living room to escape the thrumming of the hummingbirds' wings. But they are outside every window, their high cries filling the air. There are thousands of hummingbirds above our street now, the red sun flashing off their emerald bodies, each small enough to hold in a palm. You are seated at the windowsill, a shawl over your feet on the fire escape, as though you just might reach in for a second blanket against the chill. You are framed by the hummingbirds in a foliage of light. Asmahan swishes her tail on the sill beside you, mewling in imitation of the chirping.

Teta has fallen asleep in her easy chair again like a sentinel, and her brows are furrowed with the look of bad dreams. People I love are mourning what they've lost, and the city is bleeding birds. When one of the old sisters down the hall from us went into kidney failure, her sister gave her one of hers; when she passed away, a part of her sister died, too. As a teenager I learned that the body itself can be a gift, a sanctuary, a sacrifice. Satin bowerbirds will build intricate homes for their mates and decorate them with bright blue objects—bits of ribbon, stolen jay feathers, bottle caps, worn glass—before the pursuer dances for their would-be mate, displaying his feathers and his agility. The bowerbird makes a gift of itself. Maybe it's born knowing how to do this: the instinct to gather, to open, to bend. Or maybe instinct is only a name created to discount a wisdom to which one has no access.

I rearrange the blanket on Teta's lap and think of the time I asked her what it meant to love a person. It was shortly after Jiddo Jibril passed away, and though you told me Teta was grieving, she just seemed to spend a lot of time with her hands folded in thought, watching a praying mantis that had appeared on the windscreen that summer. It clung there until it froze and dropped off after one cold autumn night. Someone told me I could tell the females from the males by the number of abdominal segments, so I counted them. Female, or so it seemed. I liked being able to categorize nature more easily than I could categorize myself.

When I asked you for a definition of love, you gave me a list of agonies: depression and disfigurement, cancer and colostomy bags, amnesia, moody evenings, unemployment. It seemed then that love was the sum of what you could bear. I wondered if this was how you'd felt about my father, if you'd left because you could no longer justify carrying the burden you were supposed to let him lay on your back. But I couldn't ask you that.

The door to Teta's room is open again. A breeze enters through the window, ruffling the photos tucked into the sides of her mirror. The closet where she keeps your boxes is open a crack. I slip into the room, and you turn to watch me. I open the closet and take out your boxes of notebooks, old scarves folded thin as paper, jewelry boxes for the earrings colleagues gave you as gifts, not knowing your ears weren't pierced, useless treasures you couldn't bear to give away because they'd been given out of kindness. Now I open the boxes one by one. I take out your brooches and earrings and bracelets and lay them on Teta's bed in a line, all gold, kept carefully polished as though you were just about to wear them. You watch me from the windowsill. Hummingbirds enter the house through the tunnel in your chest, zipping around lamps and landing on the velvet back of Teta's chair as she sleeps. They hover in the doorways and crowd the air like jeweled bees.

When I asked Teta what love was, she told me a lover was not someone you were willing to die for, but a person for whom you wished good things. The definition was so simple as to be absurd. I had never imagined a lifetime could contain so many different kinds of love. But there it was.

In the last of your jewelry boxes, sealed with peeling tape that has been opened and resealed over the years, is a fat silver locket, dusty and tarnished to a greenish patina. It is like nothing you own, and by far the oldest of anything I have uncovered. No, there is no way this locket belonged to you; it is older than you are, and the way you have hidden it suggests you weren't supposed to have it at all. I turn, and you are standing in Teta's doorway. The hummingbirds flutter in after you, inspecting your jewelry, pausing at the dried flowers on Teta's dresser and Asmahan's water cup on her nightstand. I open the locket. Inside is a tightly folded square of handkerchief, once off-white, now an aged yellow, embroidered in Arabic with the name *Laila*. I unfold the square of fabric. It is dotted with brown blood.

When I look up, you and the birds are gone, and I am left with Laila's handkerchief in my hand. You knew. My entire life, you were obsessed with Laila's paintings, with her legacy, with the legends surrounding her death. But you must have found this lovers' token long ago, perhaps hidden in Teta's things. There is no other explanation: you knew Teta Badra loved her.

By midmorning, the hummingbirds have vanished. People wake and go about their day. I curl up with a heating pad while Sami puts a pot of Arabic coffee on and crushes cardamom. Reem rubs sleep out of her eyes and arranges bread and olives on a dish, swatting away her mechanical birds. Teta wakes and goes to her bedroom to change her clothes. She takes slow steps to her dresser, then picks up the silver locket lying there.

"I was going through some of Mom's things. Her old photos, her earring museum." I join her in her doorway. "I thought it was pretty."

There is panic on Teta's face. "You opened it?"

I slip my hands into the pockets of my jeans and look down. "No."

Teta runs her fingers over the locket as though reading the rings on a tree. She slips it into the pocket of her blouse and shuffles toward the closet where Jiddo's ties lay folded. She has not touched them since his death. I help her off with her cardigan and hang it in the closet. Reem comes in with a cup of coffee, and Teta drops her hand from the sagging pocket above her heart.

Dusk is falling after a day's hard work at Abu Sabah's shop, and the nightjar that has moved in on the gravel-roofed apartment building across the street is being courted by an enthusiastic male. He is doing his characteristic swooping display, making chirps and then a booming by passing air over his wings, lifting up and then diving down again, again, again. From the street, we can't see the other bird sitting on the roof, waiting. You will be watching the dark falling from your seat on the fire escape about now, your legs pulled up to your chest. Teta will have already gotten dressed for bed. She'll be murmuring her prayers from her bedroom, counting out the beads on her tasbih.

We've been working all day to fit the new glass for Abu Sabah's display window, repaint the front of the store, and gut the inside of the display case. We work in shifts, elders strolling up to meet Abu Sabah in the morning, kids and their parents stopping by after school or work. Down on Flatbush, another group is doing the same with the upstairs room of the Islamic center. They've already replaced the lock on the front door and scrubbed the entrance. During the night, the nearby synagogue has organized a group to stand watch in case the fire starters come back. At the shop, Abu Sabah has fed everyone and made round after round of coffee and black tea. I've spent the afternoon being greeted with a clap on the back or cheek kisses by people I haven't seen since you were alive, women you used to study Qur'an with, aunties who used to give me sweets on Eid.

Now Abu Sabah has laid down in the back of the shop, and Qamar has gone home for the night, so Sami, Reem, and I sit on the bench outside while Reem and Sami smoke a hand-rolled cigarette. I tug off the knit hat I usually wear to hide my haircut at the shop. I haven't figured out how to explain it to Abu Sabah yet.

Reem says between drags, "I was engaged when Mom died."

The moon rises behind the nightjars' rooftop, plump and full, a dollop of fresh labneh.

"I didn't even know you were dating someone." I side-eye her. "What do you mean *was*?"

"He was a real estate agent from Minneapolis. White guy. We met at a mixer for young professionals, one of those things you do when you're new in a city. I broke it off after Mom died. For a while I thought I was just afraid to feel anything. My friends said I was pushing people away. It was something he said that made me end it. It gnawed at me."

"What was it?"

"He kept asking what Mom did leading up to her death, like she must have done something to provoke it. He used to say the same thing about gay bashings, deportations, all kinds of stuff. He couldn't accept that something bad could happen to you unless you did something to deserve it." Reem does not look at me as she speaks, but her back shudders up and down. I cannot remember seeing her cry since she broke her leg skiing as a teenager, when I was little. Her tears scared me then, because she seemed too strong to suffer. "I stayed with him for three years trying to change his mind. Isn't that fucked up?"

"I watched Mom die." Even Teta and I have never spoken of this. "She got death threats for trying to save that building in Little Syria, especially for trying to help the Islamic center move in there.

The nest was a sign to her that she was doing the right thing. When the fire started, she put me out on the fire escape for the firefighters to take down first. But the platform buckled while they were coming back up for her. Mom slid off. I looked away before she hit the ground."

I pick at the laces of my sneakers. Sami keeps quiet. Across the street, the male nightjar swoops over his lover, a sharp dive toward the earth.

"I should have been there." It is the first time since her broken leg that I have ever heard Reem afraid enough to whisper. Beside me on the bench, she smells like detergent and lavender soap, scrubbed clean like an old woman. She has never been good at comforting people. She sets her fist palm-up on her knee and opens it, and inside is one of her mechanical birds, a black-tipped egg of wings and sparks. I take it from her. It twitches electricity into my fingers.

Sami touches the solar panels on the backs of the translucent wings. "You make these?"

"I wasn't traveling around Europe just to take selfies." Reem taps the end of the bird's tail, and it lifts its feet and hovers above my hand, giving off a faint warmth. "I liked the robotics work I did during one of my fellowships. It started as a hobby, but my ex thought it was a waste of time. Now I've got the time to do what I want, even if it's not useful."

"Why do we have to be useful?" I kick a shard of glass out from under my feet. "Is that what we're for, our usefulness?"

"Aren't we?" Reem tucks her hands into her lap, curling her fingers under her thighs. "Everybody tells you to be yourself as long as you've got value—for a job, for a man. What? You're a woman. I'm not saying anything you don't know."

"Reem, I'm—not. I'm not a woman."

I am shaking. Sami reaches over and takes my hand. He doesn't have to tell me that he knows; it isn't Sami I have to tell. My sister widens her eyes, and I remind myself that I, too, have failed to notice things because I was too close to them. In the years just after your divorce when we couldn't afford new clothes, you braided my wet hair at night and then stayed up to sew me my school dresses. You used paisley fabric I thought was ugly at the time, the fabric that would have gone to make couch cushion covers. You never let me see the bandages on your fingers. I hated those dresses. I never knew what they cost you.

I reach for her hand, but she doesn't take it. "I'm pretty sure I'm a boy." Pretty sure. I want to tell Reem that maybe I am something there is no word for, but I am afraid that I am already invisible enough to her as it is.

Reem tightens her mouth into a trembling line. "Is that why you cut your hair?"

"Yes."

Reem sets her hand on my shoulder, touching the strap of my binder. "You've been acting more like yourself these past few weeks than I've seen in years. But I always thought—"

"I'm still the same person."

"But you're not. Look at you. I'm losing my kid sister." Reem is crying. "You feel like you're different. Fine. But you don't have to throw yourself away and start over. This doesn't have to change anything."

"But it changes everything, don't you see that?" I toss the mechanical bird from my hand into the reddish light. Sami grips my hand like a rock face above a hundred-foot drop. "I'm not starting over. You're not losing me. I've been here the whole time."

Reem looks at me as though I am a wilderness.

Many species of birds have been shown to have memories of their roosting or mating sites that persist over generations. The northern bald ibis, the rarest bird in the Middle East, was once down to just three birds who continued to migrate back to Palmyra from northern Europe each spring before the war drove them to extinction in their native lands. The last bird, named Zenobia after the Palmyrene queen, hung on for a season before vanishing into clouds shredded by bombers. You spoke to me once of the bald ibis. You used to cut out conservation reports and photos of it, had written about it beside your notes in Arabic. *Nadir*, you wrote: *rare*. The word is also a masculine name. I picture Zenobia's final glorious morning of flight, perhaps in a moment of quiet between the shells that destroyed the homes she'd glided over for decades. I imagine her calling to a mate who had been so thoroughly blotted from the skies that it was as though he had never been there at all.

"I love you, Noodle. I know what it's like to want something people think is wrong." She averts her eyes. "But I have to mourn my sister."

Being mourned as though I am dead while I am standing here before her—that, more than anything else, is what lodges the knot of shame behind my chest.

Sami and I walk in silence back toward Teta's apartment, and Reem walks in the opposite direction toward her station wagon. The pain has started again, low in my belly, the pad between my legs bloated with blood.

At first it looks like the sky is full of tiny, puffed clouds, then feathers. Then the strings appear. The air is full of miniature kites in the shapes of birds, rippling like a wall of white flame over us. Everyone on the street stops, hushed, to watch the procession. The kites have been loosed into the air at sunset. As they ride the breeze, they crack the sun into a mosaic of light. For a few moments the only sound is the distant bark of horns and an ocean of fluttering paper. People slide open their windows and stand on their fire escapes to watch as the kites are carried up by the breeze, disappearing around buildings and wrapping themselves around light poles. An ancient Arab woman, easily in her nineties, stands with a middle-aged woman on a balcony on the fifth floor of an apartment building. She is crying, and the younger woman wraps a shawl around her and rubs her shoulders. In other windows, parents lift their children up to see the paper parade, and the kites cast red shadows over their faces, tiny flashlights seen through skin. I think of the glassblower dipping her rod into a furnace of molten glass and lifting out a perfect white orb, an orchid of flame dripping like a wet fist. Sami slides his hand into mine and interlaces our fingers.

The pain in my belly is a sword. I double over on the sidewalk, dragging Sami down by his hand. I lift my fingers and show him the speckle of blood between my legs.

Neither of us can afford an ambulance or an emergency room visit, so somehow Sami helps me onto the subway to get to a women's health clinic that takes walk-ins. When we're almost at the entrance, a series of strong cramps makes me sink down where I stand, and Sami picks me up and carries me inside, my face pressed to the flowers on his pink T-shirt.

He sets me down in a chair in the waiting room and consults with a receptionist, then a nurse, who informs us of what I already know: my uterus is raging against the device inside. Sami sits down beside me to wait for the doctor. We are seated across from a couple of pregnant women and their partners, who glance at us over their magazines. I can imagine that we make a strange pair, but it's the way they glare at me that makes me pause, as though I'm rude for appearing this way, with my square jaw and unreadable face, in a space where they had expected someone legible.

I lean over to whisper to Sami, who has never let go of my hand. "Ten bucks says they think we're a gay guy and the butch girl he got pregnant."

Sami pretends to be mock offended. "They think I'm pregnant?"

I muffle my laughter in his shirt, and he cracks up into the buzzed back of my head until we're both in tears. By the time we compose ourselves, the waiting room is empty. Sami wipes a tear from the corner of his eye.

My smile dissolves on my face. "Reem is probably halfway back to Boston by now."

Sami rubs my back. "Your mom would be proud of you. She wouldn't have compromised herself, either, not for anybody."

"She paid a price."

"And you've been paying yours for twenty-eight years." Sami searches my face. "Which reminds me. What do you want me to call you?"

The northern bald ibis was one of the first birds you considered when you were trying to put a name to the mating pair in Lower Manhattan. But they had never been seen west of the Atlantic, and you couldn't match their physical description to the species: the iridescent black feathers and the naked head, the red and yellow eyes. At first, this disappointed you. Looking back, maybe you wanted to believe you could save something you already loved, something you already knew to be in danger of being lost. Instead you came to love something you had never considered, and still you gave your life to protect it.

"Nadir," I say.

Sami flicks his thumb under my chin. "It's perfect."

I think of the bald ibis when I put my feet into the stirrups in the gyno's office, when I'm tempted to discard my body and never come back to it, when the doctor's gloves on my skin make me want to crawl out of myself. My blood is a fact, like my body, in a conversation that I will not always be a part of. But I hold on to my name and turn my face to the window, and trapped against the glass is the red chest feather of a ruby-throated hummingbird.

SIXTEEN / LAILA

Little wing,

After a few weeks of rest here in Dearborn, my cracked ribs have begun to heal, and I'm now left with a nasty, painful bruise that's turning green on my left side. Abu Majed has brought me a good doctor who lives here in the neighborhood, a man who was a surgeon in Syria and is still practicing medicine. Though the other families have left to return to New York, Khalto Tala and Ilyas have pledged to stay until I'm well enough to travel, and Abu Majed has welcomed us.

Being unable to leave the house to play with the children or walk down to Dix has turned me into a bit of a recluse, I'm afraid. I've become accustomed to the way the light falls on the windowpane and the view from the window in the room where I sleep, which faces the back of the house. It overlooks a small field and a shallow pond where birds like to wade, and in the mornings the long yellow grass is laden with hoarfrost, and the red-winged blackbirds call in the sedge. I wouldn't have expected such a sanctuary so close to the factory, but now I see that this place is full of pockets of greenery I overlooked.

The doctor has confined me to my bed for three weeks to let my ribs heal. He warned me that if I do too much, I risk poking a hole in my lungs, which has scared me into listening to him. That first week, when the other families from New York were still here, the other women fussed over me, feeding me and asking me about potential suitors back home, exchanging stories and news from the neighborhood while eating the leftovers of the men's meals. The women didn't trust the doctor. They brought me home remedies to supplement his pills, traditional medicine from the bilad: black seed oil for the stomach and for inflammation, chicory to boost my immune system, mallow poultices for the healing of the wound. In times of need, all of us—even Khalto Tala—trust in the remedies of our mothers and our tetas who survived by caring for one another.

Since the others left, Khalto Tala and Ilyas have been taking turns caring for Sawsan, though Ilyas often falls asleep beside me above the blankets with Sawsan on his chest, and I like to wake up to her warm body nestled in the space between us. For propriety's sake, I have to be careful to wake him before anyone comes. Here in Dearborn by our little pond, we are so far from the bustle of downtown Detroit that it's hard to imagine it even exists. After a week of this solitude, I just watched the birds calling to one another from the corners of the field: sparrows, flycatchers, and crows, and, on the pond, ruddy ducks and canvasbacks. Occasionally I catch a bobwhite quail calling from the copse of beeches at the field's edge. Ilyas has been bringing me my inks and my paints, and will even sprinkle sesame and watermelon seeds on the windowsill to attract the chickadees and thrushes, the nuthatches and the wrens, and even, once, a single purple martin.

Ilyas has been quiet these past few weeks. Sometimes I hear him downstairs, chatting or exchanging boasts with Majed and his brothers. He busies himself, helping Abu Majed clear away a fallen tree or fix a crack in the roof. It bothered me at first, the way the men seem to understand Ilyas in a way I don't, the way he sits among them and is served at dinnertime, the way they've absorbed him and treat him with an assumed respect. He inhabits a world that is closed to me, and knowing this and being unable to do anything about it stings. But Ilyas has had to navigate men in the same ways that I've had to navigate them, ways that have become much clearer to me now. The world seems full of men to be avoided and negotiated with and fled from, weapons that might accidentally go off or icebergs to be steered clear of: the men who tell me their wives are home when they aren't, the man whose living room I bolted from, leaving all my wares, when I felt his hand wandering. Sometimes I wonder at all the things Ilyas and I could have accomplished in this life were it not for the shoals of men we've had to make detours to avoid.

Ilyas has begun to remind me, in small ways, of my father, before his injury. My father's stubborn belief opened him to the knife of disappointment, and I have always secretly thought him naive. Watching Ilyas, I wonder if I judge him too harshly. Ilyas sometimes makes a plate of apples sprinkled with lemon juice and eats them beside me in bed, Sawsan twitching beside us with sleep, and I catch myself remembering that he carves each moment of joy from the jaws of a world that seeks, every day, to devour him. Sometimes I remember this is true of both of us, and then to believe in anything, let alone joy, seems a lonely tightrope walk.

Yesterday, I felt a little stronger, so I asked Ilyas to walk with me out into the field so I could watch a pair of egrets hunting for fish in the shallow pond. The spring has turned cold again here in Michigan, and the shawl around my shoulders was thin. Ilyas draped his flannel work shirt over me and rubbed the backs of my arms.

As we watched the egrets, Ilyas began, unprompted, to speak of his childhood. It was the first time he's talked about his past or his family; I've never asked him. Perhaps I've been afraid of what he would say.

He spoke of his mother, a seamstress from Tarabalus who kept silkworms, a valuable—and difficult—business. The family owned a small grove of mulberry trees, the leaves of which the silkworms ate, and harvested toutes when the berries ripened. She was a kindhearted woman, but she wanted a safe, traditional life for her child. She had laid out Ilyas's future for him since he was small: a husband with prospects, a respectable man, a marriage in the church. She told Ilyas he would have beautiful sons and taught him to plait his black hair. She bathed him in milk and scrubbed him with turmeric to give him a smooth, pale complexion, the better to attract a good husband. She had grown up in the mountains, and she was a beautiful, rugged woman, large of frame, her hair divided into two fat braids shot through with silver. When she sang, she clapped her hands, and her voice traveled for miles. She knew all the old folk songs, all the hymns, and in church on Sundays, hers was the voice the congregation listened to when they forgot the words. Her husband died during the famine that hit the mountains before I was born, after the arrival of the locusts. Ilyas's older brother had worked from a young age, and the family had only survived because of the value of their silkworms. Ilyas left his mother and brother behind when he left for Amrika, obtaining forged identification that marked him as a man. If he'd been caught dressing that way in New York, he could have been arrested for lewd behavior; with American women, the police would send them home to their parents, but far worse things would have befallen a boy like Ilyas. He'd spent most of his life unable to imagine he might survive beyond adolescence. The moment his name was recorded at Ellis Island as a man, he said, was the moment he finally began to imagine a future for himself.

The egrets had long since flown off. We stood in the cold field, the nodding heads of the grass stiff with frozen dew. A skein of ice drifted across the surface of the water. I wanted to ask Ilyas if his mother had tried to understand how he felt. But I knew as well as he did the weight of 'ayb, the shame a thing like that would bring on a family.

Ilyas plucked a stem of grass and rubbed it between his fingers. He'd gone up to Harlem once, he said, after he'd arrived, to one of the rougher speakeasies without a doorman. He was looking for others like him. Ilyas met a woman there named Duke who sang dressed in men's clothes, a tuxedo and top hat. That was the only place you could go, she told him, where nobody would take a swing at you or call you bulldagger or sissy, especially if you were Black. Ilyas started to go there every weekend to hear Duke sing. Within a couple of months, though, cops had raided the place, and the last time he'd seen Duke and his other friends, they were being dragged off in cuffs. Ilyas, terrified and ashamed, escaped out the back of the building and managed to get away with barely a word from the police. It was because he was light enough to pass, in his good clothes, for an American boy out on the town. The cops, he said, looked through him, and for that, I don't think he's ever forgiven himself.

We turned back to the house. I said nothing. I was nauseous, uneasy. In the distance, downtown Detroit was just visible. Back in New York, the recently returned will be greeted with haflehs and dancing, but the city will not notice. Migrating birds will navigate around the smoke of New York's factories. How different the world would look if it had any mercy toward migrations undertaken as a last resort against annihilation.

That night, everyone had dropped off to sleep by the time Ilyas came to my bedside with a cup of chamomile tea and a kiss on my forehead. There was no way we could sleep in the same bed at night, but he often snuck up to see me under the pretense that, should he find anyone awake, he had been checking if I needed something.

Sawsan had drunk her milk and dropped off to sleep. Ilyas sat down by the window, rubbing his shoulder. I slid out of bed and made my slow way over to him. I'm mostly healed, but I get short of breath from walking.

At the touch of my hands, Ilyas waved me away. He lifted his shirt. Underneath, he had wrapped strips of cloth tight around his chest. As he untied the knot that held them, the cloth fell to his hips in sweat-stained rings, leaving stripes of bruises on his ribs. He had left them wrapped too long.

I touched his shoulder again. He seemed as far away as a continent, beyond my power to reach, let alone comfort. He turned. His chest was bare, his brown nipples swollen violet, inflamed lines crisscrossing his skin where the tight strips of fabric had cut too deep. I reached for him and caught his eye, but he flinched and retreated from my touch.

"Don't," he said.

We were standing by the window. The waxing moon emerged from behind a cloud, illuminating the frozen field. Three shapes slid across the moon in silhouette, narrow as knives, their black wings sleek, their long, curved beaks. The birds were iridescent, huge, like my mother's stories of the birds that followed the night. As they spiraled away into the forest, I imagined that nothing, not even those moon-slicked wings, could be as lovely and true as the stories I'd been fed as a child. Nothing was ever as beautiful as it was promised.

There was a voice from the door, and Ilyas and I froze with my hand on his chest. Khalto Tala stood in the doorway, her eyes downcast, her hand on the knob. I don't remember what she said—probably she told Ilyas to put ice to his ribs. I remember she added *I'm telling you this because I care for you both,* but at the time all I felt was fear. Ilyas pulled away from me, slipped his shirt on, and left the room without a word.

I made Khalto Tala promise not to tell, but it didn't matter. She saw us, little wing, saw us on the corniche that morning in Beirut. She said she thought I was upset and confused and would perhaps outgrow what I was feeling, so she had said nothing.

Little wing, I could never outgrow you.

"Habibti"—I remember there was genuine regret in Khalto Tala's voice—"some things are possible for a woman in this world. Others are not." A woman's path is written for her and seldom escaped, she said, and not everyone was like her. The aunties and uncles might call a stranger majnouna, but family is different, and there are some things, she said, about which even she must keep silence.

I thought of the widow Haddad on the roof, tending to her pigeons. "I love him, Khalti."

She got up to shut the window that faced the pond. A strip of purplish light was growing on the horizon. Khalti told me a story.

After she had given up on her silver claim, she'd packed her things and hiked back toward the nearest town. It was miles away, and she was deep into the hills, and the snows were coming. She got lost. She stopped that night and slept the miserable sleep of an empty stomach. In the morning, she said, she awoke to a silver-black fox sitting on the ridge that overlooked her camp. He was so big that he might have been a young wolf, were it not for his black face and paws. As Khalti pulled on her boots, he rose and looked over his shoulder, as though he were leading her. It seemed a sign. She followed—like a fool, she added—leaving everything behind. The fox led her along the river, then deeper into the hills as the day grew, until she had well and truly lost her way. She began to be afraid, but continued to follow. The sun sank. The fox proceeded, always glancing back to be sure that she was there.

As the day was drawing to a close, they overtook the ridge of a low mountain. Khalto Tala stopped to catch her breath. In the valley below was the town she'd been searching for. If she descended, she would find food and shelter and return to New York the following morning. But the fox stood on the ridge, inviting her deeper into the forest. Through the trees lay a rocky path, the kind that often leads to veins of silver. Birds she'd never heard were calling in the dusk. The fox waited. But Khalto Tala went down into the town, and when she looked back, the fox had disappeared.

I asked her if she ever wondered what she would have found if she'd kept going, but Khalti shook her head. "To go on would have been foolish, selfish, maybe deadly. My loved ones were waiting to hear that I was safe. I had people counting on me that I couldn't let down."

I sat on the bed after Khalto Tala left. I, too, have loved ones waiting for me in New York, parents who are counting on me to lead a respectable life, to find a husband and become a mother, to be the face of my community in this world we now inhabit. I have a brother whose education needs financing, who will one day need a good reputation to find a wife. There has never been room in these long-laid plans for me to drink my fill of desire. There has never been room in this world for you or for me, ya habib 'albi. And now here I am on the banks of Lake Michigan, and I have still not chosen for myself, have never truly chosen, and I am still looking to the sky for signs, reading coffee grounds for something I can use as an omen.

Let the record show, little wing, that you were with me tonight in Michigan, that I carry you with me in the form of stitched feathers. Let these pages bear witness that I came to this city to follow the birds. Let them testify that on this night, I followed Khalto Tala downstairs to where Ilyas lay, rigid and awake. Let them testify that when I turned my face to the window and saw the lean black figures of the birds, I gathered my box of paints and this notebook, crossed the frozen field toward the forest, and followed.

I took Khalti's red truck and drove west following the birds. I'd only driven it once and was unsure of myself, but it was so late that there was hardly anyone on the road at all, and soon I found myself far from the city. The birds continued west for a couple of hours until a wind picked up and drove them to the north. I followed, and we continued on this northwestern route for a while longer, another hour, then two, then three. I knew eventually Ilyas would notice I was gone and would take Abu Majed's truck and come looking for me. I squinted at every set of headlights in the dark expanse behind.

The forest seemed to rise out of nothing. By the time dawn had flooded the sky with pink, I was well into wooded land, far from any town at all, and well and truly lost. At first I'd been able to stay on a worn fire road, but after a few hours the birds had veered away, and I soon found myself parking the truck by a field and crossing through the grass after them. They were traveling west again now, the wind having died down with the coming light. Beyond the field was pine forest, carpeted with dry needles. The maples and birches were still flowering, so that when the sun came out from behind the clouds everything turned green and pink, and the birches were silver columns of reflected light.

I had left the last of the farmhouses behind me more than an hour ago. Now I was deep into the Michigan forest. Occasionally I wandered through a patch of fog that had yet to burn off, so little light penetrated the canopy in places. In spite of the birds that led me, I began to feel this forest was a strange and unforgiving place from which I might never return, like the fairy tales of the jinn my mother used to tell me as a child. Then I wondered what exactly I was doing here, alone in an eerie copse of birches, the only sound the morning cacophony of jays protesting the passage of Canada geese overhead. I had made my choice: here I was. But as my legs began to tire and I realized I wouldn't know my way back to the house where I'd left Ilyas and Khalti sleeping, I wondered who I thought I was to follow.

With every step, I felt that first paintbrush in my fingers, the first time I'd spread a wash of Payne's grey across pressed paper and defied death. Now I was pressing deeper into the white pines of Michigan, more and more out of breath with each step, watching overhead for the streaks of long-bodied birds that kept me moving westward. Often I wouldn't see them for a long time, and I'd become worried. But then I would hear a strange cry, a sleek shadow would pass over me, and I would be reassured that they were there, as constant and elusive as God.

By the time I reached the river, it was past midday, and I was beginning to shake from hunger and exhaustion. There were stones visible between rushing tongues of water, but the rock was slick. As I moved to cross, my foot slipped and crashed into the current, and before I knew it my right leg was soaking wet, and I had twisted my ankle between two river stones. I winced and limped to the other side, where I wrung out the hem of my dress and waved my shoe in the breeze to dry. The sun, at least, had come out, and the clearing where I stood was warm. Still, it had been a cool spring with chill nights, and soon I would start to shiver.

Footsteps rang out behind me. Though Ilyas was close behind, I didn't turn around. I picked up my pace, knowing that when night fell again I would be exposed to the elements and that this day was my only chance at seeing the birds for myself. Of these birds, of course, I knew nothing. But I had become the selfish woman my mother had once warned me of. I'd come to feel that these birds were like me, and that if I intended to go west following the light, then I had better be sure that I was willing to accept what I would find there, for there was no going back.

The next time I caught sight of the birds, I counted more than two dozen shadows with their legs tucked under them, long beaks splitting the wind. I had not expected so many. The terrain turned rugged, and a cold wind picked up. My right shoe had not dried out. My toes stiffened, and goose bumps rose on my calves where the wet hem of my dress rubbed my skin. We'd turned due west. Nothing at all lay around me to distinguish this part of the forest: the stiff needles of white pines or the veined leaves of birches, squirrels chasing one another up the trees, the gray horizon. In spite of myself, I wished then for a road or a farmhouse, for an excuse to turn off the path, for a sign that what I was doing was foolish and unwise. But no such sign came. I understood then why my mother had wished for an angel all these years, how a faith tested by silence might begin to feel more like a burden than a balm.

Out of breath, I surmounted one final ridge. I arrived in a clearing of furled ferns and young red oaks, and the smell of wet earth was everywhere. I squinted in the falling light, and there they were: thirty arrow-shaped birds with shimmering feathers, long curved beaks, their faces shimmering iridescence. I had never seen anything like them. It seemed then that all the knowledge I considered encyclopedic had been only part of the story, and that the world was big enough to contain more than I have ever dreamed. I have learned nothing from emulating Audubon or Mrs. Theodore. Studying paintings of posed specimens has brought me no closer to the essence of things, nor has copying the patterns of spotted eggshells or the fine bones of a bird's foot. How foolish I've been to search for a sign in these things when all along, right here before me in the hush of evening, something so holy was alive without a name.

I pulled out my notebook and set my box of paints on a stone nearby. I began to sketch. Thirty shapes, three in flight and the rest on the ground, some in silhouette, some resting while another bird craned its neck to nuzzle or to inspect or to nudge, the legs extended for landing, the four toes curled. As I sketched, the hem of the sun dropped below the trees, and the birds became black sewing needles backlit by ruddy light. If my mother were here to see this, I thought, or Ilyas—but he had never been waiting for a sign. It was I who had been ambivalent. Ilyas had always pushed on, whether or not he was afraid.

I set down my brush. The birds were strolling the field in messy rows, picking at insects in the grass. I inched closer to them as I was sketching, and now I was almost among them. All along I had been searching for the remedy that would either wither the love wasting in me or make it visible. All along I had been searching for my memory of you. Only now, letting go of the dream I'd held too tight, could I lay my love for you on the broad backs of these thirty birds, wish you all the love that you deserved, and realize that another love had been waiting for me all along.

Ilyas came crashing into the clearing. The white, ibis-like shapes of the birds drifted up into the indigo evening, shimmering like curls of ribbon. Ilyas came and stood at my side. The shadow of a bird fell across his face.

"I thought you left me," he whispered.

The birds were sailing close over us, taking flight toward the west. They hid us in the shadow of their wings. When I put my arms around him, Ilyas laughed into my hair and we ducked our heads. I let go of him and took his hands in mine. Kneeling in the field under the waves of feathers, I held on to him as though he were the most beautiful of wild birds. I asked him to marry me.

"Yes," he whispered, our hands clasped tight under the winged thrum. He pressed his face to our hands and kissed them. "Yes."

When I pulled him to me in the grass, all I felt of the birds was the brush of their feathers against my hair, a thousand silk scarves.

SEVENTEEN / NADIR

We are at the shop at first light, and Abu Sabah is there to greet us with a broom and a basket of mana'eesh. No one has mentioned Reem. I haven't prayed fajr in so long that I still feel the effects of the silence and the dark and the reverberations of my prayers, like the lingering sensation of fullness hours after a meal. I haven't bled since the offending piece of plastic was removed from my body yesterday. My head is clearer, I laugh at Sami and Qamar's jokes, and I even withstand Abu Sabah's frown when I realize I've forgotten to wear my hat. Mercifully, he makes no comment. We go inside, each with a man'ousheh in hand, oil on our fingertips and our chins dusted with za'atar. We try to pretend everything is normal.

The new shop window was put in yesterday evening. Sabah, who flew into LaGuardia late last night from Detroit, comes out from the darkness of the shop to inspect it. Abu Sabah scolds us not to get our fingerprints on the glass. Sabah, who has held it together the entire time since she got the call about the attack, seems more troubled by the new glass than anything. The repair has drawn more attention to the wound than the fire itself.

Three white ibises glide over the block, reflected in the glass between our fingers, and disappear. Back in the spring of '99, I found a newspaper clipping you'd left on your desk about a fire in the Everglades that killed fifty adult white ibises, trapped on a cattail island by thick smoke. Their bodies had been found after the wind cleared the smoke away. For a few weeks after, you doodled those ibises in every margin of your sketchbook, every notepad, every napkin. You drew a series of oval faces and curved beaks, fifty V-shaped strokes of your pen in a page corner. That was around the time I started sketching my own reflection, gazing at the mirror by the door. You used to use that round, wood-framed oval to straighten your jackets and re-pin your hijab before leaving the house. After you'd clean and polish it, I'd trace my reflection. The brain, like any organ in the body, knows wordless truths, knows health from sickness, knows how to recognize self and other. Maybe it's true that the self is every artist's first obsession, that every other subject—a plate of oranges, a mountain, a lover's face—is just a recognition of the self in another form. The conceptual artist Roman Opałka's life's work, titled *1965 / 1 - ∞*, consisted of painted numbers from one to infinity, white numbers on a black background, adding one percent more white to the ground with each number he painted. In 1968, he began to take photographs of himself after each day's work. It was a way of visualizing himself in time. He went on doing it for more than forty years until he died. His final number was 5,607,249. Those last fifty marks of white paint; fifty white ibises on a sheet of paper. *A single thing*, Opałka once said, *a single life*.

From the doorway, there is an audible gasp.

"Your hair!"

Aisha is rooted to the spot, clutching a shrink-wrapped platter of chicken and basmati rice. Her hand rises to cover her mouth.

I wait for someone, anyone, to laugh off my haircut or change the subject, but that silence stretches on for what feels like minutes, and no one says anything. Sabah turns to me, waiting for my reaction, then Sami. They stare as though witnessing a head-on collision.

"I cut it." I rub my palm up the back of my buzzed head. I escape into the kitchen to put coffee on, but Aisha follows me. We've run out of coffee anyhow, so I put the kettle on instead and busy myself with counting out cups.

"But it was so beautiful," Aisha says. "Why would you . . . ?"

Sabah enters without speaking. Sami and Qamar hang back in the hallway petting the orange cat, murmuring a feigned conversation.

"I got tired of it. Short hair is less work." I turn back to the cups. The kettle will not whistle.

Sami appears at my side and fills tea eggs with rose petals and chamomile leaves. He keeps his voice low. "Nadir, you good?"

"It's just so drastic." Aisha touches her hijab where she's pinned her favorite barrette, the silver one with the rhinestone bird. "But if you start growing it out now, it'll reach your shoulders by next summer."

Qamar looks up and says, "I think it looks good short." I want to hug them.

It doesn't occur to me that Sabah has heard Sami's question until she says, "Maybe they don't want to grow it out." I realize she hasn't gendered me in conversation, not once, since she saw my haircut this morning. She made no comments, only stepped aside from names and pronouns, and now I understand that Sabah has always been paying attention in ways that had been invisible to me until the moment they were not.

At last, the whistle. I fill the cups and deposit the tea eggs, then walk back out to the front of the shop with my cup. Again I fail to escape: everyone follows me. Aisha stands at the door with her teacup in her hand and shoots me concerned, furtive glances. She is searching for the words to tell me she knows that something is wrong, but I don't want to tell her because she will think the wrong thing needs fixing. I imagine opening my mouth to say the same thing to Teta, but I can't picture it. Reem said it best: there are blueprints that have been laid out for me since before I was born.

There is a thud on the glass, and something wet splashes my cheek. I gasp and jump; Aisha lets out a muffled scream. A swallow has run into the window, leaving a smear of feathers and blood. Aisha approaches the dazed bird, scoops it up, and listens for breath. Abu Sabah brings a checkered tea towel, and she wraps it. A rectangle of golden light gleams in the new glass above the streak of blood, a block of yellow sun and a block of purple-red shadow, and this reminds me of Etel Adnan's paintings of Mount Tamalpais in California, one of the places she's lived for many years with her partner, the Syrian artist Simone Fattal. Adnan painted Tamalpais as I've painted my own face for years: in varied light, in different seasons, in shifting shades and moods. Her paintings of the mountain have a lover's touch about them, even obsession. She and Fattal made their own migrations, two women carving out a life under the silent Tamalpais. Adnan once wrote of this work, "I am making the mountain as people make a painting," and I have wished I could fashion myself in the same way ever since.

Aisha rocks the wrapped swallow in the bowl of her arms. Everything about the night you died is a blur except for this: Aisha's brown fingers around the oxygen mask the firefighters pressed to my nose and mouth, Aisha's hands cradling my face, wiping soot away with a wet wipe from her purse. Hers was the first face I saw of that new world in which you had become past tense. She was the first to see into the well of my grief. I wanted to pull away that night, wanted to slide away into oblivion and leave my body in a lump on the sidewalk, but she held my eyes fast. "Don't you look away from me," she kept saying, voice soft and hands firm. "Don't you look away." I have never looked into anyone else's eyes like that, not before or since, and maybe the terror of being seen is what keeps me silent.

Aisha rises to leave. Shifting the bird to one hand, she takes her silver barrette in the other and slips it into my own hair. She tries to smile. She fails.

"There you are," she says. "Still your mother's pretty daughter." She touches my cheek with a curled finger. There is love in this touch.

I tug off the barrette on the walk over to Qamar's place. I've tried to block out the awkward years of my puberty, but we've played this same what-if game before, you and me—what if it's just a matter of finding the right haircut, the right outfit, the right boyfriend, the right femininity. Maybe you were right in some way; you never gave in to expectations of what a woman should be. But there were other walls to the box I was in, walls beyond marriage and a child, walls beyond the raises you didn't get and the keys between your fingers late at night, walls beyond the cheaper cost of men's razors and your terrified tears when I wore a boatneck shirt with my bra straps exposed. My body came with borders. I gave up my collared shirts when my chest burst the buttons, gave up short hair after a friend's dad told me boys would call me ugly for it. I gave up my long strides when the girls at school said I walked like an elephant. I gave up going to see movies with guy friends when I figured out, after an acquaintance groped me in the dark, that I couldn't trust their judgment on whether other boys were safe. I've lost count of the times I wished I could share in sisterhood, could lay my head on an auntie's lap and know we bore the same weight. But I've borne a different burden, and I've borne it so long that, as I turn the barrette over in my hand, I don't yet have the heart to tell Aisha that I have tried all the ways I can think of to make myself fit.

I am so deep in my own well that when Qamar stares agape at their phone and stops on the sidewalk, it takes me a few steps to notice.

They lay a hand on my shoulder, trembling. "One of the foundations agreed to let us check their archive."

Qamar preps Sami and me on the way over to the archive of the Harmstead Foundation in Midtown. From everything Qamar has studied about Laila Z, their understanding is that she only worked on commission when it suited what she already had in mind. Contemporaries of hers who commented on her disappearance in the forties wrote that she could have had a lot more success if she'd tailored herself to the market, but she resisted being boxed in.

"That said"—here Qamar leans in on the subway to keep their voice down—"rumor has it she was contacted sometime in the mid-forties by a collector who wanted a book of aquatints. Now, this guy—the artists only knew him as Mr. H—he was a serious bird art collector. He knew everybody. So Laila gets back to New York, settles down, and agrees to do a series for him. The only records I've ever seen list it as the last work she sold before she disappeared.

"But this guy was eccentric—and secretive. When he passed away, his daughter discovered he had a hoard of bird art and paraphernalia: eggs, skeletons, probably more than a few things that would be illegal now. He didn't want his collection broken up, so in his will, he established a foundation. He set his daughter in charge of it and willed his entire collection to it. He just passed away recently, so the foundation is new. Apparently the daughter had no idea what he'd amassed over the years. It wasn't just about aesthetics for him—it was an obsession. His daughter felt weird about all this, of course. So she's dedicating the foundation to showcasing work by newer and lesser-known artists alongside the birds, especially women of color." They make eye contact with me, and we both know without having to say it that this does not include people like us. "Long story short, the foundation scoured Mr. H's collection, but even though they've got a letter from Laila promising an aquatint of some kind of rare bird to complete this series she made, *G. simurghus* is missing. They'd pay a lot of money to find it. In the meantime, we're welcome to look for clues."

In Midtown, the address leads us to the gilded entryway of a multiuse office building with a narrow elevator. I am the lightest of all of us, so the white doorman makes eye contact with me first, but does a double take when he fails to gender me. Before he opens his mouth, Qamar gives him a name, and he lets our little brigade pass.

Qamar takes us down two floors in the old elevator, deep into the basement. We are greeted by a nervous research assistant who explains to us that the materials we are interested in have been laid out on the table behind the movable bookshelves. She busies herself with a wall of paintings waiting to be arranged upstairs in the exhibition space. I stop and stare, stupefied. Every painting awaiting hanging is by a woman artist, from Mary Cassatt's painting of two women and a child feeding the ducks on a lake; to Orazio Gentileschi's *St Francis and the Angel,* its wings unsettlingly like those of a real bird, one of the works she painted just after sending her rapist to prison; to the abstract winged figures of Iraqi artist Madiha Omar's *Arabesques.* I stare until something in me begins to hurt. I imagine a wall of paintings by people like me, like Qamar, like Ilyas. Somehow I have never been more acutely aware of my unbelonging than this moment in which I realize that things could be different. You never know how hungry you are until you watch someone else sit down at the table.

The space at the back of the archive is bare concrete save for a clean white table on which these treasures have been laid. It is immediately obvious that Mr. H was not only obsessed, but must have bought from artists and dealers all over the world. The first species I recognize is the extinct dodo, a bird last sighted in 1662, a cast of its skeleton in white porcelain. Its form is repeated in a seventeenth-century illuminated Mughal painting of the dodo beside several other birds in an emerald forest. One corner of the table is crowded with jeweled brooches bearing painted insets depicting colorful birds, and another is taken up by a sculpture of a bright-eyed Spix's macaw, now extinct in the wild, captured in bright blue glass. From there, the collection is an explosion of canvas and paper, with oil paintings and illustrations of birds by various artists that I've seen only in your textbooks: the kakapo, the clapper rail, the California condor, the extinct passenger pigeon, the red-throated loon, the whooping crane. A box lays open beside these riches, its body and lid lined with velvet, cradling four rows of perfect blue-green heron's eggs.

"Here's the thing." Qamar clears away the paintings and sets them at the far end of the table, revealing a small book wrapped in cracked leather. Putting on a pair of white gloves provided by the assistant, they unwrap the leather to reveal a cloth-bound book with an evergreen cover and no title. They open the book to the first aquatint, a white-throated sparrow with illuminated gold margins. "The series Mr. H commissioned from Laila wasn't just a rumor."

"It's hers." I lean over the table to examine Laila's etched details and hand-watercoloring, the tufts of chest feathers, the markings around the eyes. I pull the notebook out of my bag and open it to random pages, comparing the prints to her sketches. "It's got to be hers."

"Masha'Allah," Sami says. "They're beautiful."

Qamar turns the pages like they're made of glass. "She signed each illustration, which makes this the first confirmed Laila Z anyone's found in more than two decades." Qamar reveals to us bird after bird: red-tailed hawk, fish crow, American bluebird, white ibis.

Your Laila Z is hanging in Teta's apartment, but somehow, looking at these pages is different. I set my hand on the table and find that I'm shivering. The same hands that once touched Teta's face painted these same birds. All these years, you knew. I glance up, looking for you—I expect your presence everywhere I go, and so even in the sterility of this room, I'm not surprised to find you standing at one corner of the table, resting your hand beside the porcelain skeleton of the dodo. But there's a forlorn look in your eyes. You trail your index finger along the edge of the table, passing the box of eggs and the blue macaw, keeping your eyes on the book as Qamar turns the pages. I register each bird, placing it by genus and species, waiting for the one I'm looking for. The prints are magnificent, each detail colored by a masterful hand. But then we reach the end, and you are gazing at me as though you are waiting for me to understand.

I catch Sami's eye. "It's not here."

Sami swears under his breath. "An embarrassment of riches."

Qamar closes the book. "But not what we're looking for."

I put the notebook back in my bag. At the bottom is a glint of metal, a spark. One of Reem's mechanical birds zips out, searching for the sun to recharge its wings, then fizzles out of power in my palm.

We thank the research assistant for her time. Sami takes my hand and guides me back to the elevator while the assistant and Qamar discuss the upcoming show.

"It's just a couple of birds," Sami says.

"The demolition is tomorrow night. It was on the condemnation notice." I want Sami to feel the heaviness I am feeling, the phantom of these five long years. "It's over. We failed."

"Nadir, I'm sorry." Sami tries to put his arm around my shoulders, but I am itching out of my skin. He wraps me in the canopy of his arms. "Sometimes we have to move on."

The elevator takes us back up to the lobby, and Sami and I step out into stark sunlight. The breeze is cool for the first time in months. Fall will be setting in soon with its crisp nights and steel skies, and your presence in the kitchen will become less frequent. Teta's bones will ache when the rains come. We'll spend the long nights of the winter in her apartment, listening to the drone of the television. She will ration her pills. I will always wonder if she is thinking of the lover who could've been but wasn't, and we will look at each other and see all of this and not speak a word of it. Sami's grip on my hand is loose now. He is waiting for the moment he can let go.

"If you were me," I say to Sami, "how would you explain all this to Teta?"

He looks down at our fingers interlaced. "Not everybody is going to get it, habibi."

Sami changes the subject. He gets me to agree to come out to some party tonight in Ozone Park that he and Qamar have been planning for weeks. He wants to cheer me up. I say I'll be there. Orange-bellied hawks circle above us on a gust of wind. But there is no respite for them here, no patch of green but a nearby play-ground, and soon a band of jays rises from the trees to chase them off. The world is a series of infinite migrations.

I loosen my grip on Sami's hand. "I'm tired."

Sami lets my fingers slip through his. "I know."

Sami goes home to prepare for the party, and Qamar and I walk back to the subway together before we part ways to change our clothes. On the way, we stop at a corner to watch a pair of swallow-tailed kites circle the block, their white bellies and split black tails sweeping the sky like paper planes. I have never seen one so far north in this country. During brush fires, Australian kites will sometimes take up burning branches in their beaks and drop them into new areas to spread the fire and flush out prey. They call them firebirds.

As we stand stopped, Qamar tugs their yellowed book of Attar's poetry from their pocket and strokes the leather cover, then opens to a random page. They notice me looking and offer the book to me.

Choose everything.

"Makes me feel better," Qamar says.

I take the book. Their fingers are warm, their purple nail polish just beginning to chip. Though Qamar and I have spent a lot of time together these past few weeks, this is the first time we've been alone. This is the first time I can feel the steady calm of their energy. Something about the way they look at me makes me feel that they see me for what I am. I am understood without having to explain, as though we make sense to each other, as though we speak a common language. I think to myself, It is terrifying to be visible, and then I think, I have been waiting all my life to be seen.

The kites circle lower. I run my thumb over the seam of the leather where it's been glued to the inside cover of Qamar's grandfather's book. It has the feel of something that has been loved for a long time. There is no right time for grief; I know this. It's taken me five years to go through your sketchbooks and your jewelry boxes, your earrings and your scarves. After you died, it was Sabah who came to the soot-filled apartment and went through your things, and I had to trust her to make decisions about what to keep and what to throw away. You were with me until, one day, you weren't. It took years for that day to end.

We watch the kites circling, and I imagine them setting fire to the way my life has been before this moment. I imagine the smoke reshaping me. I reimagine myself as my first work, the art that comes before all other art I might one day make, the work I fashion only for myself and for those who have the eyes to see it.

Something tears. I've pressed down with my nail at the seam of the leather, and the fragile binding has come unglued. The leather cover peels away from the book. Inside, underneath the flap of leather, the corner of a piece of paper peeks out.

"I'm so sorry," I say, "I didn't mean to—"

But Qamar and I are both studying the paper underneath. Qamar takes the book from me, peels back the leather flap covering the inside front cover, and tugs a folded piece of browned paper from beneath it. They unfold it, smooth it, hold it to the light to make out the faded ink.

"It was never just some book from school." Qamar lowers the paper from the light. "It was a gift from Laila."

Qamar hands me the letter. I am dizzy. Tucked inside the front cover of Attar's book, the paper has been pressed by time into perfect flatness. She's doodled in the margins, copied out a few of her favorite passages, and decorated the dialogues of the birds with their imagined faces. On the back of the letter is a faded pencil sketch of an ibis, marked *G. simurghus, study.* Beneath it, she has copied out one last line: *the shadows cast by that unveiling—*

Qamar and I interlace our fingers over the spine of the book, and the kite's shadows flicker across the grin on their face.

"Where there's a study," Qamar says, "there's a finished piece."

I ask Qamar if I can give them a hug. When they embrace me, I hear their heartbeat, steady and soft as the kites' feathers rustling the air.

"I know, habibi." Qamar sniffles. There is a smile in their voice. "Don't make me cry on the subway, now."

I get changed at Teta's apartment before the gathering in Ozone Park. It's already dark, and Teta's in bed. I leave the light off and listen for the rhythmic sound of her breathing. Asmahan is asleep on my bed. The humid afternoon has trapped an unbearable heat in my bedroom, so I slide open the window and breathe in. A twilight rain is coming, and the smell of lightning crackles in the air, mixing with the hot metal of subway brakes.

I go into my dresser and reach behind the first drawer, tugging out what I stuffed in there last week, a crumpled handful of spandex like a cropped tank top. I strip off my shirt and the shapewear I've been using for months. I pull the spandex binder on over my head, and it's so tight that it gets stuck around my shoulders. I grunt and roll my shoulders; the house goes silent. I hold my breath and maneuver the spandex below my shoulder blades so I can reach back and hook my thumbs under the fabric. I manage to get it down over my chest, then lay down on the bed to wriggle everything into a forward-facing position. I am already out of breath. When I sit up, it takes me a second to adjust to the feeling of compression, but then I look down, and something in my brain goes silent. My belly is visible, my hands on the waistband of my jeans. I have never experienced such clarity before, the feeling that something, at last, is right.

A shadow moves over the window, and I freeze. Teta is standing in the door, silhouetted by the nightlight in the hall. She shuffles into the dark bedroom toward me, and I reach up to cover my chest. There is nothing to cover; for the first time in years, I can lay my hand on my heart. Somehow I am more naked with the binder on than without it.

Teta lifts her hand and pats my cheek. After all the years I spent clinging to her skirt, believing her to be a leviathan of a woman, she is finally smaller than me, and this is the most painful thing of all, that Teta should grow old and have to reach up to touch my face.

"So that's what this thing is for," she says, setting her hand on my shoulder.

I take Teta's hand and place it over my heart, atop the black spandex of the binder. "It's not about this thing, Teta. I just want to be able to think about something else."

Teta sits beside me on the bed. "I knew you when you were in your mother's belly," Teta says. "Your mother swore up and down she was having a boy." Teta opens her closed fist, and the glass beads of her tasbih are curled inside. Rain patters on the sidewalk below the window, humming against the screen at my back. "But courage is the hardest blessing."

"You were in love with Laila." I wrap my arms around myself, feeling the pulse of my heartbeat. "Didn't you try to find her?"

Teta pushes herself up from the bed with difficulty, wincing and stretching her stiff back. "By the time your mother and I arrived in this country, Laila was missing already twenty years. They changed all the names on the records in those days, hayati. Even if she were alive, how could I know the name the Amrikiyyin put on her?"

The binder is a bowl holding my heart inside my chest. "In all these years, you never said a word."

Teta smooths my hair. "Not everything must be spoken to be real."

After Teta leaves the room, there is a ping on my window. The night rain has slowed to a drizzle. I lift the glass as another pebble hits the windowsill. Two figures are down on the sidewalk waving up at me, and one of them has Reem's halo of reddish hair under the streetlight.

All the way down in the elevator, my shoulders are rigid with anger and fear. I stuff my hands in my pockets when I come out to meet her. I'm still wearing Teta's old house slippers.

Sami shuffles his sneakers. "I may have texted her this time."

Reem reaches for my hands, but I don't give them. "Just hear me out, Noodle."

A wave of nausea washes over me and I know that if I don't lie down soon, I will throw up. "I don't want to talk, Reem."

"Look, if I don't say it now, I won't be able to say it at all, so just shut up and listen." When Reem uncurls her fists, her fingernails are bitten to the quick. "It only happened once, before I met the real estate agent. I didn't want things to be different. Not like *that*.

"When I got engaged, I thought my life was coming together. All the arguments, the silences—I didn't want to feel pain, so I let myself believe marriage would fix it all, and I could forget about everything that came before. It was hard to let go of the comfort of the lie. Then Mom died. I kept the secret too long. Do you know how that feels, to know I'll never be able to tell her what happened? So I told the real estate agent about the girl, even though we happened before I met him. And we never talked about it again." Reem steps toward me out of the shadows. "It wasn't anybody's business but mine. Doesn't that make sense?"

I don't want my sister to see me cry. "We don't all have that luxury, Reem."

She reaches back to tie up her hair. Not only is the tattoo on her neck visible—the silhouettes of two birds, one above and one below, turning in midair—but it's clear she's shaved an undercut around the base of her head. With her hair down, the undercut and the tattoo are both hidden, but up in a bun, there is no mistaking her or what her half-shaved head signifies. She looks entirely different with her face framed like this. Fine lines have formed around her eyes and mouth since she hit forty, and the crow's feet she gets when she smiles are more visible.

"I know privacy is a luxury," Reem says. "Don't you think I know that? Why do you think I'm telling you this?"

My sister is not young anymore. When I was a kid, I used to get mistaken for her daughter. Any beauty we have is the beauty you gave us both, just as her smell, when I hug her, is the same as yours—sandalwood and jasmine and olive oil soap. One day people will say I could have been a beautiful girl, if only I had tried harder, if only I had gone the right way, if only I'd done as I was told, if only, if only. I fold my nails into my palms and imagine that day, imagine washing my face and knowing beyond a doubt that it belongs to me, imagine their faces when I tell them my sister and I are both more beautiful than we have ever been.

EIGHTEEN / LAILA

B,

Badra,

Forgive me—

Little wing,

What a surprise to find these pages still intact after all these years. I had quite forgotten who I began writing to, then went back to the beginning and began to read, pulled out the wing I'd tucked beneath a stack of loose sketches and watercolors, touched the feathers for the first time in almost a decade. I want to say I don't know why I didn't write for so long, but the truth is that I couldn't move on until I left you behind. Even invoking you brings a sting of heat to my chest. Do you know how hard it was to write your name after Ilyas and I returned to New York with Sawsan in his arms, when Khalto Tala sewed my wedding dress from a bolt of silk and lace donated by Mr. Awad so that she could send me down the aisle with a train the length of Broadway and a floor-length veil?

In truth, it was a beautiful wedding. Ilyas and I were married on an October afternoon, with Sawsan on my mother's lap in the front pew. He met me at the front of the church in a navy suit with a white peony in his lapel. It was after the wedding, though, after the feasting and celebrating in our neighborhood was over and it seemed the whole community had eaten their fill of bitlawah and drunk three cups of coffee each, that Ilyas and I snuck out of the building in the night to promise ourselves to each other before a proper witness. We were supposed to move into our new apartment in the community house—I'd just begun my job giving arts and theater programs for the children of newly arrived families, and Mr. Shaheen's sister had come just that morning to help us move in some donated furniture and unpack the dishes my parents had gifted us for our wedding. But Ilyas and I escaped to Central Park, to the place where we'd spotted a night heron wading in the lake a few weeks before. There we whispered our own, secret vows before the divine that exists in every living thing, which was, as far as Ilyas and I were concerned, more important than the witness of any priest.

We've kept our promise to each other to raise Sawsan as our own daughter. She is eight years old now, and beautiful; sometimes I wish you could see her. She is precocious and curious, always running here and there, asking questions—why fig trees don't flower in the spring and why airplanes don't flap their wings. The purple birthmark on her cheek never did fade. Perhaps one day, when she's older and the world is different, we'll tell her how it came to be.

What else can I tell? Not everyone is with us anymore. My father passed of a heart attack one day in Central Park, not far from the lake, and sometimes I still visit the spot where Ilyas and I said our vows in the night and watch the heron glide across the water in the autumn. The widow Haddad passed away in her sleep last year. She left the pigeon coops to Khalto Tala, who gifted them to me, saying that she was an old woman and wanted the birds in young, capable hands. The neighborhood has grown and shrunk and grown again. America went to war, and Issa—who had become an American citizen by then—signed up for the Air Force. I couldn't understand his decision, nor did I agree with it. But to war he went, and by the time he came home with a steel knee and a medal for rescuing the crew of a downed plane, we had received our eviction notices.

This is why I am writing again in these pages, I'm afraid: we are to be thrown out into the street. After nearly eight years in our apartment here in the community house, I'm hard-pressed to imagine life anywhere else. Even Ilyas, who used to get so annoyed at the mold that could never quite be scrubbed away or the mice scurrying between the floors above our heads, has grown to love this place. Some of its flaws have even become dear to us. My parents gave us the leftover orange wallpaper they'd used in their own apartment, the one we first moved into with Khalto Tala in the tenement down the street, and I'll admit that the familiar water-stained color comforts me. There are two missing bricks in the wall of the bedroom, out of which cockroaches and a strange smell sometimes escaped when we first moved in. At first I liked the feel of the opening and used to put my ear to it as one might a shell, listening for the sounds of the sea. But then, after I caught Sawsan doing the same, a fear rose in me that maybe the sea really was there in that darkness, and that I was listening into the past, and that if I reached my hand inside you might reach back. I begged Ilyas to paper over it after that. But moisture would collect in the hollow and cause the paper to peel, and though he did try to glue it down, it's opened back up every time, and since then we've left the hole alone. My mother, who has been living with us the past few months since her memory has started to fade, likes to complain about it. But I've claimed the empty slot in the wall for these pages. Now that Sawsan is old enough to read and my mother has learned more English, the memory of what you meant to me would cause my family more harm than good. I keep this notebook in the wooden box Khalto Tala gave me, the one she brought with her from the bilad with its mother-of-pearl, and hide it in the hole made by the missing bricks where the sound of the sea on the corniche lives. This secret space has become as much a part of the apartment as our own bodies.

My mother has her own sacred, if not secret, space. I found a desk for her in the corner of the bedroom where she's set her candle. It even has a little drawer for her rosary, her book of hymns, the stone she took from our garden when we left—in short, her sacred objects. She rarely leaves the house anymore, except to visit my father, so she spends her time taking them out, dusting them, putting them away again. How she used to dance the dabke with us above Abu Hamdeh's shop during a hafleh! It's hard to see one's parents grow old.

I'm writing all this down to memorialize the world we know, B, which I suspect will soon be gone. For years, city officials spoke in idle terms about building a tunnel beneath the East River to connect Red Hook with Battery Park. But the entrance to the tunnel would have to be placed somewhere, and officials won't sacrifice the waterfront. Instead they chose a neighborhood only its residents will miss: ours. The Syrian Quarter is to be demolished save for half a street, protecting only St. George's Church. It seems the community house, with its medical center, its nursery, its library with more than a thousand books—all of this has already been bought by a private investor. Who knows what will become of it? The surrounding tenements will most certainly be demolished, if not now, then eventually. Without the workers of the community house handling the maintenance of the tenements, I don't see how it can be avoided.

On the night the first notices arrived, there was no song or poetry, no backgammon or bitlawah or kunafeh. There was only thick coffee that grew cold over heated discussions long into the night. But there was nothing to be done. Not long after, one man who tried to stay in protest was nearly killed when the workers swung the wrecking ball over his head, and he fled the shower of debris. Families started to flow out of our community like blood from a wound. Sawsan is still too young to be cynical, but she is old enough to understand betrayal. Having known nothing else but this country, this city, I thought she would take it the hardest, but in her own curious way, she seems to already be familiar with the way her fellow Americans view us—for how could I call Sawsan anything other than American?

It was, in fact, Issa for whom the news was most a blow. My brother always had his dreams. Like our father, he was once a seeker. But he returned from the war a different man. I gave Sawsan the seed he once gave me and told her to ask him to help her plant it, but she returned shaking her head. The next day, I found the seed on my brother's windowsill, a bit of dust clinging to its hull.

I received a letter today from my friend Dr. Benjamin Young, the ornithologist I met a lifetime ago at the New York Public Library, detailing his recent efforts to create a bird sanctuary in upstate New York. I found Benjamin's card in the move and wrote to him on a whim, including a couple of the sketches I'd done of the birds I followed into the Michigan forest. To my surprise, he wrote back to tell me he'd observed the same birds years before doing field research near Albany, headed westward. He'd tracked and studied them for weeks, finally coming to the conclusion that he'd identified a new subspecies of ibis—*Geronticus simurghus,* he called them, after the legendary bird of Attar's *Mantiq ut-Tayr,* which he'd read during university when he'd studied Persian. He'd brought his finding back to his colleagues only to be dismissed and ridiculed, though he did write to me in that first letter that it moved him to see the birds again. You can have all the truth in the world of something, he wrote to me, but the world will see what it wants to see, and maybe it's for the best to keep some beautiful things to ourselves. We've kept in touch ever since, though it's rare that our paths cross in person since we've started families of our own.

My own career has given me my share of worries over the past year. For years I supplemented Ilyas's income by selling my illustrations to the neighbors and to the occasional publisher, but the more ambitious I became, and the more I tried to get my work considered and exhibited by galleries and museums, the more I was turned away. It is no secret that women artists are not considered to be capable of real talent, but I thought—naively, I suppose—that I could prove them wrong. Day after day, I arrive at the galleries with my portfolio of aquatints, and day after day, I am turned away. Ilyas has always encouraged me, but now that the community house has been bought, he's going to lose his job as a social worker.

So when, several months ago, the same Mr. H of whom Mrs. Theodore once spoke contacted me through an intermediary, saying he'd seen some of my prints and wanted a full set for his private collection, I jumped at the chance for a commission. I envision the project as a series of aquatints, a sort of reclamation of Audubon's work, the birds drawn from life and through my eyes. But Mr. H had an unusual request: for his collection, he wanted me to include the birds I'd seen flying into the west in the forests outside of Detroit, Benjamin's elusive *G. simurghus.* Mr. H had spoken with a friend who'd seen my sketches, and was interested in this bird whose name he didn't know. The print would be the crowning jewel of his archive of rare birds.

There was something unsettling about the offer that arrived via brusque courier late one Thursday evening, but the money was good, so I agreed. I set to work trying to create an aquatint of the ibises I had seen in Michigan, but they were difficult to capture. My every effort failed my eyes, my heart, my memory. The birds curled into impossible shapes, took on elusive, iridescent colors, and nothing I created did them justice.

As the weeks went by, and Mr. H received my other prints, he grew impatient. He wanted to know where the final aquatint was and what was taking me so long. I'd been paid for the rest of the series, which Mr. H claimed would be bound into a book, but I could not complete his commission, nor earn the bonus he had promised me for this final print. I was unnerved and uncertain. One day I began to nurse a suspicion that perhaps he'd publish the book without crediting or compensating me at all, and how was I to know whether he was trustworthy or not, this obsessive billionaire? I sat in my studio, day after day, trying to capture grace, the way the light hit the birds' crests and the tips of their wings, but every attempt was plain and unsatisfying. I could not convince myself of any of it—not my work, not the project. There was always something about these creatures I could not get right. I wrote to Benjamin that I didn't know what to do. One day, procrastinating while Sawsan was in school, I went out and bought a copy of Attar's Sufi poem translated into English. It was expensive, a luxury, but I took it home and began to read it and to sketch in the margins. Of the Simorgh, the king of the birds, Attar's hoopoe says:

> *Whatsoever wears the shape of anything in existence*
> *has come from the shadow of the beautiful Simorgh.*
> *If Simorgh unveils its face to you, you will find*

that all the birds, be they thirty or forty or more,
are but the shadows cast by that unveiling . . .
Do you see?
The shadow and its maker are one and the same.

As I was reading, night began to fall. The more I read and sketched, the more difficult it became to separate myself in my mind from the birds I had followed into the forest of Michigan. Had I been following the birds, I asked myself, or had they been following me; I could not be sure then that the birds had appeared because I had been looking for them, had been waiting for them, had conjured them, or whether their appearance had changed me somehow. Perhaps I had seen them because they had willed me to see them. Perhaps, I thought, we had each willed the other into existence in order to be seen, and wasn't that the point of this too-long life?

I wrote to Benjamin that afternoon and told him that I had decided I would not give Mr. H a print of our bird. Instead, I slipped my letter and one of my illustrations into Attar's book and wrapped it as a gift for Benjamin, ripped up the last note I'd been given by Mr. H's courier, and in this way I learned that sharing a thing is not the same as keeping it alive.

Little wing,

Time is short tonight. I will need to hurry to set down everything.

Today we saw what happens to the buildings. The wrecking balls and bulldozers arrived in the morning to pull down one of the other tenements on our block, and by evening, it was as though the building had never been there at all. Tonight there seem to be no birds left in New York. Even the pigeons, save those in their dovecotes on the roof, fled the day our hope fled, too.

We are to leave tomorrow morning. I write this from the kitchen table in Khalto Tala's apartment while my mother says her prayers. We've packed the steamer trunk with her few things, her rosaries and icons and Sunday dress, and Khalto Tala has helped her wrap my father's sweaters and the tattered book of poetry he took with him from the bilad when he left. From my place at the table, I can see the orange wallpaper peeling on my old bedroom wall. Lately I've been carrying this notebook with me in my pocket, rather than leaving it in the box in its hiding place. A few days ago I found my mother inspecting the missing bricks in the bedroom, and I fear she may be looking through my things or even reading what I've written while I'm working during the day. Memory may be a sacred thing, but the words in these pages are dangerous now, and I have far more to lose than when I first began to write. Forgive me, B. I've left the box with some of my prints and your wing, but I will keep these pages with me at all times, at least until we leave this place.

We put Sawsan to bed a few hours ago. I made my last gallery visit today. As soon as I came home, Ilyas and I packed her toys and patent leather shoes along with our things and brought my mother over to Khalto Tala's. With my father gone, she wandered the place for a few moments, then sat on the fire escape watching the women hang their laundry. She is waiting for something.

After a meal of rice and eggplant, Ilyas went out to the court-yard to smoke a cigarette and give me a moment alone with my brother. I set down these lines knowing this may be the last conversation I will ever have in this apartment.

"So this is the end," Issa said into his coffee.

I scolded him for saying so. People have been setting up shop on Atlantic Avenue for months now. Half the neighborhood is there, starting over or trying to. So they've succeeded in evicting us across the river—we'd manage somehow. I'd been trying to talk my-self into this line of thinking for months, but it doesn't erase the in-justice of the thing.

"It's not home," Issa said.

We sat in silence while we drank our coffee. I began to list in my head all the families who had left New York altogether when they received their eviction notices, the sons and aunties and cousins who chose to join their families in Toledo or Dearborn or Chicago or the Twin Cities or even distant Los Angeles and Houston. This eviction is an exodus. Most of our neighbors we will never see again.

Issa began to speak of what he'd seen as a pilot during the war. Once, he'd had two planes on his tail in cloud cover so thick it might as well have been Khalti's lentil soup. He was close to the Alps, and he was afraid that he would crash into an outcropping. But an ibis appeared, large with a long, sleek body, its color difficult to determine because of the iridescence of its feathers and the play of the clouds. Tricks of the light, he'd thought at the time, or the adrenaline. Still, the shimmer of the sun on its back had calmed my brother, and so he'd followed it, banking when it banked, flying higher when it rose on an updraft. And before he knew it, the ibis had steered him clear of both the mountain and the planes tailing him. When he emerged from the cloud cover, it was gone.

Below us on the street, one of the widow Haddad's pigeons pecked at an eviction notice before fluttering up to join its siblings on the roof.

I told him we should stay.

"You saw what happened to Abu Anas." Ilyas came in, folded his jacket over a chair, and sat down. The past eight years have aged him, etching new lines across his face, turning his hair silver at his temples. He still has the boyish look he's always had, but he's fought his own battles, most of which he will never utter. Unlike my father or my brother, Ilyas has always known the world was an unjust place, and even though he believes in the hope he's made for himself, he has never pretended otherwise.

My mother stoked the kitchen fire, silent and brooding. Khalto

Tala entered the room and began to fill the dish bucket with water. She's suffered a double loss in the last year: the loss of the widow Haddad and then the loss of the neighborhood. Khalto Tala has built a life here far longer than we have; she's lived in this community for more than twenty years. She only just last year opened her own linen shop, a dream she's had since she arrived at Ellis Island with only the dress on her back and a gold necklace to pawn. We've talked about it since I was a girl. Khalto Tala and I even came up with a name during our time on the road: Khoury's Linens and Laces. Her shop has been one of the few still operating in the neighborhood over the last few weeks, defying the eviction notices, but we had to close it, too, earlier this afternoon, emptying out the inventory and transferring it over to the new building on Atlantic Avenue. Khalto Tala was lucky to have the money for a new location; not everyone does. Still, she's taken it hard. I was sweeping the empty shop this afternoon and came out to lock up for the last time when I saw her behind the building, smoking a cigarette and wiping her face. Khalti has never, as long as I've known her, let anyone see her cry. I slipped back inside and left her alone.

After Issa had gone, Khalto Tala pulled a stool up to the table and sat down as she washed the dishes. She confronted me without ceremony about the gallerist I'd spoken to that day. She knew right away that he'd said no. I didn't bother telling Khalto Tala the rest of what he'd said: that if indeed I came from the Holy Land, then I should follow the example of Our Lady and focus on my duties as a mother rather than wasting my time with my paints.

More and more since I refused to give Mr. H the print of *G. simurghus*, I've been considering giving up painting. I complained to Khalto Tala tonight, not for the first time, that the only thing I was allowed to paint as a woman were birds, landscapes, copies of Audubon and other painters with something between their legs. Eight years ago that was enough for me. But if I want to do something else, something bigger, something perhaps even bigger than painting, I'll be shunned as a woman who doesn't know the first thing about art, as though having a womb precludes my having eyes or a brain.

Ilyas set his hand on my forearm, and his wedding band was a reassuring heat. "They wouldn't know art if it chewed their balls off," he said.

Khalto Tala tried to comfort me with the reminder that women writers in the nineteenth century used to write under the names of men in order to be published. Where would the state of science or the arts be, she said, without women? It had been a Muslim woman who had opened the oldest existing, continually operating university in the world, after all, al-Qarawiyyin in Fes. Khalti meant it as a consolation, but as she spoke, a spark came into Ilyas's face.

"You could do it," he said.

His plan is simple: there's no reason I have to present my paintings in person to the galleries. If I have someone to represent me to gallerists and museum curators, they never have to know who I am. I can take on a man's name, or at least an ambiguous one; Ilyas can represent me to the galleries; and their assumptions will take care of the rest. As long as I never appear in person, no one will be the wiser.

The artist without a face. I'll admit the thrill of the idea appealed to me right away, ludicrous as it was. I said to Ilyas that I would give it a try, as I had little to lose, and right away I knew what name I would take on: the family name, Zeytouneh. The Americans wouldn't know my gender from such a name. If I started producing new work, something entirely different from what I had done before, the art world—in which I'd been only marginally known—would assume I was a man, new to the market, perhaps, but maybe, considering the scraps of success I'd gleaned as a woman, talented enough to invest in.

Behind the cracked bedroom door, my mother knelt beside the

bed to pray. I turned my coffee cup over. The grounds had settled into two wheels with melting spokes and a cloud of brown foam above them. It didn't occur to me until later, when I had snuck out to wait for the night heron in the spot where my father's body had touched the earth, that it reminded me of someone I had known, an ocean ago.

NINETEEN / NADIR

THE FOUR OF US get on the A train to Ozone Park close to midnight.
Reem has her hair up, rocking her tattoo and her undercut. We
aren't far from the house Sami once shared with his mother. A small
group of people is gathered outside of the 80th Street stop. Sami
and Qamar greet them one by one, including Yara and Malik and
half a dozen other folks I don't know at all. Sami tells us we're supposed to walk in groups of two or three down the street, following
the organizers, until we come to the entrance of the event space.
Reem and Qamar and I walk in a cluster of three, following a few
paces behind Yara and another woman who hold hands, and Sami
and Malik ahead of them with their arms around each other. Somehow, walking together in relaxed silence makes this walk feel like an
act of love. Gradually, it dawns on me that I am marching between
some of the same people I danced with at the bar in Bushwick. We
are a chain of Black and brown friends and lovers dressed in glitter,

leather, and purple hair, holding hands without regard to who is watching us from the sidewalk.

Ahead of us, the clumps of people begin to disappear one by one. We stop, and Sami points without a word to an open manhole in the ground. Yara grabs the ladder and lowers herself down into the darkness. Malik follows, and soon Sami is waving his hand for me to drop down into the circle of shadow.

At first I balk at this, but there's no time to argue. I step on the first bar, then the third, then grab the ladder with my hand. The fear of slipping seizes me. The ladder is damp and cold, but I keep going, fifth rung and seventh, ninth, eleventh. I shiver as the sunlight becomes a window above me. "Go, go!" someone whispers above me, and I tap my toe on the rung below and climb down into the cloying dark.

Hands pat my back and guide me to the ground. I've reached the bottom. The only light down here is a handful of candles, which someone is touching with a lighter in the dark canyon of the concrete room. I am handed a candle. As my eyes adjust, the others emerge from the shadows. We meet one another's eyes and nod without speaking. The crowd mills about the tunnel that disappears into shadow. Soon Qamar and Reem are beside me; Sami has gone off somewhere in the dark. Qamar gives Yara a fist bump, a grin plastered on their face. Reem's face, on the other hand, is stone, and I know her well enough to know that this is her defense mechanism against terror. I squeeze her elbow. She turns to me, deadpan, and says, "We're all getting arrested."

In the dark, the faces are my neighbors, my cousins, my aunties, my friends' parents. Some of them are yours. Above us, someone slides the manhole cover shut, and we are left in darkness. Then music starts up from farther down the unfinished tunnel, distorted by the curve in the concrete and the cavernous echo. The crowd surges toward the music. Soon we are walking in a procession down the tunnel, each with our candles in our hands. There are at least a couple dozen of us, more than I realized when we gathered at the A stop. To my right, two brown men are holding hands; to my left, a tall Black person in a leather harness has dyed their dreads ocean blue and green. Reem's curls transform themselves into garnet in the candlelight.

Over the heads of the people in front of me is a ring of candles on a concrete subway platform, the edge dropping into debris-strewn darkness. In the middle of the ring Sami sits playing his oud, the red silk knot of memory swinging with the movements of his fingers. He is hunched over his instrument, listening for its hidden language as though none of us are here, as though tonight, of all nights, he might finally summon the ghost he's been looking for.

A drumbeat joins Sami's rhythm, the crowd ripples and separates, and soon we are dancing. Here in this place the city carved out and abandoned, there is only movement and heat and darkness. I can't see my body, or Reem's, or Sami's, or anyone's. I can only feel my hips moving the stale air and listen to the rise and fall of the feet of those around me.

I have been taught all my life that masculinity means short hair and square-toed shoes, taking up space, raising one's voice. To be soft is to be less of a man. To be gentle, to laugh, to create art, to bleed between the legs—I have been taught that these things make me a woman. I have been taught all my life that to dance is to be vulnerable, and that the world will crush the vulnerable. I was taught to equate invincibility with being worthy of love. But here in the darkness of this abandoned subway platform, I can almost imagine a world big enough for boys like Sami and me to love each other, to dance and let the pain out of our bodies, to breathe and make love and be enough and be enough and be enough. Tomorrow, Sami and I will tie a green silk knot around the elm tree in front of Aisha's sanctuary, and Sabah's father will sweep bits of glass from the floor of his shop that we missed. But for now, Sami comes toward me through the crowd carrying his oud, and the light in our faces is the only thing we know of ourselves.

We face each other, two candles flickering. Sami's sweat smells of chamomile and musk. When we dance, I am a bird shaking loose the night from its wings. I kiss him, my hand behind his jaw, his hands in my hair. He gasps into my mouth and goes soft as water, our bodies molten glass that I am shaping with my kiss, and I wonder if it's true that there is nothing on this earth that is not born of the sweet ache of flame.

A couple hours later, we assemble at the ladder and climb back up into the night, then scatter like a network of veins. Reem and Sami fall asleep on each of my shoulders on the subway ride home, Reem with her hand curled around Qamar's, who stretches out with their combat boots on an empty seat and lays their head in Reem's lap.

At Teta's apartment, Qamar and Reem fall exhausted into bed, but Sami and I are still so wired that we go up to the roof with a blanket and a sleeping bag and sandwich ourselves between the covers against the predawn chill. Teta's plants have been forgotten up here, creating a makeshift garden. A late drizzle has transformed the firepit into a lunar reflecting pool.

Sami's arm is a ghostly heat on mine. He reaches over with his pinky finger to stroke the back of my hand. "You know," he says, "I never came out to my mom. I always thought she kinda knew, seeing the friends I invited over. But I thought we had more time."

I lay my head on Sami's shoulder. "She would have understood."

"Maybe I'm just telling myself that." Sami pulls a snapped rubber band out of his pocket and twists it as though he is braiding dough. He is tying yet another knot, repeating a rhythm he can't escape. "I don't want to rewrite history just to spare myself the truth.

People can be okay with something in theory, but when it's their own family, they freak out."

I've spent so long trying to forget that Sami's enchantment to keep memory alive feels alien. I spent so much time wishing I could rewrite the past that I never allowed myself to imagine what might come after it. But if I think of your notes, of Laila's notebook, or of Teta's handkerchief, the past seems so much more complex than I could have ever imagined. I am a fool. I spent so many years feeling alone, not knowing how to ask the right questions. Even now, if I admit that I have spent a lifetime denying myself, I will also have to grieve the time I lost trying to become someone else.

I place my hands over the rubber band in Sami's hand. "You're gonna run out of places to put those."

He doesn't move away. Warmth pools in the pit of my stomach. To my surprise, he is trembling.

A shape no bigger than my palm sails down to the edge of the roof and perches there, preening its gray wings. It's a Kirtland's warbler, with a golden face and belly and a gray-green back scaled with black stripes. I've never seen one; their habitat is in Michigan, and they're incredibly rare. This one must have lost its way, or been drawn, maybe, like the others. The silence up on the roof, unusual in this neighborhood at any time of night, is foreboding. Tonight's the night: any minute now, they should be setting up the explosives for the demolition of the building on Washington Street. It's a clear night. From up here, we might even be able to see the cloud of dust dissolve over Lower Manhattan. The warbler preens itself. Sami squeezes my fingers.

"Would you look at that," I say. The warbler hops along the ledge, showing us its golden belly. "Lots of birders go their whole life without seeing one."

Sami laughs. "We found you a rare bird. Just not the one you were looking for."

"I don't know what I'm looking for anymore." I shiver under the blankets. "Maybe I just wanted a reason to be brave."

"Ya Nadir," Sami says, touching my knee, "brave is one thing you have always been."

I take Sami's face in my hands and lower him to the blanket. He takes off his shirt and unfurls himself under the moon. I tell him I want him, and he whispers that he wants me, too. We roll through the dark, I on top of him and he on top of me as though we are wrestling gravity. We begin from our hands rather than between our legs—our hands entangled, my hands in his hair, his hands crumpling the blanket when I move my lips below his collarbone. The condom in his pocket is a ring against my thigh. When he is inside me for the first time, I cry. It is the first time I've made love to a boy as a boy, which is to say that this is the first time in my life that I have been naked and not been invisible. When I roll him onto his back, he is not inside of me. I am inside of him somehow, rocking into him like the tide, and when he touches my face and asks me if I find him beautiful, I tell him he is the most beautiful creature I have ever seen.

Afterward, we dress each other in the chill, sneak downstairs to pee, and come back up to the roof with snacks. By now the sky is streaked with dark blue clouds, and the moon is seated low on the horizon. I touch Sami's cheek, and he strokes my face with the back of his hand.

"I see you," he whispers.

I put my arm around his shoulders, and he snuggles into the crook of my armpit. I laugh into his curls. "Imagine if they hadn't been able to open the manhole."

Sami laughs. "Fuck."

"I finished Laila's notebook last night." I trace spirals across his shoulder. "They'll be bringing the community house down this morning."

Sami kisses my neck, but he knows better than to try to make me feel better. A breeze forms an arrow of ripples across the rain-water that has collected in the firepit. "I don't know why we don't use this spot more often," he says.

He's right, of course. You used to talk about making a little space for us up here, a small garden, a few cushions. But we never found the time, and so we never claimed a space for ourselves. I think of Laila, the desk she gave her mother so she'd have some-where to pray, a place to put her things. The body itself should be a sacred space.

Something could be built here, I think, something resembling a family. If an object can become sacred by placing it on a table and calling it an altar, then who is to say we cannot sanctify our own bodies? When I touched those eggs in the nest, I understood that to love something, even oneself, is its own terrifying act of faith. Years ago, Laila placed my teta's wing in a box with her own aqua-tints, set it in a hole in the wall, and stopped fearing the sound of the sea. In the same room, her mother guarded her own secret life in the drawer in her desk, and she may as well have been as far away as Saturn.

I sit up, rigid. Across the river, there's still no dust cloud over Little Syria. The building is still there, though not for much longer.

Sami sits up. "What's wrong?"

I pull Sami up by the hand. "I know where the missing bird is."

TWENTY / LAILA

I SHOULD HAVE KNOWN she'd found it when I saw her stoking the fire last night, should have known it by her silence, or by the way she looked at me, or by the way she snapped at me when I asked her if she'd gotten all her things from our apartment. My mother knows who you are, B, and there is no hiding it now that she's taken the box with your wing, not to mention the other pieces I'd been keeping in there. It's all gone now, all of it. I don't know how she managed to smuggle it out of the apartment without my noticing. She must have taken it while I was out at the galleries and hid it in her trunk.

I saw that the hole in the wall was empty as soon as I came back from Khalto Tala's apartment. I went to confront her. When I arrived, my mother was poking through the cinders of a fire, which is how I knew she had burned everything—your wing, my illustrations. She wouldn't admit to it, didn't want to talk, just shook her head with furious tears until it all came tumbling out: that she had read my notebook before I removed it from the box and had waited for me to leave the house before taking everything.

"Tuyour, tuyour, tuyour," she cried. Just birds, birds, birds, each one a symbol of you.

I was so angry that I burst into tears and screamed at her in English. "You witch," I cried, and called her names she didn't understand. I took a power from her then that she could never take back. English itself had carved a canyon between us, and you were only a part of that canyon, B. The truth is that I knew exactly who I was writing to when I picked up this notebook after all those years, remembered every word I'd set down, every word I'd scratched out because I couldn't risk being seen.

I brandished my English against my mother like a weapon. Afterward, I returned to this apartment and wept for the fact that, no matter how many blessings I might have in my life, my mother has finally succeeded in closing the wound of you, the one wound I hoped would never heal.

TWENTY-ONE / NADIR

It's still a couple of hours before dawn by the time I jolt Reem and Qamar awake and we arrive, breathless, at the community house on Washington Street. We leave Reem's station wagon a few blocks away and post up in the alley behind the building, watching the work crew roll up with their demolition equipment and discuss how to set the charges. Most buildings are brought down these days with a minimum of ceremony, the building imploding rather than exploding, falling into its own footprint to avoid damaging the structures around it.

"We've got some time, but not much. Less than twenty minutes to be safe." Reem walks to the back door, locked but not as securely as the front, and heaves down the bag she pulled out of the trunk with a clank. "I'm not much of a lockpick, but let's see what we've got."

"Whatever you do, hurry." I peer back through the alley. The work site is being taped off and potential traffic diverted with orange cones, though no one is driving down here at this hour.

While Sami and Qamar keep watch, Reem fiddles with a pin in the lock, but it's no use. She grimaces and tries again with a second pin, then shakes her head.

"Forget it." I scout the side of the building for windows I can pull the boards off of. "We don't have time for this."

"I figured you'd say that, so I brought this." Reem turns to rummage for something in her bag, then turns back to us with a metal rod in her hand.

Sami steps back. "Is that—a crowbar?"

Reem pulls her curls into a high, round bun. "I'm full of surprises." She uses her body weight to put torque on the crowbar, and with a crack, the lock flies off the door and into the wall of the neighboring building. We duck our heads, and when we look up, Reem is kicking the door. Qamar joins her, and the door bursts in.

When I give them an open-mouthed look, Reem and Qamar grin. Qamar stifles a giggle. "I've always wanted to do that," Reem says.

Sami catches my arm. "You don't need to do this."

I touch the curls at the back of his neck. "I'll be right back. You all keep watch."

Inside, the construction crew's voices are a muffled murmur from the front of the building. I keep to the shadows and head for the staircase. Others must have broken the glass and gotten inside since the last time I was here. The living room ceiling has crumbled onto the hardwood, and the walls are covered with spray-painted tags. The floorboards groan with my weight, so there must be a cellar below. I raise the flashlight on my phone to a patch of plaster that is missing above my head, revealing exposed wiring. The electrical system in this old building has been eaten away over the years, making it vulnerable to catching fire and earning it a condemnation notice. Easier to tear down than to repair.

I head up to the floor where I found Laila's notebook. Here, I pick out her apartment by the orange wallpaper in the bedroom. The old bedframe pushed up against the wall is still there. The wallpaper has peeled in the humid nights since the last time I was up here, and spider carcasses hang by their cobwebs from the dried glue.

I run my light over the floor and over to the upended desk in the corner of the room. I kneel and tug on the jammed drawer, but it doesn't budge. I brace myself against the wall and pull until the wood begins to give, then wiggle the drawer back and forth until it unsticks from the desk. At last it slams out, and something hard inside smacks my fingers. I wince and lift up a wooden box about the size of a backgammon board inlaid with eight-pointed stars and diamonds in mother-of-pearl, its rusty tin clasp still tightly shut.

There's a loud pop, and a vibration spreads across the floor. I drop to my knees. The smell of burning reaches me from the walls. Downstairs, the workers are shouting. Something is wrong. It's far too early to start a detonation, not with the crew still on-site.

I cough and raise myself up on the corner of the desk, waving away a string of smoke that escapes from behind the wallpaper.

I shove the desk aside and grope the wallpaper with my fingers. The brick behind it is hot to the touch. Where the wallpaper covers lines of electrical wire, it smokes and melts.

"Nadir!" One of Reem's mechanical birds zips into the room a second before Sami appears in the doorway, coughing and waving smoke out of the air. Behind him, the stairwell is gray, as though full of fog. "One of the charges malfunctioned. A spark got into the walls. Yalla, let's get out of here."

"I found it!" I grab Sami and move for the door. The smell of smoke is undeniable. The fire is spreading through the wiring, through the ceiling and up inside the walls. We reach the stairwell, but it's already full of smoke. As we reach the steps, one of the walls bulges, then disintegrates, and flames spread across the stairs.

We run back into the apartment, looking for another way out. I try to force the window open, but it's stuck and won't budge. I heave my weight against it—nothing. The room begins to fill with smoke.

"Fuck," Sami says, hacking. "Fuck."

You were the one who had the courage to push us both out onto the fire escape the night of the fire. When I saw the fire trucks arriving, I thought everything would be okay. But then you tipped me into the firefighter's arms, and as we descended you became smaller and smaller, and the platform didn't hold, and all the power I attributed to you was stripped away. Every ground looks solid until the rains come.

If someone finds me here after the fire has parched my body, will they see the resemblance I bear to you? Once, on an autumn afternoon, we stumbled upon an owl perched on a fence in upstate New York that had died in its sleep. It looked nothing but peaceful. If I find death now, it will not be because I've gone looking for it. I am a lifetime away from the forty-eight sparrows above Teta's rooftop.

I harden my fists and turn my knuckles toward the glass. I step back, take a breath, and charge forward, throwing my shoulder to the pane. My weight shatters the glass, and I drop, bloodied, onto the fire escape. My shoulder hits the chipped iron hard enough to cut.

"Nadir! Sami!" Reem and Qamar stand below us in the alley behind the building. Qamar shouts up, "Get out of there!"

"We have to climb down one at a time." I shove Sami toward the ladder. "What are you waiting for? Go!"

He grabs me with both hands. "I'm not leaving you."

I hold his face between my palms. I taste his tears on his lips. "I love you. Go." I push him toward the ladder, forcing him to grab the railing and put a foot on the rung below.

He looks up at me, terror in his eyes, but he begins to descend.

His old knee injury makes his steps shaky. On the seventh step, the ladder sways, and his foot slips off.

Reem positions herself below the fire escape. "You're almost there, Shaaban."

Qamar calls, "Keep going. We got you."

Sami reaches the second platform and starts down the final ladder, but as he prepares to drop, there's another loud pop, and the window above the second platform explodes. All of us scream. The ladder wrenches free of the fire escape, and Sami drops to the ground, knocking Qamar and Reem down in the process.

I clear the smoke in the window and try to make out the rest of the apartment. Flames have chewed through the staircase from the front of the building, leaving a gaping mouth of charred wood and smoke. There's no way back now. The heat from the window, even on the platform, is suffocating. My eyes tear from the smoke. I take off my jacket and hold it over my nose and mouth. Sweat runs down the cleft in my lower back. The hairs in my nose burn and turn bitter.

"You gotta jump," Sami calls up. "We'll catch you."

But they are twenty feet below, and all I can see is you sliding from the fire escape half a decade ago. Behind me, the fire reaches the window. Flames press their way through the broken glass and lick my back.

When you fell from the fire escape, you spread your arms. Astaghfirullah. In your final moments, you, too, became a bird.

A shadow passes overhead. A dark arrow slips between the moon and me, the feathers of its wings an iridescent flash, its curved beak pointed toward the west where the night is retreating.

I climb over the railing of the fire escape and open my arms to gravity.

TWENTY-TWO / LAILA

LITTLE WING,

I sit writing this in Ilyas's and my bedroom in the community house, now emptied, the bedframe and this old desk with the remnants of my mother's candle the only things left. A line of blackbirds perched on the demolition equipment this morning. The wrecking balls are waiting, the dynamite ready. The work crews are shuffling toward the work sites, as they call what will become of our homes.

This last morning dawned pink and long. I went up to the roof of my mother's building just before sunup to release the pigeons from their dovecotes. Ilyas stopped by my mother's apartment to take her steamer trunk with him to our new apartment in Brooklyn, but I went straight up to the roof. I didn't want to speak to her. From the rooftop of the tenement, I looked down across the courtyard and into the window of the apartment. She was sitting there watching me, seated on the windowsill. She has a relationship with these walls. The past few days she's been speaking strangely, telling me my father is in the sitting room or telling me to go down to the village oven to bake bread as though we're still in the bilad. She lies awake at night and speaks of time passing as though it were a rope tied to itself. It's the leaving that's unraveled her memory this way. She once begged God to spare one of his angels for her. But time has passed, and no angels are coming.

The last of the stars and a sliver of moon were still visible. The last of the cool spring nights are now behind us. The pigeons shook the chill out of their wings, fluffing their leg feathers for warmth. As I reached to open the dovecotes, they squawked and hopped. They knew something was coming.

The machines roared to life, the first of the dynamite less than a block away. Metal and brick shrieked as the building two doors from ours came down. I hurried to undo the latches of the coops, and the doves took to the air all at once. Startled by the noise of the machines, they bolted from the dovecotes with such a hum that I covered my face. In our old apartment, my mother remained rigid in the window, squinting at the birds against the sun. Dawn had just broken and flooded the courtyard with light. She shielded her eyes, then pressed her fingers to her lips. She fell against the windowpane and wept, mouthing one word in Arabic again and again: malayika, malayika. Angels, angels. My mother had not seen doves.

Afterward, she followed me back to the community house, but I closed myself in this bedroom to spend the last few moments alone. She's jammed her desk drawer shut, so I'll leave this notebook in its place in the wall where it belongs, and I'll try to move on. She is knocking frantically now, but Ilyas is reassuring her that we've forgotten nothing. She's convinced we've left something behind. Maybe we have.

Maybe she was right to burn my things, little wing. I loved you once, and I love you still, but not all migrations end with a return home. Even memory begins to cut if you hold on to it too tight. I don't know anymore if I believe in angels and signs. Perhaps we are the miraculous creatures my mother was looking for.

TWENTY-THREE / NADIR

I KNOCK REEM, QAMAR, and Sami to the ground when I land, and we fall in a tangle in the alley, coughing and groaning. Sami checks me for injuries, kissing the tips of my fingers and the dark smears of ash on my face. Qamar and Reem wrap their arms around us, and Reem squeezes me to her, laughing a terrified, relieved laugh. She doesn't want me to see her crying.

I grope around on the ground. The wooden box has landed nearby, denting one corner. The lid has popped open. I pry it off and pull out an odd-shaped package wrapped in burlap. There are no pages here, no papers, no rolled-up canvas. There are no illustrations.

Qamar picks up the burlap-clad object and unwraps it. "Are those feathers?"

I take the burlap from them. Inside is something comma-shaped and soft. A wing.

"Wait a minute," Reem says. The burlap is stamped with the name and address of a business on Washington Street: *Khoury's Linens and Laces*. "Isn't there a Khoury's fabric shop on Atlantic?"

Brooklyn. Brooklyn, all this time. I underline the text with my finger, then weigh the wing in my other hand. The longest contour feather is embroidered with delicate thread, the stitched handwriting so small that I have to hold the wing beneath a streetlight to make it out.

You are altogether beautiful, my darling. There is no flaw in you.

I've been here before, when the kites were in the air, when the streets opened their sails to the wind. We follow the address to a fifth-floor apartment above Khoury's Fabrics, the same balcony where an old woman and her daughter watched the kites pass. The hallway stinks of clove cigarette smoke, lined with a stained rug that was once red but is now brown. In one of the apartments down the hall, a father is shouting at his child, and elsewhere a television drones daytime shopping. Teta is on my arm as we ring the bell, her cane in her hand. She knows who we are here to see. This morning, she was quiet as I prepared coffee, quiet when the owl alighted on the sill as usual, quiet as we piled into a cab to take us the ten blocks to the building we presumed was Laila's apartment.

I straighten my shirt and tug the fabric away from my binder. I count each passing second. Under my arm is Laila's notebook, an unsent confession to Teta Badra but which Teta has never read. Sami and Reem wait with their hands in their pockets, and Qamar shares their headphones with me so that the sound of Umm Kulthum's voice comforts us while we wait. Teta coughs. Reem clears her throat.

A scraping announces the pulling back of the chain lock. The door opens to reveal a light-skinned, barefoot girl in her early twenties with chestnut hair, her pink sweater embroidered with the word *Mondays*.

"Sorry to bother you." I peek around the girl into the apartment. "Does Laila Zeytouneh live here?"

The girl looks me up and down a moment before peering out of the door to study the rest of our entourage. "She doesn't normally take visitors."

"I think we have something that belongs to her. I'd like to give it back."

The girl is nonplussed. "One sec." The door closes again, and we are left in the hallway, fidgeting.

Just as I am about to turn away, the door opens and the girl beckons us inside the apartment. Books and papers lie tossed about everywhere, piles of stretched canvas and tins of watercolor, yellow legal pads covered with doodles of garlic with the shadows blocked in, open boxes of Conté crayon covered in reddish dust. White folds of what look like origami hang from strings throughout the apartment, suspended confetti. The girl pads across the carpet to lead us into the living room, where she drops onto the sofa beside a woman who looks to be at least in her mid-nineties, sitting by the window stirring a cup of hibiscus tea.

After a few awkward moments, the girl says, "This is Nadir. He and his friends are here to see you." She pauses and surveys us, then pops up from the couch. "I'll make some more tea."

Laila squints at us. "You are who?"

"My mom was a big fan of yours," I say, and that is all it takes to conjure you. I notice you when I turn my head, seated in an easy chair in the corner of the room in a shaft of sunlight. You observe the proceedings with a nervous detachment, smoothing your dress pants, the white pair you used to wear to research conferences with your navy jacket and hijab. Someone has dressed Laila in your style: a matching pink sweater and pants set, a chiffon scarf in a floral print that she has tangled around her wrist. She sets down her teacup on the table beside her.

"Does she like birds?" Laila turns toward the kitchen and shouts to the girl, who I surmise is her granddaughter. "Grace, where's your mother?"

"She's getting dressed, Grandma, I told you." Grace comes back with two cups of tea in each hand.

Laila says, "Show them the kites."

"Kites?" I look around at the corners of the room and realize that what I took for origami are the bird-shaped kites we saw floating over Atlantic Avenue. They are scattered about the apartment now, hanging from the ceiling by their kite strings. "That was your work?"

"It was her pet project for, like, a decade." Grace tugs one of the kites down and holds it out for me to examine. "The kites tell the story of something that happened to her in the thirties when she was out in Michigan. Mom found the funding, and we all helped. They released the kites to commemorate the year Little Syria was demolished."

I take the kite from her. "You said—Mom?"

Laila picks up her empty teacup. "Habibti, get me a tea," she says. "I haven't had one all morning. Wallahi, my mouth is so dry." Then she turns to me as though just processing my comment and gasps. She reaches out her hands, then motions for me to come closer. "Where have you been, ya Ilyas?"

Laila touches my face, and I glance over at Grace for an explanation. She gives me a helpless, embarrassed look, and it dawns on me at last: Laila has end-stage Alzheimer's. She was crying at the kites that day because they were beautiful. She had forgotten they were hers.

My fingers wilt on the notebook. Teta plasters a tight smile onto her face. She is drinking Laila in, though Laila has no idea who she is.

"Jiddo Ilyas passed away a few years ago," Grace says so Laila doesn't hear. "He told the best stories."

The bedroom door opens, and a steel-haired woman enters the room, a red shawl wrapped around her shoulders. On her cheek is a purple birthmark the size and shape of a fingerprint.

"Mama, you've got guests." Sawsan greets us each with cheek kisses. "This isn't Baba, this is—?"

"Nadir." I finger the notebook under my arm. "I found something that belongs to your mother." It is difficult for me to relinquish Laila's diary. You rise from the easy chair in the corner and sit on the couch beside me. The sunlight follows you.

Sawsan takes the diary and studies it. Laila only furrows her brow, then takes the cup of hibiscus tea Grace offers her. "Where did you find this?"

"I rescued it before they demolished the community house." I turn to Laila, but she seems to have forgotten me again, murmuring to herself.

Sawsan smiles and pats her mother's knee. "Please accept my thanks on her behalf."

"It's nothing." I look down at my hands. I don't know how to continue. My voice falters. "We were—my mom was an ornithologist, and—I don't know if you heard, but they found a book of illustrations Laila made for a private collector, a long time ago."

"Mr. H. Whatever happened to him?" Laila snaps to attention. She seems so lucid that it's hard to believe she mistook me for Ilyas. "He owes me three hundred dollars."

I turn from Sawsan to Laila. "There was one print missing."

Laila laughs. "That's because I haven't finished it yet."

Sami, Qamar, Reem, and I exchange confused looks. Laila rises from her chair, beckoning Grace over to help her up.

I stand. "What do you mean?"

"Come with me." Laila leads us all to the spare bedroom, and Sawsan opens the door. Inside is a studio strewn with white drop cloth, a single easel and an ergonomic desk chair in the middle of the room. All around these things, the room is filled floor to ceiling with canvases and papers, oil paintings and illustrations, piles of sketchbooks and spare frames, mountains of drawings. All these works have a single subject—*G. simurghus,* your birds. Laila has varied their features, sometimes giving them white wings and sometimes making them dark, allowing the sun to bring out the iridescence of their feathers, positioning them with wings spread or heads cocked, walking a field after dusk or taking flight. The detailed etching she is known for is here, too, the fine tufts of feathers above the birds' legs and on the crests behind their heads, the dots of light in each of their pupils. In one corner of the room are an array of small prints of the birds with gold foil laid painstakingly into individual feathers. This is not a room; it is a menagerie, and standing in the midst of it, I am one of its birds. Beside me at the door, Qamar is weeping, and I am trembling like a person in snow. One day, someone will try to explain us as they once tried to explain this, and they will not have the words.

"I never finished it," Laila says. She picks up an exquisite aquatint of two *simurghus* ibises, one perched with wings extended, the other hidden in its shadow, and holds it out to me. "Take it," she says, "if that's what you were seeking. There's no need to hold on to it now. As for what the others will think—tfeh. People see only what they are ready to see."

I take the painting and put my hand to my heart by way of thanks. It is in this moment, when I hold the painting in my hands and understand what it represents, not only to me and to my friends but to everyone we love, that it finally dawns on me what it means to compromise for your own survival. Yes, it is painful to imagine releasing my grip, relinquishing the painting to Sabah or to Mr. H's daughter. But then I remember what Laila's work has meant to me all along, how many times I longed to see her in a gal-

lery, and I realize what a profound gift this will be for so many people, if I can let it go.

Laila pats the painting like an old, beloved friend. "I release
you to the light."

"Auntie." Qamar touches the crest of one of the painted birds.
"If you never gave it to Mr. H, then who were you keeping it for?"

Laila sits down in front of the easel. An aquatint is half-
finished there of one of the ibises with wings extended, the deli-
cately inked feathers hand-painted with watercolor. You slip
between us to join her. The sun is in that rare hour now when it
pierces the canyons of apartment buildings, and you bring the light
to warm the silver hairs on Laila's arms.

"I was in love with her once," Laila says. "She wore her hair in
two braids. Her mother lost a child one night. I remember. I was
there."

Beside me, the scarf Teta has folded in her hands is dotted and
damp. She is fingering the locket in the breast pocket of her jacket.

From beside the easel, your ghost motions to the last object in
my hands.

"Auntie." I hold my hand out to Laila. "I think this is yours."

Laila takes Teta's wing. She runs her fingers over the silver-
and-white feathers. Her face blossoms, her eyes widen, and then,
like a person just waking, she turns from the easel to offer Teta her
hands.

"Ta'burni," Laila cries.

I try to picture Teta through Laila's eyes, young and black-haired
and a little shy. She would have had her ears pierced then. As far
back as I can remember, Teta has never again worn earrings.

Teta takes slow steps toward Laila. She has forgotten her cane
in the other room, but with each step she becomes surer of herself.
When she reaches the easel, she bends down to wrap her arms
around Laila, who has grown small with age. Laila strokes Teta's
back with her swollen hands, and Teta rocks her, whispering some-

thing only the two of them can hear. Hidden in the blanket of Teta's arms, Laila weeps.

You move to the window, slipping yourself into a shaft of light. The owl will not visit Teta this night or any other. The next morning, I will rise to watch the light fall across Teta's kitchen, and you will not be waiting for me at the table.

TWENTY-FOUR / NADIR

ONE BRIGHT MORNING, I gather my paints, and the four of us head over to Laila's building. Grace has asked the owner for permission, so we bring all the materials we think we will need: ladders, masks, brooms topped with foam paint rollers. Over the course of a week, Sami, Qamar, Reem, and I paint a mural. It's our own interpretation of the birds that follow the night, their contour feathers iridescent, their faces turned toward the east. When we've finished, I add a smaller bird in the corner, a white-throated sparrow, by way of a signature. We add our names to the mural. I sign it *Nadir*.

The night after the painting is finished, we all go up to the roof of Teta's apartment. We light a fire in the firepit, arrange Teta's plants, and watch the sunset. I've already laid out Teta's pills for this coming week; she hasn't cut them in half in months. Aisha will come over tomorrow, after she's finished getting everything ready for the reopening of the sanctuary next week, to check on her. We are all surviving, however tenuous our grip. From this high up, the last light hits the wing feathers of our birds on the brick wall of Khoury's. Sami takes out his oud and plays, setting the red knot swinging. Reem gets up to dance. The fire crackles, and the mural dissolves into the dusk. The Canada geese are migrating this time of year, winging over New York like single-engine planes. I get up and walk to the ledge to study the arrow of their flight. By the fire pit, Qamar cracks a joke, and Sami interrupts his playing to laugh.

"Ya Nadir," Sami calls to me. "Ya habib 'albi."

When I glance back, my friends are beckoning me to them. I step back from the ledge and turn my face from Brooklyn's silhouette. There is a new moon tonight, revealing Deneb low in the sky. On the edge of the city, planes are landing from Beirut and from Cairo, angling their enormous wings.

ACKNOWLEDGMENTS

FOR THIS JOURNEY, ALHAMDULILLAH.

I want to acknowledge the Lenape, Paugussett, Wappinger, Fox, Miami, Anishinaabe, Peoria, Sauk, Potawatomi, and Ohlone peoples, on whose ancestral homelands the majority of this book was written.

Thank you to everyone who made this book possible. Thank you to Trish Todd, for giving this project the care necessary to bring it to fruition. Thank you to Kaitlin Olson, Megan Rudloff, Abigail Novak, Laywan Kwan, and the entire Atria team for the support they have shown me and my work. Thank you to Michelle Brower for always believing in my words. Thank you to Danya Kukafka, Kate Mack, Chelsey Heller, Esmond Harmsworth, and everyone at Aevitas Creative Management for their tireless support.

Thank you to those who provided me with the time and space

to write this book over the past four years. Thank you to Lori Wood, Donna Conwell, Kelly Sicat, Andrea Blum, and everyone at Montalvo Arts Center's Lucas Artists Residency Program, where I was lucky enough to be a 2017–2020 fellow in fiction. You may never fully know how precious the time and space you gave me were, but my time at Montalvo changed the direction of my creative work and of my life, and for that I will be forever grateful.

Thank you to Ryah Aqel, Kirsten Terry-Murphy, Matthew Jaber Stiffler, and the folks at the Arab American National Museum, where I spent two months in residency in 2019 holding workshops for marginalized writers and researching large portions of this book, including the sections in Little Syria and in Dearborn. The AANM's oral history archives of the stories of Arab Americans during the first half of the twentieth century helped to shape this work in crucial ways.

Thank you to Nour Balout and Detroit Grinds for the coffee and friendship. Thank you to Randa Jarrar and the Radius of Arab American Writers for believing in me and for creating a space where I was able to connect with my community. Thank you to Beit al-Atlas in Beirut and to the Fes Medina Project, where I spent time in residency from 2017 to 2019 writing and rewriting sections of this book. Thank you to *Winter Tangerine* for their "When the Moon Walks" and "Open By Riot Laughter" online workshops, during which various scenes in this book were first drafted. Grazie mille to Cherimus for the physical and emotional space you gave me in Sardegna during multiple revisions of this book: to Emiliana Sabiu, Matteo Rubbi, Carlo Spiga, Derek Maria Francesco Di Fabio, Fiammetta Caime, and all the artists I was lucky enough to meet there.

Thank you to *Shenandoah* for publishing an excerpt of the first chapter of this book in vol. 68, no. 2 (2019).

Thank you to those who read and provided feedback on parts of this novel, or whose conversations helped to shape the story: to

Lori Wood, Ibrahim Nahme, Matteo Rubbi, Alex Chee, Elmaz Abinader, Cinelle Barnes, Sarah González, Arla Shephard Bull, Nour an-Naas, John Joo, Devi S. Laskar, Soniya Munshi, Jai Dulani, Tina Zafreen Alam, ZZ Packer, Maya Beck, Naomi Jackson, Adrienne Robillard, Sandra Sarr, Leah Schnelbach, Emily Atkinson, Emily Kiernan, Jacqueline Adomeit, Joyce Li, Liz Harmer, Natalie McAllister Jackson, Sarah Fuchs, Raad Rahman, Mom-Mom, and Mae Smith.

Thank you to the Washington Street Historical Society for the work they do to preserve the cultural legacy of the neighborhood of Little Syria, including their work to protect its three remaining buildings: St. George's Syrian Catholic Church (a New York City landmark), the Downtown Community House, and the 109 Washington Street tenement. I have taken some liberties with the condition and placement of these buildings in the text for the sake of the plot, some of which reflect their precarious situation and the importance of protecting these buildings and their history.

Thank you also to the many writers, researchers, and historians whose works informed and influenced this novel, particularly Gregory Orfalea, Alixa Naff, Evelyn Shakir, Samir Abu Absi, Anan Ameri, Yvonne Lockwood, James A. Reilly, and Sholeh Wolpé, whose gorgeous English-language translation of Farid ud-Din Attar's *The Conference of the Birds* (*Man-tiq ut-tayr*) is briefly quoted in this book.

Thank you to my mom, Dana, and to my teta Zeynab. Thank you to my chosen family. Thank you to the communities that hold me and uplift me and help me dream a better world. Thank you to the ones who refuse to make themselves legible and the ones who remain unnamed. Thank you to my person, Matteo Rubbi, for the October sky, for being my brightest star, and for reminding me always that we are enough.

ABOUT THE AUTHOR

ZEYN JOUKHADAR IS THE author of *The Map of Salt and Stars* and *The Thirty Names of Night*. He is a member of the Radius of Arab American Writers (RAWI) and of American Mensa. Joukhadar's writing has appeared in *Salon*, the *Paris Review*, the *Kenyon Review*, and elsewhere, and has been nominated for a Pushcart Prize and the Best of the Net. *The Map of Salt and Stars* was a 2018 Middle East Book Award winner in Youth Literature, a 2018 Goodreads Choice Awards Finalist in Historical Fiction, and was shortlisted for the Wilbur Smith Adventure Writing Prize. He has received fellowships from the Montalvo Arts Center, the Arab American National Museum, the Bread Loaf Writers' Conference, the Camargo Foundation, and the Josef and Anni Albers Foundation.